JESSICA BENSON

Much Obliged

ZEBRA BOOKS
Kensington Publishing Corp.
www.kensingtonbooks.com

Prologue

Ah, Monday.

The notoriously stiff-rumped Dowager Lady Elsingham opened her *Morning Post* with a zeal not entirely attributable to the lengthy front-page article on the upcoming visit of the Duchess of Oldenburg. She, in fact, skipped the entire front page in favor of turning farther back, which business she pursued with an alacrity that could only have been deemed notable.

This piece of business accomplished, she read eagerly for a few minutes, twice pausing to exclaim, "Oh, my!"

She then bobbed her properly capped, crimped head around the corner of her paper and bellowed to her companion, the mousy, spinsterish Sophronia Pettiford, "Dear me! But you must read this, Sophronia. Really!"

"Eh, what?" returned Sophronia, at nothing less than a shout, as she, although she never would have admitted it, was no less hard-of-hearing than her employer.

"Pardon?"

"I said, 'EH, WHAT?' " Sophronia roared.

"So you did. I said, 'READ THIS,' " roared Lady Elsingham in reply, further making her point by handing the folded paper across the table.

"THE BOXING COLUMN, IS IT, AGAIN, CORABEL?" Miss Pettiford reached for her spectacles, and finding them missing, as usual, pressed the paper hard against her nose and began to read. After a few moments, she too put it down, and entirely unaware that her somewhat lengthy nose was now smudged with ink, pressed a hand to her admittedly scanty bosom. "Well!" she breathed. "Well! I must say!"

"EXACTLY," boomed Lady Elsingham. "MY THOUGHTS EXACTLY, SOPHRONIA!" She nodded vigorously to underscore her agreement. "You understand, Sophronia," she began, forgetting momentarily to bellow.

Until, that is, her companion yelled, "SPEAK UP, CORABEL. IF THERE IS ONE THING I LOATHE, IT IS A MEALY MOUTHED WHISPERER."

" 'YOU UNDERSTAND, SOPHRONIA,' I SAID."

"I DO!"

"THAT I, NATURALLY, AS MUST ANY PERSON OF REFINEMENT, CAN ONLY ABHOR THE SPORT—"

"NATURALLY," Miss Pettiford agreed with a firm nod.

"BUT REALLY! THE THOUGHT OF CLAREMONT 'STRIPPING,' IF YOU WILL, DOES GIVE ONE QUITE A FRISSON! DOES IT NOT?"

To this, Miss Pettiford tittered her ladylike agreement.

And then, both ladies, quite exhausted by the effort of such extensive conversation at such an early hour, retired to their bedchambers to rest.

Chapter 1

In fact, Claremont himself, otherwise known as John Fitzwilliam, fourth Earl of Claremont, counted himself about the only person in London who was looking forward with something less than enthusiasm to the day's edition of the *Morning Post*. He had even, he discovered, developed a sudden, and possibly excessive, interest in the plans for the Duchess's upcoming visit, going so far as to peruse that particular article a second time.

He was seated in the breakfast room of his house in Berkeley Square, taking his breakfast at his customary hour of nine of the clock, when he was interrupted by the arrival of his friend, Drew Mannering. In point of fact, it should be noted that at the time of Mr. Mannering's entrance, Claremont was actually doing very little eating. He was, through sitting at his table, the sun streaming in the windows offering a counterpoint to the scowl darkening his handsome brow, whilst his eggs cooled on his plate and his coffee did likewise in his cup. With one hand, he held a cool compress to his left eye, and with his other, made a botched attempt at turning the unwieldy pages of the *Post*. At Drew's entrance, he barely looked up long enough to bestow a glare on the new arrival before returning to these efforts.

" 'Morning, Fitz,'' ventured Drew in amiable tones.

A black look came his way in response to this inoffensive greeting. A look that Drew, in characteristically cheerful fashion, stoutly ignored as he strolled to the table.

His glare apparently having missed its mark in an exceedingly vexing fashion, Fitzwilliam ceased his efforts with the paper to snap, "If you must show up at my breakfast table, Drew, you needn't affront me by being so bloody cheerful!"

Drew raised a sandy brow as he took a seat. "Eye still troubling you, I collect?" he queried equably as, uninvited, he helped himself to coffee.

"There's no need, no need at all to use such a barking loud voice either. My ears, you know, escaped remarkably intact," Fitzwilliam complained.

"Well the same obviously cannot be said for your civility," Drew parried, taking a sip. He made a face. "Coffee's gone cold," he observed, as if that were his most pressing concern.

Fitzwilliam shrugged but nonetheless summoned his butler.

"My lord?" asked Simms, appearing instantly.

"Hot coffee, please, Simms."

"Y'never know, p'raps some would even improve *his* mood," Drew said happily to Simms.

Fitzwilliam, meanwhile, had resumed his one-handed attempts to open the newspaper, but was only succeeding in mauling the front page beyond recognition.

"And some eggs, I think," Drew added. "If you would be so good, Simms."

"Certainly, sir," answered Simms. "Permit me, my lord," he said as he crossed to Fitzwilliam's side and took the paper, opening it precisely to the sixth page. "Are they to be shirred this morning, sir? Or coddled?" he asked Drew as he expertly smoothed the paper and handed it back to his employer.

"Shirred," Drew replied after but a moment's consideration. "And some ham, I think. And perhaps some toast."

"Your quick decision on the style of the eggs shows a

firmness of mind one can but envy, Drew. Some buttered mushrooms, perhaps? As a complement to your meal?'' Fitzwilliam's tone was dry, but his expression was less thunderous as he raised the paper.

''Excellent suggestion! Don't you agree, Simms?''

''Unquestionably, sir.''

''Wouldn't do to forget your veggies,'' Fitzwilliam mumbled from behind his paper. ''My nanny was always wont to say they were essential in the aid of proper digestion.''

Drew grinned. ''So was mine! I wonder if all nannies say that.''

''Was there ever anyone upon whom irony was so wasted?'' inquired Fitzwilliam, still from behind his paper.

''Me? Or my nanny?'' Drew asked, before once again bestowing his sunny smile upon Simms and thanking him.

Simms bowed, saying in response, ''Very good, sir. One should always listen to one's nanny!'' before departing.

''Gudgeon!'' said Fitzwilliam, lowering the paper.

''Simms?'' asked Drew, his brow raised in mock surprise. ''I've always thought him an excellent fellow.''

Fitzwilliam heaved a sigh. ''Correct me if I am wrong, Drew, but don't you have your own house? Not at all far from here, in fact?''

''Ain't nearly so well run as your place, doncha know,'' Drew replied, eyeing Fitzwilliam's plate with a keen interest. ''As I was just saying, excellent man, Simms. Keeps things running smoothly. You planning to eat your eggs?'' he asked.

''Take 'em,'' replied Fitzwilliam, putting the paper down and pushing his plate across the table with his free hand. ''One can only hope they'll hold you until your own arrive. What's got you so bloody cheerful, anyway?'' he inquired.

'' 'M'always cheerful,'' responded Drew, as best his full mouth would allow.

''I suppose that's true,'' Fitzwilliam allowed. ''But that defect in your personality rarely grates so glaringly on my nerves as this morning.''

''Perhaps I'd do better to ask what's put *you* in such a rotten temper," said Drew, frowning across the table. "Not like you, Fitz," he added, with perhaps a touch of reproach.

Fitzwilliam tossed the folded paper at him. "This," he grunted. "Might as well read it aloud. I make no doubt I'm prominently featured."

But before Drew could reply, Simms reentered trailing a footman bearing new coffee and Drew's breakfast. In his own hand, the butler carried a silver tray with a fresh compress, which he proceeded to offer Fitzwilliam, who wordlessly accepted it and handed back the used one.

Drew stopped shoveling in food, long enough to observe. "Eye does still look pretty rough," he ventured, as he took in the purple swelling that marred his friend's countenance. "Lucky that's the worst you sustained though, what with the way things were going."

"Thank you. You are ever a comfort in my darkest moments, Drew."

"Anyway, all the dashed females will no doubt think it only serves to make you even more rakishly attractive, Drew complained as he looked at his friend's chiseled features. "In fact, with the way they sigh over your eyes," he said gloomily, "it's only justice if you end up with just the one." He frowned at the memory of how only yesterday those very eyes had been sickeningly and inaccurately—if one were to be a stickler— described by Miss Emily Soamesworth as *azure pools in which it would be simply too heavenly to drown.* "Not, mind you, that I care anymore," he remembered, and brightening, resumed eating, "about the fact that you monopolize all the female attention wherever you go."

Fitzwilliam raised a brow.

"That's why I came by—"

"And to think! I'd believed it for the breakfast."

"You malign me! Was to tell you the news. 'M' in love."

"Ah. Again?"

"Truly, this time."

Fitzwilliam smiled carefully. "Truly more than last time, then?" he asked.

Drew glowered. "Last time," he snapped, "was nothing."

"And the, ah, time before?" Fitzwilliam asked in amiable tones. "If I collect properly, that was with—no, no, she was the time before that. Last time would have been Perdita Richmond? Or was she—"

"You've made your point, Fitz," Drew conceded, his smile returning. "But when a fellow meets his true love it ain't fair to throw his past in his face—"

"I apologize. But you must admit that you do fall in love rather a lot," Fitzwilliam pointed out.

Which reasonable retort Drew ignored.

"Why, if I was to do that to you, throw *your* past in your face . . ." He trailed off for a moment. "Well, it really doesn't bear thinking about, does it?"

"No, it certainly doesn't." Fitzwilliam gave pause to consider this and shook his head. "Not at all. But I've long given up hope of meeting my true love, you know, Drew. I *am* pleased for you, though," he added.

"Thank you." Drew, unable to sustain his outrage, smiled his open smile again. "And I am assured that if you were to meet someone as lovely, as exquisite as she is—" He broke off frowning. "Truly, Fitz, I cannot understand why someone hasn't snatched her up already. In fact"—his frown deepened—"I can't really understand why it took *me* so long to fall in love with her. Why, I've known her practically forever—for that matter, so've you—and I've only just come to realize that she's so clearly the very epitome of female loveliness and grace. A treasure beyond compare, in fact."

"In that case, I might want her for myself," said Fitzwilliam, a mischievous grin lighting his face.

The horror in Drew's expression was almost comical. "You wouldn't!" he exclaimed.

"Drew! Of course I wouldn't," Fitzwilliam reassured him, shaking his head, not for the first time, at the foolishness of love. "But please, put me out of this misery of anticipation. Who *is* this paragon beneath our very noses?"

"Miss Winstead," breathed Drew, as if overcome by saying

ier very name. "I don't know how I could have overlooked for all these years that it is clearly the loveliest, most elegant name ever to grace the loveliest, most elegant female. . . ." His voice trailed off when he saw what was on Fitzwilliam's face. And by this he was so stricken that he broke off, even going so far as to put down his fork in his horror. "Don't tell me that you—that you've—"

"Good heavens, no!" Fitzwilliam replied hurriedly. "You need have no fear on that score, Drew."

Drew picked up his fork and resumed eating, his smile returning. "Thought for a second that you and—that Justine, er, Miss Winstead and you had um—"

"*Justine* Winstead!" interrupted Fitzwilliam with a shaky laugh. "You are head over heels for *Justine* Winstead."

"Yes," replied Drew somewhat beadily. "Yes, I am. Didn't seem likely to be one of your conquests, mind you."

Fitzwilliam, completely recovered from his momentary surprise, smiled lightly. "No. Not exactly the type of young woman one would set up as a flirt."

"I should say not!" Drew responded hotly. "But with you one never knows."

"Even *I* am hardly in the habit of setting up innocent young damsels, Drew."

"Sorry, Fitz. 'Course not. It's just that even the most well-bred young ladies have a way of losing their good sense entirely around you, Fitz. I've seen the iciest maidens and the most hardened spinsterish ape-leaders flirt and simper and throw themselves at your head."

"It's hardly *that* extreme, Drew. And entirely beside the point, since Justine Winstead has never—not once!—flirted, simpered, *or* thrown herself at my head! Most lowering, I don't mind telling you."

"Don't mind me." Drew had the grace to look sheepish. "It is just that Miss Winstead has the most *speaking* eyes and—"

"Naturally." Fitzwilliam's tone was dry. "What would a true love be without speaking eyes?"

"No need to be snappish, Fitz."

"I'm sorry, Drew." Fitzwilliam's look was genuinely contrite as he apologized. "Forgive my cynical, jaded outlook. But what of the lovely Justine? Does she return your regard, do you think?"

Drew actually blushed as he nodded.

"And how did this come about, so suddenly?" Fitzwilliam inquired.

"Well, it's not as if we haven't met countless times before, of course," Drew explained, his eyes misting at the memory, "but when we took the floor together at the Trelawnys' ball the other night, we looked into each other's eyes at the same time." He shook his head with the recalling of such an astonishing moment. "Well, it simply *happened*. The proverbial thunderclap. And we stood stock-still on the floor, just staring at each other until old Barnacles Barclay bellowed that we were holding up the figures and we'd best get moving before his wooden leg grew back into part of the floor and . . ." He trailed off again in recollection. "But *how* could such an angel still be unspoken for?" he finished, as he recalled himself.

Fitzwilliam's tone was dry in contrast to Drew's mooning. "Her family is no doubt waiting for her older sister to wed first," he replied briskly.

"Addie?" Drew asked, his brow furrowed. "No expectations there at the moment, I shouldn't think. And surely, she'd already be bracketed if she was of a mind to be? She's got to be six-and-twenty if she's a day."

"Four-and-twenty, actually."

"Point is, she passed her first blush years ago, and it's not as if she hasn't had offers. No stunner like her sister, s'truth, but well enough. I know both Winters and then later Raines showed a marked interest in that direction, but in the end neither made a match of it."

"Neither would have suited. Winters is a twit and Raines is a fool," Fitzwilliam said shortly. "A paltry, pompous fool."

Drew leveled a surprised look at his friend's vehemence. "True enough, but since when has that stopped a fellow being considered a highly eligible *parti*? I mean, look at that coxcomb

Whittaker. . . . Well, anyway, wonder what she's waiting for?'' he mused.

"Now that you mention it," Fitzwilliam replied, his tone once again light, "I think the elder Miss Winstead *does* have expectations."

"Really?" Drew looked up with interest. "She does? Expectations of whom?"

Fitzwilliam's gaze was fixed on the window overlooking Berkeley Square with what Drew considered excessive interest for a man who saw the same vista every morning. "Me, actually," he said so quietly that Drew wasn't certain he had heard correctly.

"Did you say—" began Drew, before stopping, unsure of how to proceed.

"Close your mouth, Drew," Fitzwilliam suggested. "Along with *eat your veggies,* did your nanny not instruct you that gaping is rude?"

"Sorry. But what exactly did you just say?" Drew asked, shaking his head as if to clear it.

Fitzwilliam's tone was light but deliberate. "I said," he reiterated, "that she has expectations of *me.*"

"Of you what?"

Fitzwilliam looked patiently at the ceiling for a moment. "Coming up to scratch."

"You?" Drew could not help but goggle again. "Of *you* coming up to scratch! Thought that was what you'd said. Well she'll catch cold at *that!''*

Fitzwilliam raised a brow.

"You are going to marry Addie Winstead? Is that what you're saying?" Drew demanded.

"No, no. Well, yes. I have no plans to do so," Fitzwilliam mumbled. "But I suppose so. Eventually."

"Fitzwilliam? What on earth are you talking about?" Drew demanded.

Fitzwilliam sighed and threw down his compress. "Be a good fellow, Drew. Pour me some fresh coffee—as I can barely lift my right arm—and then, as I can barely open my left eye, read me the boxing column. And after, once I can rest easy in knowing the extent of my humiliation in the eyes of the world, I will tell you the whole of it concerning Addie Winstead.''

"You are ever a man of surprises, Fitz,'' Drew said. "But I can hardly turn down that offer, can I?'' Accepting that he would have to be patient, he poured out the coffee. "Cream?'' he inquired. "Sugar?''

"Thanks, but I think black and bitter would best suit what I am about to hear,'' Fitzwilliam answered, taking his cup and leaning back in his chair. "I am all ears.''

"You ain't going to like this, Fitz,'' cautioned Drew, who had been skimming ahead.

"Don't worry. I am laboring under no illusions. Just read it.''

"All right.'' Drew frowned. "This fellow—whoever he is—writes,

'A certain gentleman about town, whom we shall call "Lord C.," known to be a formidable sportsman—a veritable Corinthian, if you will—currently sporting a badly damaged left peeper, as those amongst us possessed of keen powers of observation will have noted, is reputed to have been seen a goodly amount, of late, in the company of one of Covent Garden's finest dancers. Little was it known until yesterday when he, for the first time, entered the ring at Jackson's Rooms—against an opponent to be hereafter referred to as "Lord T."—that the fair charmer could surely best him in any contest in the ring.' ''

Drew broke off, laughing. "Sorry, Fitz,'' he gasped, trying to compose himself. "Just the image of you milling with Bella and coming up the loser . . . well, it's ludicrous.''

"I know what it is, Drew,'' replied Fitzwilliam, coolly, lifting his coffee cup in his good hand. "And believe me, I'd be laughing myself, as I have many a morning, if it were some other unfortunate being skewered by this cowardly fellow. Who *is* he? And why on earth would he be so craven that he would need to hide behind this anonymous column, do you suppose?''

"Hardly because he's afraid of you, I shouldn't think. At least, not based on what I saw yesterday,'' replied Drew beginning to laugh again. "Dashed clever with a phrase, though. And invariably dead-on in his observations."

Fitzwilliam glared. "No need to sing his praises. Just go on."

Drew took a deep breath and continued. " *'At a first look, Lord C. appears possessed of all the athletic requisites that constitute the beau ideal of perfect manhood. And on stripping, appearances were certainly greatly in his favor as he stood a good four inches taller and approximately two stone lighter— and one hesitates to mention, a good ten years younger—than his worthy opponent. On these merits alone, odds were given at two to one in his favor.'* "

Drew stopped reading and glared at Fitzwilliam for a moment. "Almost forgot. Lost a monkey on you, myself, Fitz," he complained. "Who'd have thought that old Truesdale would've—"

"Read, Drew," interrupted Fitzwilliam. "And please, spare me the editorializing. This blasted fellow does enough of that on his own."

"Right." Drew focussed his attention back on the paper. "He goes on to say, *'To call it a battle, however, is to disgrace the synonym of fight. It was a most unequal match.'* I'll say! Sure you want to relive this further?" he asked, looking up, a questioning expression in his eyes.

Fitzwilliam contented himself with another black look.

"Right-o." Drew went back to reading. " *'Round one. The instant Lord T. shook hands, he stepped back and assumed the attitude, before Lord C. had even managed the withdrawal of his hand. Short sparring ensued—or in the case of Lord C., a short bout of flailing about—and Lord T. put in a severe hit under the left ear of Lord C.'* "

Drew fought his urge to look up to catch Fitzwilliam's expression as he continued. "He goes on to say of round two, *'Lord C., finding he could not get at his steady and formidable opponent—although against a man of even a modest degree of science he would have been barely competent—hopped and danced about the ring. At some times falling down, and at*

others jigging around in the style of an Otaheitan dance.'
Lord!'' Drew was clearly hard-pressed to suppress a smirk at
the memory.

" *'Round Three. Lord C. actually succeeded in the delivery
of a half-arm hit with his right on Lord T.'s left side! But in
doing so made the classic error of leaving himself unguarded.
And Lord T., a man of barely average quickness, managed to
take advantage to the extent of putting in two severe blows
upon Lord C.'s head.'*

"Thought for sure you were dead. Harry Crenshaw said it
might be more fortunate for you overall if you were," Drew
couldn't resist adding as an aside. "Then you wouldn't have
to live down the humiliation!"

"Read!"

" *'Round Four. Lord C. attempted to land a blow, which
was parried and Lord T. put in a dreadful blow on Lord C.'s
left eye and in closing hit him twice in the body. The knowing
ones were at this period of the battle rather at a standstill with
regard to sporting their blunt. Lord C., it was certain by his
appearance, had received severe punishment, but not enough
to dissuade his backers entirely. Dear Reader. This author
cannot, under the circumstances, credit these backers with the
sense with which all men are alleged to be born!'*

" *'Round Five. Lord T. put in two weak blows and Lord C.,
already limp as an old sack after but five minutes of sparring,
fell upon the ropes and gave up the contest.'* "

Drew stopped reading and looked at Fitzwilliam who had
buried his head in his arms on the table. "Fellow about sums
it up exactly as I remember it. Bit about the Otaheitan dance
was a little harsh, though, I grant you. Thought it looked more
like an Irish jig, myself."

Fitzwilliam lifted his head. "Ah, Drew, the comfort you
bring!" He dropped his head again.

Drew ignored the sarcasm in Fitzwilliam's tone. "I thought
you told me your boxing had improved since Oxford," he said
accusingly.

"Sadly, it has," mumbled Fitzwilliam.

"Best stick to riding or racing or fencing or shooting or catching females, then, all of which you excel at to a disgusting degree," Drew advised.

"Believe me, Drew, I intend to. In fact, this very morning I shall be seen culping wafers at Manton's, followed by crossing swords at Angelo's, followed by driving through Hyde Park making an excellent show of handling the ribbons of those two mettlesome grays. Then, I daresay, my reputation will once again be intact enough to allow me to venture into White's with some degree of equanimity that I shan't be refused service, nor disallowed the bow window."

Drew laughed. "I take leave to doubt it's as black as that. No more plans to enter the ring, then?"

"None whatsoever," Fitzwilliam replied with a shudder.

"Good. We can all rest easy then." Drew poured himself more coffee. "Now," he said, leaning back comfortably with the air of a man about to be well entertained. "Tell me about Addie Winstead."

Chapter 2

By rights, Addie Winstead's ears should have been burning at that moment. Had they been, however, she would probably not have noticed, engrossed as she was in the document she was writing. Even *her* concentration, though, could not withstand the screech that echoed from the doorway to the drawing room.

"Adelaide! Whatever are you about?" Honoria Winstead shrieked, upon having entered the room and seeing her niece engaged thusly. She followed up the shriek by leaning weakly against the wall.

The object of her wrath looked up and smiled at her aunt's dramatics. "I was just taking a moment before we leave for the shops to jot down a few notes, Honny. I need to finish the column by first thing tomorrow morning."

At her words, Honoria abandoned her pose of horror, which, in addition to seeking the support of the wall, had consisted of clasping her hands to her face, making, she rather thought, a nice dramatic gesture, and gave a moan. "Refrain from even mentioning that revolting *thing* you scribble at while in my presence, if you please, Adelaide," she begged. "I am perilously close to succumbing to a faint and would likely do so were I not so very afraid of the effects such an action would have upon my new dress." She smoothed the decidedly uncreased garment in question.

Addie laughed and laid down her quill on the little mother-of-pearl-inlaid writing table at which she sat. "I beg you will refrain. I am done for now, Honny," she said, stretching out her hands to prove they were devoid of writing implements. "Truly, I am."

"Well, thank goodness for that, anyway," her aunt replied as she sunk comfortably onto the yellow and black gilt-wood chaise longue. She adjusted her fetching little lace cap and waved a languid hand. "Pour me some tea, then, my love," she said. "Justine looks to be an age, so we might as well take some refreshment before we go. Goodness knows it does answer to be well fortified before going shopping with *her*. And now that she and Mannering are all sheep's eyes at each other . . . Well, she's bound to be even dreamier than usual. Mother's a lovely gel, of course," she added, with one of her leaps of logic that would have confounded many. "We shall just have to wait and see if it lasts more than a sennight."

"The Dowager Lady Ardean is, and has always been, extremely pleasant and surely can have no objection to Justine as a match for her son," replied Addie, who was skilled at following her aunt's conversational twists and turns with a semblance of understanding. She rose from the desk and crossed to the sofa table to pour tea. After handing her aunt a cup she poured herself one before settling in a Trafalger chair. "I know that Justine falls in love at the drop of a hat," she said consideringly, "but Mr. Mannering might just have the perfect disposition for her."

Honoria could not resist. "Not to mention the perfect best friend?" she said.

Addie did not reply, but stirred a chunk of sugar into her cup.

Having failed to elicit a rise from her niece, Honoria continued with a sigh. "A younger son, though, Drew Mannering."

"Indubitably."

"Not what I had hoped for," confessed Honoria, still in sighing mode.

"A younger son who might well treat Justine with the love and respect that she deserves, Honny," Addie pointed out.

At this, her aunt turned a gimlet eye to her niece. "Now if you and—"

"No, Honny," Addie interrupted. "We are talking of Justine."

"Were we?"

"Yes."

"Well, *she* was upstairs mooning into the mirror when I passed by on my way down. I vow, the girl takes an age to get ready. And you! You barely do more than pass a brush through your hair!"

"Actually, I am not sure that I even remembered to do *that* this morning, Aunt," retorted Addie. Which was not strictly true, but she never could resist teasing Honoria. It served her right. *Drew Mannering is possessed of the perfect best friend, indeed!*

For once her aunt, apparently taking a leaf from Addie's book, failed to rise to the bait, instead casting a keen eye over her eldest niece's neat but otherwise unexceptionable appearance. She was quick, but Addie knew that every detail had been noted. From the plain, smooth knot of brown hair on the back of her head to the simple lines of her dove gray gown.

"Well, it's hardly any wonder, my girl, that Fitzwilliam has yet to come up to scratch, then, is it?" Honoria said, setting her teacup down with a decisive, yet ladylike, clink.

"Please, Honny—"

"Not, mind you," Honoria continued on, "that your appearance can account wholly for his failure."

Addie's tone was dry. "No. Indeed, I should think it is more the appearances of the Divine Bella Carstairs and possibly the rest of the Covent Garden Opera chorus that account for it," she replied.

This time Honoria's gasp was genuine. "Adelaide! I will

not have you talking of such things. If you cannot keep a civil tongue, I shall put a stop to this ... *occupation* of yours on the instant! It is outside of enough that you can even bring yourself to *go* to That Place, let alone—well, I can't even bring myself to say it!'' huffed her aunt. ''But if it is going to cause you to lose all sense of propriety! Well, that is another question altogether.''

Addie smiled to show that she did not take her aunt's pronouncement entirely seriously. But when she spoke, her tone was gentle. ''You know as well as I do, Honny, that we have no choice. This''—she motioned about her at the small but luxuriously appointed sitting room of their town house—''costs a veritable fortune to maintain. A fortune, which I hardly need remind you, we do not actually possess. If we wish to remain in anything above and beyond food and apple wood for the fire—not to mention staff and shopping expeditions—it is the only answer.''

''You would be quite amazed at how frugal we can be,'' replied her aunt. ''Why, this very gown? A bargain beyond compare,'' she assured her niece, smoothing the skirt of her new flounced jonquille silk walking dress. ''Madame Boucharde said that it was so perfectly *me* and no one else—no one else, at all—that she would give me a special price rather than see it end up on someone entirely wrong for it. She quite dotes on her fabrics, you know! And Justine's new gowns were also exceedingly reasonable, which, of course, is why we need to shop for shawls and slippers today.''

''Of course.''

''So how on earth could we economize more? But I beg anyway that you will desist altogether from continuing this discussion as it is vulgar beyond all things to discuss Financial Matters,'' Honoria finished in accusatory tones.

''Not as vulgar as it is to have none to discuss,'' retorted the ever-practical Addie. ''Which is exactly the position in which we shall find ourselves almost on the instant should my income cease and your economies continue! The annuity from my mother, you well know, does not stretch much beyond the necessities, Honny."

Honoria glared. "You have only yourself to blame for this mess, Adelaide," she said.

"Me? I hardly see that it can be laid at *my* feet that father lost everything on which he could lay his hands to that foolish venture. Who, with any degree of sense, could honestly have believed that tea plants could possibly thrive in Lapland?"

"That is not what I meant, and you well know it."

"Honny, please don't—"

"Why," demanded Honoria, overriding her niece's words, "if you won't tell Fitzwilliam what kind of straits your father left us in, won't you at least allow me to do so?"

"No!"

"There is no need to be so stubborn, you know, Adelaide," said Honoria, bending her eagle eye to the sudden flush of color that suffused Addie's face. Really, the girl was more than passably attractive—lovely, expressive gray eyes, nice hair, although, admittedly, not in a fashionable profusion of curls, good nose, nicely shaped mouth, excellent complexion, good figure, Honoria reflected—or would be if she didn't insist on styling herself so plainly. "You and he both know as well as I do that he will eventually do what's right. Why wait?"

"There is no reason why Fitzwilliam should marry me, Aunt. Nor I him," replied Addie in what she hoped was a quelling tone.

"There is every reason. Your fathers agreed before you were even born, missy, that the first son and the first daughter would make a match of it. And well both of you know it! And now they are both gone on to their heavenly reward, and Fitzwilliam all but promised your poor, dear papa that he would honor the agreement. He's thirty if he's a day, long past the age where he should be settled and done with this rackety behavior. Opera dancers! Refusing to be addressed by his title! Curricle races! Wagers! Honestly. What is the man waiting for? The Thames to freeze over?" She paused to consider the implausibility of

this ever coming to pass. "Really, he has been Most Remiss!"
she finished.

"Are you quite through?" inquired Addie, politely, as Honoria subsided, breathing heavily from her indignation.

"More or less."

"Good. Then I will tell you, not for the first time, that I refuse to hold the man to what is tantamount to an extorted deathbed promise. Besides," she added, wishing her face didn't feel quite so hot, "we don't *wish* to marry each other."

"And exactly who are you to make that decision?" inquired Honoria in dangerous tones.

"Nobody at all, I suppose," sighed Addie, putting down her cup and rising. She well knew the futility of pursuing this particular line of conversation. "I'll just run up and prod Justine along, or the Burlington Arcade will be closed before we've so much as left the house," she said, as she made her escape.

No sooner had she affected her departure, but Honoria had risen and crossed the room to the writing table. She picked up the sheet of foolscap on which Addie had been scribbling and held it up. With aplomb that would have surprised any observer, she skimmed over the words.

> *Few, if any, who were ringside at Jackson's Rooms on Tuesday last would have guessed that the quiet M of E. would prove himself to be such a first-rater in the ring. Although of such an unassuming and gentle demeanor that he stammered quite unintelligibly when inviting Miss R. to take the floor at Almack's, he is the surprising possessor of a goodly supply of the home-brewed as well as the talent with which to put it to good use. . . .*

Here, judging by the sudden ending, her own appearance had interrupted her niece's scribblings. Honoria replaced the page as she had found it. Really, she thought, the girl *was* remarkable. How many other young women of gentle birth would have had either the ability or inclination to support a family by taking up writing, after all? And about boxing of all things! Although most of them, to be fair, would not even dream of possessing a degree of knowledge about such a coarsely *masculine* sport as to make such a thing possible. Not, of course, that Honoria could approve for an instant of her brother's rackety decision to have allowed—no, worse, encouraged— such knowledge in his daughter!

John "Gentleman" Jackson, the former champion fighter and owner of the esteemed boxing salon that bore his name, had in fact been bosom bows with Addie's late father. When Eliot Winstead had died, leaving his family alarmingly close to the River Tick, Honny herself had fretted helplessly, and waited equally helplessly for Fitzwilliam to do his duty. But Addie, not one to wait idly, had approached Jackson with a plan. At first Jackson had refused, making it clear that he would be excessively happy to lend the little family whatever monetary assistance was necessary. Addie, however, had adamantly refused to hear of such a thing, and had remained insistent that the only help she could possibly accept was his assistance in secretly establishing herself as a boxing commentator. So determined was she to accept no other assistance, he had eventually capitulated and given his reluctant agreement to the scheme. Which is how they had ended up in this coil: with Addie, dressed as a maid, sneaking into his rooms several mornings a week. Thus unnoticed by both his noble patrons and the staff, she would observe the action in order that she could write about it.

Honoria recalled herself with a sniff. In the meantime, it could not be denied that the income was sorely needed. And in addition to putting the occasional frivolous bonnet on their heads, the columns, which had spun off into a slim but moderately profitable volume entitled, *The Compleat Fistic Annals of Jackson's Rooms, or, Gentlemen in the Ring,* had become wildly fashionable. In fact, Honoria was uneasily aware that, as often as not, they provided the *on-dit* of the day, with all of fashionable London speculating as to the identity and methods of the mysterious author.

A few wags, a minority, it should be pointed out, believed Jackson himself to be the author, but most acknowledged that that gentleman, known for his reluctance to offend his customers, would never be so indiscreet. He, for his part, professed complete—and fairly convincing—bafflement not only as to the identity of the mysterious scribbler, but also as to how the fellow got his intelligence. He was, however, wont to say that he had rarely met anyone with such a keen insight into the sport and professed a deep and abiding desire to make such fellow's acquaintance should he ever come forward and make himself known.

Honestly, thought Honoria, she *was* quite proud of the girl's enterprise. But still, this would never do! That the girl could even think quite calmly of gentlemen behaving thusly *and* of Covent Garden opera dancers, when most gently bred young women would become vaporish—and quite properly so!—at the mention of either, was a case in point. *I cannot like this. No. I cannot at all,* she thought.

Chapter 3

"D'you mean to say that your fathers made an agreement between them before you were even born?" Drew demanded once he had heard Fitzwilliam's tale.

"In a word, yes."

"How medieval! And you promised Mr. Winstead as he was dying that you would honor it?"

Fitzwilliam nodded, and with his free hand absently crumbled a piece of toast onto his plate. "More or less."

"By Jove!" Drew exclaimed. "Knew you'd grown up together, of course. But I'd no idea there was anything like this in your closet. How'd'you keep it to yourself all these years? The lady must be unusually discreet!"

Fitzwilliam nodded. "She is. And *I* was hardly disposed to discuss it, even with—forgive me, Drew—you. The odd thing is that I got the impression that Eliot Winstead was quite concerned for their financial security. I remember talk that he'd been involved in some very questionable business dealings and ended up all but losing his shirt not long before his death."

"Well, why haven't you then? Married her, I mean?" Drew asked.

"As it's turned out, I don't seem to be the marrying type," Fitzwilliam drawled. His tone was light, but his good eye, as it met Drew's gaze from across the table, was troubled. "And, before you can take me to task on it, yes, I've kept an eye on the ladies, but they seem to go on very comfortably. I assume that Winstead, in his concern for his family, exaggerated their circumstances."

Drew said nothing but raised a brow.

Fitzwilliam hurried to say, "Don't worry your overactive conscience over it though. I plan to do right by her when the time comes. It just hasn't come yet."

"Well, what are you waiting for? The Thames to freeze over?"

"Something like that, I suppose. Addie's pleasant enough— a right one, in fact. I always have enjoyed her company, and we had some outrageous larks growing up when she used to trail around behind me. She was a frightful tomboy."

"Addie Winstead was a tomboy?" Drew asked, his face disbelieving. "Hard to envision. She's so ladylike and proper."

"Now she is," Fitzwilliam replied. "In fact, she's one of the most decorous people I know. Which, it seems to me, is half the problem with the match. There's not been even a trace of a spark between us as adults. It would be duty, pure and simple. And I haven't been able to resign myself to that just yet."

Drew looked at him consideringly. "You do realize, putting all consideration of your morals and ethics aside, for the moment, Fitz, that you may be all that stands between me and the woman I love, do you not?"

"Perhaps love is coming it too strong, Drew," Fitzwilliam suggested, reaching for another piece of toast to mangle. "I'd suggest dancing with Justine a few more times before you make that decision."

"That statement shows exactly how little you do understand, Fitz," snapped Drew, an unusual edge of temper surfacing. "It is not a decision. I am in love with Miss Winstead—the *younger*

Miss Winstead—and dancing with her a thousand times ain't going to alter that.''

Fitzwilliam crossed his arms and gazed evenly across the table. ''Are you suggesting, then, that I marry just to smooth your way into the family?'' he inquired in tones that were amiable, but held an undertone of steel. ''Because if you are, Drew, I think you outstep the bounds of even our friendship.''

For just a moment Drew was uncomfortably aware of the undertone. ''You said yourself you would marry Addie eventually,'' he pointed out in reasonable accents. ''Don't want to wait until she's too old to breed, you know.''

''She's not a horse, Drew.''

''And well I know that,'' Drew retorted. ''But you're the one who can't think of a single other reason to enter the married state. If I've heard you say once, I've heard you say a thousand times that heirs are the only reason you would wed.''

''And I stand by that. Not in your case, perhaps. But in mine? Certainly. I've nothing else to gain and everything else to lose.''

''What about love?''

''Love does not seem to factor into any of these arrangements for me,'' Fitzwilliam said lightly. ''In its absence, however, I have found that fun and variety make an exceedingly satisfactory substitute. And I've no intention of giving them up.'' He drew a deep breath. ''No, Drew, not even for you will I marry before I am ready.''

''Then, perhaps, you could talk to her aunt for me,'' Drew suggested, backing down from what looked to be his first true argument with Fitzwilliam in all the years they had known each other. ''Maybe she is not so firm in the idea that Addie must marry first. I know that is the strict order of things, but times have changed, and she might allow me to pay my addresses to Justine regardless.''

''I suppose I could do that much,'' replied Fitzwilliam slowly. ''I could mention it to Addie first. Find out her thinking.''

''Can't make them much of a settlement, of course.'' Drew

looked truly gloomy for perhaps the first time in Fitzwilliam's memory.

"As I said, they seem to go on quite comfortably, so Winstead must have left them better situated than I'd assumed."

"I can assure them that she'll never go wanting, at least." Drew said, brightening.

"I am certain that will be enough, Drew. Addie, after all, does have reason to . . ." He trailed off. "Anyway, talking with her about your suit would force me, you know, to lay my cards on the table. To tell her that I've no intention of settling down anytime soon."

"It might be best anyway. Free her up to accept someone else if she wishes. Seems she's already sent two suitors packing on your account," Drew pointed out.

"Raines and Winters, do you mean?"

Drew nodded.

"On my account! I should think she sent them packing on her own account," Fitzwilliam said. "She's a thousand times above their touch." Drew looked at him with interest, as he continued, "But you're right, Drew. I can just tell her that if, when I'm ready for the parson's mousetrap—say in five or ten years—she's still unattached, I'll honor the agreement. But that in the meantime, she should feel free to go ahead an ally herself with someone else should she wish it. Addie's a good sort, she'll understand."

"In other words, don't turn anyone away on your account?"

"Exactly!"

"Because you just might be willing to wed her after she's past her last prayers and has completely lost her chances of bringing anyone else up to scratch, but in all honesty, you'd just as soon not? You might try to be a tad more diplomatic," Drew advised. "Don't sound much like the kind of thing females care to hear."

"Addie's very practical," Fitzwilliam assured him. "She's not in the least romantic. Shouldn't mind at all. In fact"—he looked up, much struck by his idea—"I think I'll engage to escort the ladies to the Winter Festival at Vauxhall two Saturdays from now. There should be plenty of opportunity to sneak a private word there without arousing expectations. Don't suppose you'd care to make up one of the party, Drew?''

"You know I would," Drew replied. "But, Fitz?"

Fitzwilliam raised a brow in question.

"Be gentle with her."

"I am not a complete fool, Drew. And please, give me *some* credit when it comes to managing females."

"Of your ability to manage females to the extent of having them fall at your feet and into your bed, I am in no doubt," Drew retorted. "It is your ability to manage *ladies,* and ladies who have reason to have hopes in your direction, that I am in concern of."

Fitzwilliam, confidence restored, gave a dazzling smile. "Don't worry on that score, Drew. I shall let her down gently enough. Now, let us talk of something else." His hand went to his eye. "Who on earth do you think this boxing fellow is? Jackson swears he has no idea, but Crenshaw thinks it has to be Pierce Egan."

Drew shook his head. "Surely Egan would simply put his name to it? That makes no sense."

And so, they were off, companionably debating London's favorite topic du jour, the problem of the Winstead ladies put aside for the moment.

Chapter 4

It would be another hour before dawn would even begin to touch the sky over London, and Addie groaned as she dragged herself from her warm bed. Outside, even through the closed windows, she could hear the whoops and yells of one or two young bucks just now making their way home through the still-dark streets after a night of carousing. Thus far, she had been lucky enough not to run into any of them, she thought with a shiver not entirely attributable to the chill of the early morning. She lit the bedside candle against the darkness, and allowing herself only one last longing look at the enticing jumble of bedclothes, marched herself firmly across the floor to her clothes press.

Nellie, her maid, would have been more than glad to assist her on these mornings, but Addie, on the grounds that the fewer specifics anyone knew about her activities, the better off they all were, had flatly refused her help. Although Nellie had long since given up hope of having her curiosity satisfied as to Addie's mysterious early morning departures, she persisted in offering hopefully from time to time.

Still shivering, as no Nellie meant no fire, Addie located a burlap bag in the back of the clothes press and emptied it onto the bed. Out fell her plain brown, much-mended dress, and she picked it up and shook it out. She endured a quick wash in the basin of cold water, and then slipped the dress over her head and tied on the none-too-clean apron. Standing in front of the glass, she brushed her hair back, catching it up in her customary plain knot. After adding her cap, she studied herself and decided that her transformation from Addie Winstead, young woman of admittedly little fashion but excellent birth, to nameless servant girl was depressingly easy to complete.

She crossed once again to the clothes press to retrieve her cloak. It hung in its muddy, patched drabness next to the blazing glory of her newly purchased Hungarian wrap. *One of Honny's economies,* she thought with a smile, unable to resist pulling out the new garment. Addie had not thought to buy anything for herself on their little shopping expedition the other day, but Honny had insisted that the deep red velvet with the sapphire silk lining and luxurious ermine trim was absolutely *her*. Justine and Madame Boucharde had added their voices to the chorus of encouragement. And Addie, for some reason that she still could not figure, had gone against the grain of her usually frugal nature and agreed not only to its purchase, but to that of the matching ermine muff, without even so much as *asking* the price beforehand. And now she could not help but be glad she had, since Fitzwilliam had sent a note round that very night, inviting the ladies to accompany him to the Winter Festival at Vauxhall Gardens.

Not, of course, that she could have any interest in trying to impress Fitzwilliam! Which was a very good thing, she decided wryly, as with his obvious taste for flashy, voluptuous, sophisticated women, she stood about as much chance of that as of flying to Jackson's like a London pigeon.

Still lost in thought, she replaced the glorious new cloak and wrapped herself in the dreary brown. Fitzwilliam's invitation had come as a surprise, to say the least. True, he danced with her very properly at assemblies and the like, and occasionally paid a morning call, but the man was hardly in the habit of

escorting them about town. Honny, of course, had immediately
jumped to her own conclusions about the matter, the thought
of which made Addie sigh again. It would take weeks to disabuse her aunt of the notions that were currently taking root.
But when the missive had gone on to mention that Fitzwilliam's
friend, Mr. Mannering, would make up one of the party, Addie
had understood the intent behind the invitation. At least Fitzwilliam was good enough to try to help his friend's case, she
thought, trying to be charitable, if not to do what he himself
ought.

Not, of course, that she would want him that way, Addie
reminded herself, as she silently descended the rather faded
Turkish-carpeted stairs, being certain to avoid the creaky one,
fourth from the bottom. Could there be anything on this earth
more foolish than her nurturing a passion for John Fitzwilliam,
Earl of Claremont? she asked herself, for what must amount
to the thousandth time. As usual the answer was a resounding,
disappointing, *No*. If she held her peace, she knew that he
would eventually marry her. But marrying her and wanting
to marry her were entirely different things. And that kind of
marriage, to him, she had decided long ago, would be more
than she could bear.

Wrenching her mind away from Fitzwilliam and back to the
business at hand, Addie opened the door to the servants'
entrance and raised her hood to conceal her face.

Thus cloaked, she made her way down the back steps and
into the darkness of Curzon Street. As was her custom on these
mornings, she walked quickly. Crossing Half Moon and Clarges
Streets, avoiding heavily trafficked Picadilly, generally keeping
to the smaller, and at this hour, more deserted streets to accomplish the short walk to No. 13 Old Bond Street. As she walked,
her mind drifted. She never would have admitted to Honny
how much she enjoyed these early mornings. It was a dangerous
game, she knew, in that should her identity be discovered, the
same society that relished each and every word of the columns,
the society in which Addie had traveled all her life, would
ostracize the entire Winstead family in an instant. But not only

did they desperately need the tidy little income her writing brought in, there was just something about freeing herself from the person of Addie Winstead—conventional, on-the-shelf, properly raised young lady of good birth—that was exhilarating. And she was actually writing about boxing! Where others could see only coarseness and blood, Addie could see science and footwork and artistry. And happy days with her father, as he imparted his love of the ring to her. *Poor father,* she thought. *He really should have had sons.*

As she rounded the corner to Hay Hill Street and walked the block to Dover, Addie let a smile drift across her face as she recalled writing the column about Fitzwilliam. She knew she shouldn't have allowed herself, but it had felt in some way like revenge. *It is unworthy of me,* she reminded herself, *to think that way. And besides, revenge for what? For not loving me as I do him? For leaving me so very disturbed at the sight of his bared torso?* Addie, who at this point was well used to half-naked male bodies, had been trembling as she left Jackson's. Even now she could see the broad shoulders and tapering waist, the sculpted, fluid muscles, as if the picture was engraved in her mind. She stopped for a moment and considered the unsettling possibility that that had been her motive. How awful! But most likely true, she had to concede, if she were going to be honest.

But he had been truly, unspeakably, dreadfully . . . well, *dreadful* in the ring, she recalled, her grin returning. Still lost in the gratifying memory of his pummeling at Lord Truesdale's hands, Addie prepared to cross Dover Street. But before she could step out from the curb, she heard behind her the telltale notes of a song that indicated yet more young bucks on their way home from a night of debauchery. Quickly, she stepped back and into the shadows of a building, walking as inconspicuously as possible. She knew she was being overly cautious. *They won't even notice me,* she assured herself.

> *"Drink, my boys, and ne'er give o'er,*
> *Drink until you can't drink no more,*

For the Frenchmen are coming for a fresh supply,
And they swear they'll drink little England dry.''

The words of the song drifted closer as two sets of unsteady footsteps clattered along. Addie's heart felt as though it was in her throat. The quiet streets, which had recently seemed so reassuringly empty of people who might recognize her, suddenly felt menacingly deserted.

''Paddie, widdie, waddle, widdie, bow, wow, wow,
Paddle, widdie, waddie, widdie, bow, wow, wow
For the Frenchmen are coming with a fresh supply,
And they swear they'll drink little England dry.''

Replied a second voice.
Breathe. Walk. Keep your head down like a servant. Pay them no attention, Addie commanded herself.

''They may come, the frogs of France,
But we'll teach them a new-fashioned dance,
For we'll pepper their jackets most ter-ri-bully,
Afore they—''

''Well!'' Suddenly, the footsteps halted and Addie's blood pounded through her veins.

''What have we here?'' a slurred voice—Addie thought the first singer—asked from too close behind her. ''Look, Tom, a wench! Is not that fortunate? Just the very thing!''

''Don't, Raymond,'' pleaded the second voice.

Addie willed herself not to look back and not to run. Surely, to do either would only serve to encourage him further.

''I'll bloody well do what I wish,'' replied the first, as, judging by the sound of his booted footsteps, he resumed walking and, despite his drunkenness, gained on Addie at an alarming rate. She could feel his nearness now. Just as she was about to give in to terror and run, he grabbed her by the arm.

''Well let's have a look, love,'' he said as he swung her

around. When he did so, she caught sight of his face, and almost groaned aloud. *Just my luck,* she thought wryly, her fear giving way to terror of an entirely different sort—she knew her assailant. It was Raymond Walters. The youngest son of a prominent family, he was little known to London society, having only recently returned from a lengthy spell at his family's Barbadian plantation. His blond good-looks, deep pockets, and easy charm had made him a welcome addition to every hostess's ballroom, and recently, even to the sacred rooms of Almack's. He had made a point of securing an introduction to Justine, and had even led her out on several occasions. But fortunately, as far as Addie's current predicament was concerned, he had thus far neglected to bestow his attentions on the older, plainer, Winstead sibling.

"No, Raymond," begged his friend, catching up to them, just as Addie began to struggle against his grip. A struggle she knew instantly to be fruitless. He might have been drunk as the proverbial lord, but his grip was iron.

He faced his friend without loosening his hand. His fingers bit into the flesh of her arm. "I don't want to hear any of your scruples, Tom," he snapped. "If I've a mind to take a servant girl, I shall. When and where I please. Make no mistake. If I decide I want her right here, you'll have nothing to say about it. You ain't my conscience, y'know."

"Please, sir," begged Addie, forgetting, in the face of the very real terror that was stealing through her at his coldly issued words, to disguise her accent.

Her mistake was instantly borne in on her as he whirled back to face her, his eyes glittering with curiosity. "My, my. What exceedingly refined tones you possess, my dear, for such a poorly dressed servant girl!" Even Tom stopped his protestations and stared. "Fallen on hard times, have you? Let me see you," Walters said, his face descending even closer. Addie could see signs of dissipation marring his looks that one would not notice from more of a distance. Red, spidery veins were beginning to develop, crisscrossing his nose and cheeks. His blue eyes were red-rimmed and puffy. And his complexion held an unappealing coarseness and pallor. He smelled quite appallingly unwashed and of strong spirits.

Almost involuntarily, Addie turned her head away from the smell. "I shall scream," she threatened, wondering even as she said it if she would have the resolve. It might save her from Raymond Walters, but it could easily result in her unmasking.

"Oh, no, you won't," he said pulling her roughly toward him. "Let me see your face and then I shall decide if I want you," he said, as he pushed her hood away from her face and looked down at her in the rapidly lightening dawn. Addie held her breath, waiting for the dreaded sign of recognition to flicker in his eyes. But blessedly, there was none. "My what smooth, well-tended skin you have for such a lowly servant," he remarked instead. As his eyes traveled slowly, insultingly, down her face to her heavily draped body, Addie's face flamed. "And I wonder what delights lie under that cloak. What do you think, Tom?" he asked without taking his eyes off of her.

"I think that you're foxed and this is a dangerous game, Raymond. Let us go home," pleaded Tom, "and you can sleep it off and—"

"No!" Walters interrupted. "Don't you see? She's much too finely cared for to be a maid. She's a whore, Tom. A lightskirt. Looking for a new protector, are you, my dear?"

"Now *that* is enough!" snapped Addie, her natural demeanor beginning to surface despite her fear.

He raised a brow. "A rather high-handed manner from a servant girl, doncha think? Or, even, come to think of it, a lightskirt," he said, flatly. " 'S'enough. Now, let's have a look at the rest of you." With one surprisingly economical motion, he pulled open her cloak. Despite her heavy, patched woolens, Addie had the feeling he could see right through her clothing. As she struggled fruitlessly against his grip, he ran a careless, appraising hand down her body. Addie, who had never had closer physical contact with a gentleman than a young lady of her station should, was horrified. She ceased her struggles and tried to contain the tears of revulsion and humiliation that threatened.

"My, but she's a fine one," remarked Walters, apparently having finished his shaming inventory. "A little thin, but everything's there. I've half a mind to set her up."

For a moment, a terrible silence hung in the air. And then, miraculously, ponderous footsteps could be heard turning the corner from Grafton Street.

"The Watch!" gasped Tom. "It's the bloody Watch, Ray."

"Damn!" grated Walters. "What a pity. I was really going to enjoy this one, but fact is, there's plenty more and willing, too, where you come from, love. And who knows? Perhaps, we'll meet again," he said, as, kissing his fingers toward her, he turned and ran in the direction of Stafford Street.

Addie, unable to believe for a moment that they were truly gone, just stood, immobile. Then, it dawned on her that the last thing she wanted was to have to explain anything to the Watch, so she began to walk at a rapid clip, back up the street.

Just another servant girl on her way to work. No doubt lazy and late, thought the policeman as he watched her go.

As soon as she had turned the corner into Albemarle Street, Addie found a quiet doorway, and sank down. Her heart was hammering and she was distressingly close to giving way to those tears. She had been cavalier about the possibility that she could be unmasked, but when it had come down to it, it was very nearly as terrifying as her near escape from Raymond Walters's hands. And what of Mr. Walters? Would he recognize her when next they met at some social function, as they were bound to? Or providentially, had he been too foxed and she too insignificant? And what of the hapless Tom. Would he recall her?

London was beginning to wake around her. She was sorely tempted to turn around and creep back into her bed. Just this once. Suddenly, Addie thought of her role as sole supporter of her little family with more of a sense of fear than adventure. Should she have to stop, what would become of them? And the consequences to Justine ... Perhaps she should have accepted one of her offers of marriage, she thought, giving the idea serious consideration for the first time. Both were reasonable enough suitors from an eligibility standpoint. But, in truth, she was inclined to think Lord Winters a twit and Mr. Raines a fool. And besides, every time she was with one of them, an image of Fitzwilliam, exuding that carefree life and vitality, intruded. No. She could never have accepted either of them. And Justine? Well, there was simply no question there. Justine would marry for love, she thought fiercely, as she picked herself up on her still-shaking legs.

Work, she decided, was the only answer to this uncharacteristic fit of the dismals that threatened to engulf her. Besides, the Viscount Sandringham, a dab hand in the ring, was scheduled against none other than Jackson himself. A matchup that, under any other circumstances, she would have been agog to see. So she collected herself and set off in the breaking light of day.

Chapter 5

The pluck of Sandringham was to be much admired, Addie thought as she stared unseeing into her mirror while Nellie fussed with her hair.

"Some left loose around your face, Miss Addie?" Nellie asked as she began to twine a wreath of silk flowers around the smoothly coiled knot in the back.

Addie nodded absently. The quality of Jackson's blow truly was unmatched, she thought, even now that he was well into his fourth decade. Six-and-forty to be exact. It was said that it was only observable in effect—that it literally came like lightning, and was felt before it was seen. Even so, Sandringham had remained game as a pebble through what could only have been a most demanding—

"Well? How do I look?" demanded Justine, appearing in Addie's dressing room and interrupting her sister's reverie. It was Saturday night, and the Winstead women were making themselves ready for the Winter Festival. "Stop your woolgathering about dreadful blows and spouting claret and take a look."

Addie laughed as she saw Nellie's eyes meet Justine's in the mirror. "Don't distress yourself, Nellie. I was attending

enough to know I agreed to some left loose around my face.''
Still laughing she turned toward Justine, only to have Nellie pull
her head back. "Turn around," she commanded her sister.

Justine did a graceful pirouette as Addie watched in the mirror
and then faced her sister, a slight frown crossing her face. "Well?"
she asked. "And why did you have me turn around?"

"Because that's what Honoria does, of course. I've no idea
what she looks for, as you are always lovely from any angle,
but it seems a good enough idea," admitted Addie beginning
to giggle.

"If you could just see your way clear to holding still a moment,
Miss Addie, I might finish tonight," Nellie complained.

"Sorry, Nellie. You, Justine, are a vision, as usual," Addie
replied. And she was. From the toes of her little boots to the
soft rose wool of her gown. But the clothes, fine as they were,
paled in comparison to the loveliness of her sister's countenance, Addie thought fondly.

"You might too, Miss Addie—be a vision, I mean—if you
would only see your way clear to letting me cut your hair and
give you some curls," Nellie said, with a meaningful glance
at Justine's modish blond ringlets.

"You know as well as I do, Nellie, that Justine's curls are
so glorious because they are natural. Were I to let you do mine,
I should only end up with a head full of crimped frizz!"

"Oh, Addie," said Justine, beginning to laugh also. "Stand
up, let me see your gown."

"Just you wait one more second, Miss Addie, or all this
work on your hair will be for naught. And I, for one, have no
intention of hearing what Miss Honoria would have to say
about that!" cautioned Nellie.

"Nor I!" Addie assured her, doing as she was bid, until
Nellie pronounced her done and stepped back to admire her
handiwork.

"Good. Now don't you two muss yourselves. I shall just
run up and put the finishing touches on Miss Winstead," said
Nellie, bustling out in the direction of Honoria's rooms.

"Now, *you* stand and turn, Adelaide," commanded Justine.

And Addie, with a grin, did just that.

"That color looks good on you," Justine said, admiring the deceptive simplicity of Addie's new white dress, set off with equally simple diamond drops at the neck and ears. "And it will look splendid with your new cloak. Honoria is bound to scold you, though, as diamonds, you must know, are all exploded this year!" They both laughed at this, and Justine continued. "Fitzwilliam cannot help but notice how lovely you look!"

Addie stopped, midturn, her laughter gone. "And why should I care about that?" she demanded, an uncharacteristic edge to her voice.

"Not that you should. Of course you would not. It is only that I thought—"

"Never mind, Justine. I shall do my best to forget entirely that you said it. We are undoubtedly invited *only* because Mr. Mannering desires to further his acquaintance with you! Honny has already decided to overlook that fact. Please, don't you also."

"All that you would need to do is tell Fitzwilliam, you know, that the time has come," said Justine gently, sitting down on the sofa and drawing Addie down next to her. "He can hardly refuse to honor his promise."

"Oh, Justine," Addie said, so sadly that her sister was startled. "I'd assumed that you, of all people, would understand. I could never bear to have him that way. Could you?"

Justine took her hand. "I do not know, love. Some might say that any way was preferable to none."

Addie shook her head. "Don't you see? To see him day after day, to live with him, to have his children, knowing that he did not care for me? That he was forced into it by a sense of obligation? To go through life wondering whenever he was out if he was with Bella Carstairs, or whoever her successor of the moment might be?" She shook her head. "No. I could not live that way."

"Is it so impossible to imagine that in time love would come, Ad?" Justine ventured.

Addie smiled, but without gaiety. "How is it that you have become so wise, Justine?" she asked. "I have always been accustomed to think you the flighty one and myself the thinking one."

"Well, perhaps I shall give you a surprise," Justine said, releasing her hand with a grin. "I am thinking of turning over an entirely new leaf and becoming quite solemn and serious!"

Addie did laugh at this. "Please, I beg you will not. We should miss your gaiety and joy immensely, my dear. And think what your Mr. Mannering would say to find you become prim and prune-faced!" They laughed at this, and Addie continued, "But only imagine being married to him where there was affection on your part and resentment on his, Justine," she said, turning serious again.

"I cannot believe there is truly no affection on Fitzwilliam's part, Addie," replied Justine, equally seriously. "You used to be the best of friends as children."

"No. He *tolerated* a tomboy six years his junior dogging his every footstep."

"Tolerated? He adored it," Justine insisted.

"Well I am no longer a tomboy trailing adoringly in his wake," Addie pointed out.

"Not on the surface, perhaps," Justine agreed with a grin, "but deep down—"

"*Very* deep down!"

"Besides, it seems to me that the two of you are quite well suited," Justine continued.

"How can you think that?" demanded Addie, beginning absently to finger the fabric of her gown. "He is some type of exotic beast. An untamable panther! And I am, well, I'm a plain old English house cat," she finished.

Justine smiled gently. "But don't you see that you're both, apparently—although I confess I had not previously been aware of it—felines. And as such, there must be *some* common ground. And then, perhaps, Addie, he is not as exotic or untamable and you are not so plain and domestic as you seem to believe."

Addie was saved from having to take that suggestion under consideration as just then Honoria burst in. "Look at the time!"

she cried. "And the two of you! Sitting and chatting quite as if we had all day! Well, we do not! I have just been informed that the gentlemen are indeed arrived and are waiting below stairs. How gratifyingly prompt they are, to be sure! Addie! You are wearing *diamonds!*" she wailed. "They are *quite, quite* exploded this season, you know. I cannot like it, but never mind! We shall not keep them waiting as one can only think that is what ruined Dahlia's chances with Alistair back in 'seventy-four! And then she married that *most unsuitable* merchant. And there was that whole *Unfortunate Business* that I shall decline to go into altogether, and which, one hates to say, one can only *assume* could have been avoided *entirely* had she only not been so intent on the placement of the feathers!"

Addie and Justine, well practiced as they were in the art of not breaking down entirely in the face of their aunt's conversation, avoided catching each other's eye. Recalled to the moment by the sight of her two nieces, still sitting, side by side, Honoria ceased her reminiscence and continued. "At least, you are both ready," she cried. "Unsuitable as some of your accessories may be. But oh, my loves! You are *sitting!* What *can* you be thinking? Have you given no thought to creases? Obviously not!" she continued, not bothering to wait for an answer, as she was so often wont to do. "Stand, stand," she shooed.

They did as they were told, with Addie saying wryly, "Are we to suppose we are not allowed to sit all night, Honny? Surely, the gentlemen will think it odd if we stand in the carriage!"

"Don't be pert, Addie. It is a most unattractive quality," Honoria chided. "Now, quickly, before we go downstairs! Turn! Quickly. Both of you," she commanded, waving her arms in a circle. "Why are you laughing? Whatever has gotten into the two of you tonight?"

"I don't know, Honny," Justine said giggling, then finished her graceful turn. "It must be the air. Anyway, d'you suppose Fitzwilliam's *peeper* has healed?" she asked, setting them off laughing yet again as, with Honny scolding them, they headed for the stairs.

Chapter 6

In point of fact, it *had* healed. And very nicely indeed, Addie thought, as they descended the stairs to greet their escorts who waited below in the hall. Fitzwilliam, in fact, looked his usual, all too devastating self. He was dressed in the darkest navy blue with only the stark white of his shirt for counterpoint. The expert tailoring of his jacket emphasized his lean strength, and his brown hair fell slightly over his forehead. The blue of his clothing only served to heighten the almost startling blue of his eyes.

He, in his turn, looked up at the little trio descending and decided that Addie, who was still recovering from her fit of the giggles, looked quite unaccountably lovely tonight. Her almost austere white dress, the stark diamond drops, and the silver flowers in her simply dressed hair suited her, he thought.

He had just bought Bella some diamond eardrops, but she had sent them back to Rundell and Bridge, complaining that they were so plain they made her eyes hurt, and besides, didn't he realize diamonds were exploded this year? He had, of course, but had liked this pair regardless. They would have looked exceptional on Addie, he found himself thinking. Startled by his train of thought, and somehow disturbed by the realization that he was thinking of her as an attractive woman, he assumed a bland mien just as her gaze slid to his.

Looking away from Fitzwilliam's painfully flat expression, Addie glanced at Mr. Mannering. He was watching Justine's descent as if she were the only person in the house, quite obviously overcome by her presence. Although shorter and stockier than Fitzwilliam, he somehow seemed to gain in stature as Justine came toward him, smiling shyly in his direction. *If only Fitzwilliam would look at me with that light in his eyes just once*, Addie thought, *I would at least know what it feels like. But, of course, he never will.* Before she had any time to refine upon that lowering thought, however, they had come to the bottom of the stairs and were engaged in a polite flurry of greetings.

"It is positively bone chilling out tonight," Mr. Mannering cautioned them. "As all the festivities are to be held out of doors, you would do well to bundle up."

The ladies thanked him most graciously for this intelligence, although they of course had planned in advance, down to the last detail, what they would be wearing. In fact, Sprague, the butler, waited discreetly next to the door, a footman at the ready next to him, their wraps already piled in his arms.

"I confess, I can hardly wait to see the Gardens. Honny has never allowed us to attend at night before, and I understand they shall be particularly fabulous tonight," said Justine with a smile. "I have even heard that the Regent may be there!"

"Well, let us not tarry, then," exclaimed Honoria. "Goodness. You know how he always creates a huge *crush* of carriages with that great entourage of his! Indeed, we may well have to turn around and come home without ever entering the Gardens at all. And what a shame that would be. Quite like the time we were absolutely unable to get into that ball at the Leopolds'—or was it the Jerseys'? I quite forget. At any rate, we waited for *at least* two hours in the carriage. Do you not recall, girls?" Without waiting for their nods she burbled on. "The horses practically dozed on their feet—and our gowns! Well, *they,* I must confess, were in a sad state. All creased and rumpled. *Entirely* ruined by sitting for so long, you must know! Well, what are we waiting for?'' She looked around at the assembled company as if they had kept her waiting. ''Sprague!''

''Madam.'' The butler stepped out and, taking the wraps from the footman, began to assist the ladies into them. Mr. Mannering instantly took Justine's from his hands and helped her on with it in what could only be considered a most gratifyingly proprietary manner. She dimpled up at him, and Addie saw a look of shared amusement at Honoria's prattle pass between them. It seemed somehow more intimate than any physical contact—a meeting of minds, and that stabbed at her a little. Chiding herself for what she could only consider her most unattractive burst of envy, she looked quickly at Fitzwilliam as he took Honoria's arm, but his gaze when it met hers was still bland, devoid of humor or any particular emotion except politeness. Alas, no meeting of minds there. She allowed herself a small sigh as Sprague helped her on with her own wrap.

The wrap, at least, was as glorious as she had remembered. Addie's clothing was always of the highest quality—Honoria, naturally, would allow nothing less. But rarely did she indulge in such elegance or luxury. The deep red velvet fell in a heavy drape, and the sapphire satin lining slipped over her dress with a whisper. She left the face-framing ermine-trimmed hood down for the moment—as Honoria had issued the firmest strictures about leaving it off to show her coiffure, regardless of the weather—but accepted from Sprague the matching ermine muff. Perhaps Justine and Honoria were in the right of it: clothes *could* make the woman, Addie thought, suddenly feeling uncommonly fine. Fitzwilliam's face, however, was still loweringly devoid of admiration as he ushered them out the door to his waiting barouche.

''What an elegant equipage, Fitzwilliam,'' commented Honoria, as they were settled into the luxuriously upholstered carriage bearing his crest, the ladies on one side and the gentlemen facing them.

The well-sprung vehicle started smoothly forward, and Fitzwilliam replied, equally smoothly, "It is only what is fitting for escorting three of the most elegant ladies of my acquaintance, Honoria."

Justine smiled prettily at what Addie could only judge to be a specious compliment, as she knew with certainty that she was anything but one of the most elegant ladies of his acquaintance. Her eyes narrowed a little at him.

Honoria, apparently oblivious to her niece's uncharitable thoughts, began an anecdote about how in 'seventy-one Marjorie Marston (daughter of the third son of Viscount Cranleigh) had criticized the ride in Edward Armistead's carriage and he, in return, had issued her the Cut Direct, and *who* would have thought that her son would eventually marry his daughter?

Addie stared out the window as they passed house after house ablaze with lights. She let her aunt's chatter wash over her as her glance strayed to Fitzwilliam, who showed no awareness whatsoever of her presence. He sat relaxed on the seat, his long legs sprawled out in front of him, giving every appearance of listening attentively to Honoria, smiling and responding at the appropriate places. But his eyes were flat, Addie noticed. No true spark of interest or appreciation reached them. His polite smile, a product only of the centuries of good manners that had been bred into him, no doubt masked intense boredom, both with the company and with the entire expedition, Addie was certain.

In truth, he was not so oblivious to her presence as Addie believed. Behind his bland facade, he was indeed aware of her, and had not missed her narrowed eyes at his facile words about the three most elegant ladies of his aquaintance. He hadn't meant them, and he knew she knew it. Which made him feel somehow . . . shabby.

At her reaction, he had recalled one reason he so assiduously avoided spending an excessive amount of time in Addie's company. It was her eyes. They were large and gray and fringed with long dark lashes. An extraordinary feature in an otherwise unexceptional face. They gave him the feeling that they saw things in him he would altogether rather they not. And he was uncomfortably aware of what he saw in that reflection. A man, he thought, with a sudden surge of guilt, could, for example, never be married to Addie and keep a *chère-amie* on the side.

He covertly examined her face as she gazed out the window. For some reason that he could not pinpoint, she did look uncommonly fine tonight. He took in the firm chin and her small, straight nose. Her lips were perhaps a little thin for true beauty, but beautifully shaped, and even with the wreath of silver flowers, her hair was styled extremely plainly with none of the ringlets and curls affected so fetchingly by her sister and indeed, most of the young women of his acquaintance. It looked good on her somehow, though. Justine was all softness and curls, a lovely girl. But Addie, with her air of calm and simplicity seemed, well, a woman, he thought with surprise. Not at all the child he had grown up with and was still accustomed to thinking her. Suddenly the odd notion came into his mind that the little diamond eardrops that had been his mother's favorites would suit her better than Bella's rejected ones. As he examined this idea, Addie, seemingly feeling his scrutiny, turned toward him.

He gave her a brief smile and she responded in kind.

Suddenly, the air-clearing chat he had so looked forward to seemed infinitely more complicated and much less appealing.

"Oh, my goodness, dears, we are arrived!" trilled Honoria as they approached the famous pleasure gardens. "And to think I have been chattering on the entire ride. How mortifying. Whatever must you young people think of me!"

"Nonsense, Honoria," Fitzwilliam assured her, collecting himself from his woolgathering, as the others chimed in their agreement. "We all enjoyed your story enormously. Why, the drive seemed to pass in a trice!" After which bouncer he deemed it much the best thing not to even look in Addie's direction.

* * *

"Oh, but *look*," breathed Justine as Mr. Mannering solicitously handed her down from the carriage.

The Gardens were indeed transformed. The trees, of course,
given the season, were barren of their leaves, but lanterns and
torches blazed, lighting the famed walkways. Bonfires burned.
In a large clearing, there was a dance floor. There was even
an orchestra. And everywhere there were people. Glittering,
richly dressed people in satins and wools and furs. Addie
hugged her cloak about her, glad once again for its opulence
and warmth, as she surveyed the scene. On the dance floor,
ladies and gentlemen moved gracefully. Waiters and footmen
dispensed cups of steaming mulled wine and plates of delicacies.

Despite the Gardens' slightly rakish reputation the faces
above the cloaks were the same faces that graced every ball
and amusement during the Season.

"It is almost as though Almack's were simply relocated out
of doors," Fitzwilliam said in dry tones as he returned Mrs.
Drummond Burrell's salute. "One would think the patronesses
should melt in horror at the thought of entering Vauxhall. But
all the tabbies are here."

Addie giggled. It was true. But still, somehow, the night felt
different. Magical. As if the possibilities were limitless.

"Would you ladies care to join the dancers?" asked Mr.
Mannering.

Justine smiled dreamily at him.

"Of course the girls would," Honoria replied. "For myself,
I plan to sit and have a nice comfortable, if chilly, coze with
Sally. But first, a word with you, Adelaide, if you would be
so good," she said in tones that brooked no cavil, as she took
her eldest niece's arm and drew her back a few paces from the
others.

"Honny, should we not—" began Addie.

"No!" Honoria replied without waiting for her to finish. "I
have every intention of allowing Justine and Mr. Mannering a

little freedom in which to get to know one another this evening. I am indeed convinced that he is an excellent match for her, but I want her to be certain.''

"But you always adhere to the strictest propriety,'' Addie objected.

Honny looked offended. "Well of course I do! But *that* is because the situation has always called for it before! Tonight is different. And you—''

"I intend to adhere to the strictest propriety.''

"I should expect nothing less, naturally. But do not play gooseberry to Justine.'' She looked around and pulled her own wrap a little closer. "There is something in the air tonight, you may depend on it.''

"This does seem somehow to be a magical place,'' agreed Addie.

"Then perhaps Fitzwilliam will finally do as he ought and propose,'' Honny said baldly. "You look very well, Addie. Despite the diamonds! One can only hope they have not given him a disgust of you. Now! Remember, no matter how cold you might get, do not, *under any circumstances,* put up your hood!''

Addie laughed, but without much mirth. "I understand many a gentleman has been put off from proposing to the love of his life by the sight of her in diamonds and a hood!''

Honny shot her a look. "Never mind your levity. Just be prepared for a proposal.''

"I do believe,'' Addie said, shaking her head, "that your imagination, or possibly the cold, has gotten the better of you, Honny. Surely it is clear even to a blind optimist such as yourself that the man is utterly indifferent to my existence.''

"Then, make him different,'' responded her aunt, waving gaily to her bosom bow, Emily Cowper.

"I hardly think different is the opposite of indifferent,'' began Addie, stopping to ponder that question, before she noticed that Honny had gone on ahead.

* * *

"Be a dear, Fitzwilliam," that lady was saying, when Addie caught up, "and procure some punch for my gels to keep them warm." At his nod of acquiescence, she paused to whisper to Justine not to put up her hood, before gliding off in Sally Jersey's direction and, Addie thought, abdicating her responsibilities entirely.

As Addie and Justine exchanged bemused glances at the vagaries of their aunt's behavior, Fitzwilliam, as ordered, hailed a passing waiter. He handed around the four glasses of steaming wine punch and they all stood in an awkward little group with no one speaking, Drew and Justine apparently being content to gaze besottedly at each other.

Across what passed for the dance floor, Fitzwilliam could see a merry throng of young bucks gathered. In their midst, was Bella Carstairs, attired in an amazingly transparent silver tissue gown. She was laughing and flirting with what looked like at least five admirers. Her long red hair was dressed in a froth of ringlets, and her ample curves offered the tantalizing threat that she might spill entirely out of the inadequate gown at any moment. *She must be freezing,* he thought with amusement. But freezing or not, she certainly was lovely. And, for the moment, anyway, she was his. He felt not even an iota of jealousy to see her cavorting with such an admiring audience. It was, indeed, the perfect relationship, he decided with satisfaction, catching her eye and throwing her a wink to let her know that he would visit her later that night. That, at least, would give him something to look forward to.

"May I beg the pleasure of the next dance, Miss Winstead?" Drew, apparently having gathered his wits, asked Justine with a slight bow.

Justine looked to Addie for permission in Honoria's absence. Addie smiled. "Of course. And very properly done, sir."

Drew smiled, and Addie decided that he really did have the most contagious grin.

Justine curtsied. "I should be honored, then."

"Excellent!" replied Drew, taking her still-full cup and placing in on a footman's tray, before leading her out, leaving Addie and Fitzwilliam alone.

Addie, in fact, had been following the direction of Fitzwilliam's gaze, and, having divined with some accuracy his thoughts, suddenly found herself feeling out of reason cross with her companion.

As though realizing that it was incumbent on him to play host, Fitzwilliam dragged his attention back and set himself to being attentive. "Are you feeling, shall we say, a trifle *de trop*," he asked, with his most charming smile.

Addie raised a brow. "Indeed," she replied, her accents chilly, and those eyes, to Fitzwilliam's way of thinking, accusing.

"I was *speaking*," he said, setting himself to charm, "of Drew and Justine."

"Of course."

"One has the feeling we could have both been struck down by fits of apoplexy under their noses and they would not have noticed."

At this, Addie laughed, thawing a little toward him, and some of the awkwardness seemed to evaporate. "In that case I fear as chaperons we should prove ourselves to be almost as woefully inadequate as my aunt has turned out to be, my lord."

"My lord?" He looked down at her, as she sipped her punch, cradling the cup in both hands for warmth. "I realize, Addie, that we have not seen a great deal of each other of late," he said, "but we have known each other all our lives. Please call me by my name, as you are accustomed to do. It makes me feel quite forbidding to be addressed otherwise by you."

"If you insist, Fitzwilliam."

"I do. I really do. In fact"—he smiled down at her again. Addie's breathing constricted a little, and the thaw was reluctantly completed. Really, it was most unfair of her father to have matched her with this man—"my name is John, and well you know it."

Indeed I do. John Henry Edmund Churchill Fitzwilliam,

Addie thought, but she said, only, "And it would give Honoria fits were she to hear that from my lips."

He grinned. "I suppose then that Fitzwilliam will have to do. But no Claremonts, my lords, or sirs, Addie," he said severely. "Do we understand one another?"

"We do," she said with a trace of a grin, and Fitzwilliam found himself intrigued by a small dimple in her right cheek.

He swallowed. "And speaking of Honoria," he said, forcing himself to look away from the dimple, "I doubt that she intends for us to dog Drew and Justine's every footstep. Your sister, I assure you, is well looked after. So what do you think, Addie? Will you do *me* the honor?"

"You are no doubt right about Honoria's intent, and dancing sounds like an exceedingly good idea, *Fitzwilliam,*" she replied with a ghost of a smile, handing her empty cup to a waiter and accepting Fitzwilliam's proffered arm.

Across the dance floor, Honoria listened idly to Sally Jersey's unfaltering burble of chatter—*really the woman talks entirely too much!*—while scanning the floor for her charges. Seeing both of them out there, executing the lively steps of a quadrille, she smiled.

"I'm sorry, Sally," she said, turning back to her companion. "What was that you said about Claremont's *mug* being *pinked* at Jackson's Rooms? Sally! I never thought I'd live to see the day that *you*, of all people, would be rattling on about *claret* flowing from gentlemen's *potato traps!* Really! It is quite as if all of London has gone mad!"

Chapter 7

When the dance had drawn to a close, Fitzwilliam again took Addie by the arm and escorted her to the side.

"One hardly notices the cold with such exertion. What a clever idea this Winter Festival is, to be sure," she said breathlessly, as, standing on tiptoe, she looked for Justine.

"There they are," said Fitzwilliam, who stood considerably taller, correctly surmising her glance around. "About to join the next set. A reel, I think. Do we join them and dance again, Addie? Or have some refreshment? Or perhaps stroll the Gardens?"

At his words, Addie realized with a little shock that Honoria was indeed correct. It might look like Almack's in the snow, but tonight the rules were completely different. Not only were Bella Carstairs, and surely others like her, clearly being accepted here, but gentlemen did not in the ordinary run of things lead young ladies out for two dances in a row. Nor did they offer to take them walking in darkened, secluded gardens. Such behavior would generally have sent tongues wagging, but tonight, no one seemed to care. Even the notoriously proper Mrs. Drummond Burrell was laughing aloud. And with quite unladylike abandon.

"A walk. Please," she replied. "Since you have assured me that Justine is in good hands, and I confess, I should love to see the rest of the grounds."

Fitzwilliam smiled at her, albeit with a sinking heart. A walk meant a tête-à-tête. Which meant he had absolutely no excuse for not telling her straight out that he had no intention of settling down to marriage in the near future. He had spoken cavalierly to Drew of his ability to do just that, but now that she had fallen so neatly in with his plans, he was feeling considerably less sanguine. Not that Addie would enact any tragedies—there was no question of that. But the idea that it might wound her feelings had taken hold, and he was finding himself strangely out of countenance at the thought.

"Then, walk we shall," he said, offering his arm with a little sigh at how disturbed he felt.

Addie, who had sized up his reluctance, heard his sigh and surmised that he was desirous of being out of her company. "Actually, Fitzwilliam," she said, stopping and letting go of his arm, "I have just remembered that I have something I really should discuss with Honny and Lady Jersey. If you would be so good as to escort me to them?"

He looked at her. "You would deprive me of your company, Addie?" he asked, realizing with surprise that loath as he was to break his news, he was oddly reluctant to give her up. *You cannot have it both ways,* he scolded himself, then said, "I was looking forward to a stroll of the grounds. And surely this night feels too extraordinary to fill with Sally's prattle?"

Addie stood looking up at him for a moment, completely confused. She could have sworn that he was impatient to be rid of her, yet now he seemed reluctant to seize his chance. She nodded. "Indeed it is," she said, and then added in an undertone, with a little sideways glance that made him laugh, "but then, so are most."

Still laughing, he took her arm again and tucked her hand beneath it, saying, "Careful, Addie, you shall lose your vouchers! No more stale cakes. No more insipid lemonade. No more gangly green youths stepping on your hems!"

"To think! Perhaps I should say it more loudly," she responded, which made him laugh harder.

"If it succeeds, I shall have to say it, too! Come then, let us walk. And, please, no more talk of Almack's."

And so, they meandered side by side down the spacious Grand Cross Walk in what felt to both of them a surprisingly companionable state. Addie made polite conversation about the beauty of the grounds, and Fitzwilliam, in his turn, brought up the unusual coldness of the winter. They passed other couples similarly engaged and, here and there, little groups of revelers.

Addie looked up at Fitzwilliam's almost heartbreakingly handsome profile beside her and felt a little smile tug at her mouth. "Your left eye appears a little swollen, Fitzwilliam. Is something amiss?" she could not resist querying in her most dulcet tones.

He looked down sharply, and was surprised to see an expression of barely restrained laughter in her eyes. "Just a trifle," he replied, his hand straying to his eye almost of its own accord—he could have sworn it was healed enough to be all but invisible. "I had an, er, a blacked eye," he explained.

"However did you come by such an injury?" She was all polite concern, but still Fitzwilliam could have sworn her expression held a trace of mockery.

Was it possible that serious, ladylike Addie Winstead read that dratted fellow's boxing column? With the exception of John Jackson—and the bedamned *Anonymous*, he reminded himself—her father had possessed a higher degree of knowledge about the sport than any other man he had ever known. Still, it was most unlikely, he decided. "Er, a foolish accident," he lied. "Indeed it is very nearly healed altogether."

"Ah, foolish accidents can be the very devil, can they not? How fortunate that it is so very nearly healed!"

He glanced at her again, but her expression was quite serious. He must have imagined her undertone, but still, somehow he couldn't shake the unsettling idea that she had been having a quiet laugh at his expense. For some reason, the thought of her doing something so out of character and downright frivolous as reading the boxing column amused him. They had reached the point where the wide, well-lit Grand Cross Walk intersected with the much less acceptable Dark Walk, and he turned toward her. "Do you care to walk more?" he asked as they stood.

"I should love to," she replied with such enthusiasm that he laughed and forgot his suspicions as he led her to the new path.

It was considerably more secluded than the one they had been on previously, and Fitzwilliam was willing to bet that Addie had no idea it was commonly referred to as Lovers' Walk. There were numerous spots along it that he had reason to know were perfect venues for private conversation. The thought of which put him in mind of other activities, of a considerably less conversational nature, he had conducted there once or twice. *Goodness knows,* he thought, *I should be in a tearing hurry to have done with this entire business so I can go see Bella.* Indeed, the thought of her working her expert skills on him in that soft, perfumed bed should have had him escorting the ladies back to Curzon Street at the first possible moment, but he found himself curiously unwilling to bring things to a close. *I am becoming a coward,* he scolded himself.

But to Addie he only said, "Are you not cold? Drew was right. It truly is bone chilling tonight."

Addie was wondering where they were headed and exactly what his motivation for this private little stroll was. She sincerely doubted it was a fierce desire for her company. But all the same her heart thumped painfully. *It is all Honoria's fault,* she decided, *if I am having fanciful notions.* "Not particularly," she said as she smiled up at him. "As I said, the exercise of the dancing and now the walking have left me quite warm. Although, I must confess—despite my conviction that it is less than ladylike to complain of such things—my ears *do* feel as if they are about to freeze off my head!"

He stopped and faced her. There was no getting around it, she *did* look somehow different tonight. Or maybe he was just seeing her differently. He saw no trace of the decorous, ladylike little mouse he had described to Drew. Her cheeks were flushed from the bite of the night air and the dancing, and her eyes once again held what he could have sworn was an almost wicked sparkle instead of their usual demure look. Her hair, with the wreath of silver flowers twined in it, was gently falling out of its knot. And her lips, although they, like everything about her, were thinner and somehow more graceful than Bella's, were an appealing rosy color. For a mad instant, he found himself wondering if they would taste of the spiced wine she had drunk. He swallowed, and said lightly, with a smile, "If your ears are cold, Addie, you should put up your hood. Surely, charming though it is, it cannot be merely decorative?"

She replied with a laugh, "Of course it is not. Aunt Honoria, however, warned me in no uncertain terms that it is more than my life is worth to put it up, as it will serve to disarrange my coiffure."

By what seemed mutual accord, they resumed walking.

Fitzwilliam refrained from telling her that if her advice was on his account, Honoria had misjudged male tastes—or his, at least. He much preferred this somehow looser, softer Addie. Which might, in fact, account in some part for his sudden desire to keep her in his company. He was poignantly reminded tonight of the times they had spent together as children. And the memory—so far from anything in his life now—was somehow . . . *relaxing,* he thought with surprise.

"Well, goodness knows there is no need to stand on ceremony with me, Addie," he said with a grin. "I've seen you in much worse states when we were children! If Honoria gives you trouble I shall simply tell her about all the torn petticoats and skinned knees I have witnessed."

"The very thought would send her to bed with the vapors. For days. So, indeed, Fitzwilliam, I must beg that you refrain! Besides," she continued, "it is monstrous ungentlemanly of you to remind me!"

He laughed. "But are they not good memories, Addie? In fact, sometimes it is hard to believe that we are all grown up and become so very proper."

And distant, she wanted to say, but did not, saying instead, "Even Justine is a woman grown now."

He wondered, glancing at her, if she had deliberately given him an opportunity. "Indeed. And a very lovely one. Drew, you must know, has fallen head over ears for her," he ventured.

"And she for him," Addie responded with a little smile, as they walked down the narrowing path. "We all think he seems an exceptional young man."

"Oh, he is. He is amiable and constant and good-hearted," Fitzwilliam replied with sincerity. "He would very much like the chance to make Justine happy," he said quietly.

"Then, I shall be happy for her," Addie responded with equal sincerity.

"I know it seems precipitous, but he has been in, and equally quickly, out of love with enough regularity these past several years that I have complete faith in his ability to recognize the true thing," Fitzwilliam said on a laugh. He looked down intently to see if he could read anything of Addie's thoughts.

But her face was too shadowed for him to see, as she replied lightly, "Oh, dear. Then they *are* well suited it seems. Justine, you know, has lost her heart at least a dozen times this past year, none of them lasting more than three days. Her infatuation with Mr. Mannering is something of a record, actually, having survived two sennights." They had reached the clearing where a little stone bench sat. Addie stopped walking, and they once again stood facing each other. She continued, saying bluntly, "We have no objection to Justine wedding before me, you know, Fitzwilliam, as long as it is indeed the true thing. Honoria would be thrilled to receive him—even she no longer clings to so strict and outmoded a notion of propriety that the oldest must wed first. So I beg you will tell Mr. Mannering that he is welcome, if that is what you are wondering." Her tone was matter-of-fact, but her expression was still unreadable.

"Thank you. I only hope I can convince him to wait a respectable amount of time before paying his addresses. I give you fair warning that having opened that door you will be fortunate if he does not come belting over before the dawn and throwing himself on bended knee. It has been his fondest hope that she might return his regard,'' he replied, knowing Addie had provided him his opening but reluctant to take it. This new and surprising ease between them should have made his task easier. But somehow, combined with his odd notion of a few moments ago to kiss her, it only served to make it harder.

''I can assure you that he needs have no fear in that regard.''

Fitzwilliam smiled briefly. ''I will tell him, then, and try to convince him that it would at least be proper to wait until after breakfast to call on Honoria. Drew, you should know, does have a penchant for showing up at the breakfast table and eating his way through one's kitchen.'' Addie laughed, as he had intended her to, and Fitzwilliam continued. ''I know it is not considered the thing to speak of such matters, but he cannot offer much in the way of a settlement.''

''We had assumed as much,'' Addie replied calmly, hoping her sinking heart was not visible.

''She can still accept him, then? Even if—''

Smiling as brightly as she was able, Addie cut him off before he had a chance to articulate anything that could only embarrass them both. ''We go on quite comfortably,'' she lied, knowing as she did that she was forfeiting her opportunity to tell him the truth.

''Truly?''

''Truly.''

He took a breath. ''Addie, I-I . . .'' he began.

She looked up at him, quietly. Waiting. Could Honny have been right?

''I, er, think you should know, ah . . .''

She had to fight the urge to prompt him. Help him over his difficulty. She took a breath and schooled herself to impassivity. Polite interest. And an instant later was glad that she had.

''That I've no intention of settling down anytime soon,'' he blurted out. ''So, please, feel free to accept another offer.'' *Damn!* Had those odious-sounding words truly come out of his mouth? He, with his legendary silver tongue, had made a worse hash out of this business than even Drew could have imagined.

But Addie, despite the blood pounding in her ears, had prepared herself too well for this moment to show her chagrin. "Thank you, Fitzwilliam. I will," was all she said on the topic. "Shall we walk some more?"

He breathed with relief as he nodded. "But first, Addie, I really must insist that you put up your hood," he said softly, guilt roiling though him in wake of the relief. "It is freezing and there is no one about to see you except me."

She smiled, fighting the impulse to ask who else could possibly be important. "You are bareheaded," she pointed out.

"I am a man," he said simply. "You are a woman, and as such are a frail and delicate creature."

They both laughed at this. "Stuff," she replied. "I am every bit as sturdy as you, and well you know it, Fitzwilliam." *Sturdier, in fact,* she thought, *because I have just been delivered a body blow and am still able to stand here smiling and bantering.*

"Humor me, then," he replied.

"Very well." She was about to take her hands out of her muff to pull up the hood, but his hands went to her arms, stilling them.

"Let me," he said softly, still holding her arms. "You keep your hands warm."

Addie's heart lurched. She stood, looking up at him in the moonlight, not at all certain what was going on. Fitzwilliam had just made it clear in no uncertain terms how vastly relieved he would be if she were to bracket herself to someone else and release him, and now he was . . . He was what exactly?

He removed his hands from her arms and very gently put up her hood, pulling it around her face. Addie's eyes, he thought, looked almost silver in the glow of the luminous full moon. Again he was possessed of the incredible notion to taste her lips, but this time it was even stronger. In all the years he had known her, he had never before been subject to even the slightest inclination to kiss Addie Winstead. And making it even more scandalous was the fact that she had just pleasantly agreed to release him from any obligation toward her. *It must be the air. There is something in the air,* he thought wildly, in the second before he bent his head and brushed his lips chastely across hers.

Addie gasped. Whether in surprise or horror, Fitzwilliam could not have said. He was about to release her, when her lips moved tentatively under his.

It may have been an innocent kiss, but to Addie, it felt electric. Her heart raced and her blood surged.

Fitzwilliam's hands still gently held her hood on either side of her face. He raised his head and looked down into her eyes. What she expected to see in his, she was not sure. Mockery. Or regret, perhaps. But what she did see was surprise.

"Addie—" he began, ready to embark on an apology. Then he stopped. "I have known you nearly all my life, but have I ever really looked at your eyes, thought about them, before tonight?" he heard himself asking.

It was an effort to catch her breath to speak. Actually, she was surprised that her knees hadn't given way entirely. "I don't know, Fitzwilliam, have you?" she returned softly.

"I'm not sure," he admitted, still looking into them. "But I am now."

She smiled her sweet smile, and it seemed to reach and warm some mysterious part of him. Still not letting go of her hood where he held it under her chin, he pulled her down on the little stone bench. *This is reckless and foolish and dangerous and ruinous and heartless.* And *this bench is cold,* he told himself sternly, waiting for her to voice proper objection or his common sense to reassert itself. But she remained quiet, and common sense had clearly deserted him altogether. Somehow, all he could think about was tasting her lips more deeply. He released her hood and slid his hands onto the satin skin of her face beneath it. He moved his lips against hers again, ever so gently. They felt warm and pliable. Her mouth, as he had guessed it would, tasted sweet and a little spicy from the punch. He tentatively ran the tip of his tongue along her top lip. She drew in a sharp breath at the sensation. He pulled her closer against his chest and slanted his firm lips over hers in earnest.

An explosion seemed to rock them both, and they pulled apart to look at each other in amazement. Realizing simultaneously that it was the celebrated Vauxhall fireworks being launched, they began to laugh.

Fitzwilliam sobered first, and began to kiss her again. He feathered gentle kisses against her lips, and when she made a little noise, opened his lips against hers. She followed his lead, and for a moment, he was completely lost in the taste and feel of her. The only thought in his head was that he did not want to stop.

Addie, for her part, too, felt as if she never wanted the moment to end. Being kissed by Fitzwilliam was far and away more wonderful than she had ever even imagined. And, if she were to be strictly honest with herself, she had certainly imagined it. The fantasy had been nice. But the reality was something entirely different. It was spice and heat and electricity coursing to her very fingertips. It was . . . well, what, exactly? She was suddenly intensely aware of the sensuous feel of the cool air on her burning face and the satin lining of her cloak where it brushed her skin. *No wonder,* she thought fuzzily, *he can command any woman in London, if he can do this with a mere kiss.* And then, shamefully, an image of how Fitzwilliam had looked, stripped to the waist at Jackson's, drifted through her mind. And she shivered. For reasons having nothing at all to do with the cold.

He kissed her again and Addie began to think she might simply melt into a pool of liquid sensation.

Fitzwilliam felt no desire to take things further. On this very bench at other times, with other women, he had been in a tearing hurry to move matters along. For some reason, now, with Addie, he felt he could be content to sit and kiss her for hours. She felt so sweet. Unexpected. Like something to be savored. He murmured a sigh of pleasure, and she felt the electricity igniting into a shower of sparks.

Engaged as they were, neither of them noticed the sound of nearing footsteps until the other couple was almost upon them.

* * *

"Here, my little love," came a slurred voice. "If I remember properly there sh-sh-should," it hiccuped, getting the words correct at last, "be a little shtone—I mean stone—bench where you can give me a sample of your favors."

Addie and Fitzwilliam sprang apart just as a staggering Raymond Walters and a woman of obviously easy virtue, entered the clearing.

"Fitshwullium. Er, Claremont. Sh-shorry old man," slurred Walters, letting go of his companion's hand and lurching toward the stricken couple on the bench. "Din't know you were here firsht. Obviously. Or never would have been so gauche as to interrupt. But per-perhapsh the *ladies* know each other?" He giggled. Before Fitzwilliam had a chance to respond, Walters turned to the woman with him and drew her forward. "Shorry, love. Forget your name, et cetera. Be a shweet-be a, er, introduce yourself."

The little improbable blond, shivering in a flimsy gown, made a slight curtsy. "Oi don't believe we've 'ad the pleasure," she said with a saucy smile in Fitzwilliam's direction. "But Oi know who you are. Oo doesn't? Orelia Azure. At your service, my lord." She giggled.

Addie's heart, which had hammered so delightfully but a few moments ago, now tripped in terror. *This is the second time,* she thought with some annoyance, *that Raymond Walters is responsible for scaring and insulting me beyond any decency.* She was too outraged and upset even to find amusement in his companion's wildly improbable name.

"Well, love," Raymond said, turning to Addie. "Don't be shy. No need for that. Tell the lovely Or-Orel-er, girl, your name." When Addie stood silent, he turned to Fitzwilliam. "Yoursh ish a shy little thing, Claremont. Shomething to be shaid for that, though. Far cry from your Bella, eh? Looks to be a del-del a de-lec-ta-ble"—he grinned in triumph at having articulated the word—"armful, Bella, but prefer the quiet type m'self. P'raps we should trade—Hey!" He broke off and stared at Addie, her face framed by her hood, whose heart sank. ''I know you! Just din't recognishe you in your finery, what hey? So you found yourshelf a protector after all. And a top-o-the-trees one. At that! By Jove, that was quick. Told you we'd meet again. Knew you wash too fine to be a sherv—a shervant!'' he finished triumphantly, with a gigantic hiccup.

''I can only assume you mistake yourself, Walters,'' Fitzwilliam drawled lightly, stepping between Addie and Raymond Walters.

''No mistake. May be in my cups, but not so cast away that I don't recognize 'er.''

Fitzwilliam heard his voice say, coolly, ''Well, then, you insult my future wife, Mr. Walters. Addie, you apparently are unacquainted with Mr. Walters? Raymond Walters, *Miss* Adelaide Winstead. I'd suggest, Walters, that you apologize to the lady.''

Raymond Walters, who was too cupshot to recognize the deadly light behind Fitzwilliam's calm demeanor, laughed. ''Apologize? Lady? Not too bloody likely. That ain't your fiancée, Claremont. That's a doxy. Tried to solicit my cushtom the other morning, in fact,'' he said, embroidering considerably on the circumstances.

Addie gasped, and Fitzwilliam put her more firmly behind him.

''Consider yourself fortunate, Walters,'' he said, ''that since I am reluctant to sully the lady further by keeping her in your company so much as a moment longer, I won't take the time to kill you now.'' In a swift movement, he reached out his free hand and grabbed Raymond Walters by his ridiculous cravat. His tone was still conversational as he said, ''Rest assured, that is the only reason. And should you so much as *mention* Miss Winstead's name in connection with this evening—''

Orelia uttered an excited little shriek at the prospect of bloodshed.

Fitzwilliam ignored it. ''You shall answer to me.'' He let go of Walters, and the fellow reeled back and fell heavily on the ground.

"Hey!" he yelped, staggering up, rubbing his seat. "You have insulted *me* now, Claremont, and *you* shall answer to *me* for that!"

"Not afraid to meet me, Walters?" Fitzwilliam asked.

"Not a bit."

"Send your second to call on me in the morning, then." Fitzwilliam's words seemed to hang frozen in the clear air.

"By rights you name the weapons," Raymond Walters replied, sounding considerably sobered now.

"By rights I do. But do you know, Walters, I can't think of a single one that's not too good to waste on the likes of you. I bid you good evening. Come, Addie." And with that, he took Addie by the arm and led her away, not sparing a backward glance.

Raymond Walters stood, gaping disbelievingly at their backs.

Chapter 8

The walk back was accomplished in a fraction of the time that the walk there had taken. There was no companionable meandering this time. No dallying. No conversation, even. Fitzwilliam marched along furiously, wordless. And Addie gamely kept pace. And held her peace.

As they approached the dancers, they could hear the strains of the orchestra. He stopped suddenly and faced her, his abrupt halt almost sending her sprawling. He steadied her with his hand. "Addie . . ." he began, not letting go of her arm.

"It's not necessary," she interrupted, withdrawing her arm and trying to catch her breath. "Truly, I am greatly appreciative of your protection of my name, Fitzwilliam. But I am well convinced that Mr. Walters was so far in his altitudes that he not only had no idea what he was saying, but will have forgotten the entire incident by morning! So let us do the same." She only wished she felt as confident as her words. Something told her that Raymond Walters was not a man to let such a thing slide.

Fitzwilliam looked down at her. How was it that everything about Addie was surprising him tonight? Would he ever understand this woman? Or for that matter, himself? She had every right to expect him to wed her as he had given his word to her dying father he would. And tonight he had all but told her that he had little intention of honoring that promise. And then he had kissed her. And she had kissed him back. And before either of them had been able to examine their reaction to those kisses, they had been thrust into a position that would have had any other woman of his acquaintance hauling him to the altar in no time.

But here she was, again, offering to release him. Was it possible that she did not even *want* to marry him? That she would be as relieved as he to be free of their fathers' agreement? He looked into her eyes, searching for a clue. But for once they told him nothing. He wished he were less a gentleman. That he could take her at her word. Instead, he suggested, "Let us say no more for tonight. I will take you home and come to call tomorrow."

She forced a smile. "That sounds by far the most sensible approach."

He knew he should apologize for kissing her. For propelling them both into a compromising situation. But somehow, he couldn't bring himself to utter the words. Even now, even given the outcome, he was not convinced entirely that it had been a mistake. He wasn't sure that he had ever experienced a moment so sweet. But what about Addie? Had she felt it? He forced an answering smile. "Indeed," he said. "Most females would be completely overset by what happened, Addie. It is all things fortunate you are so sensible."

She turned away so he wouldn't see her flush. Sensible! Why did it sound so insulting? "I am rarely overset, Fitzwilliam."

He smiled again. "I know that." On impulse, he tilted her chin up with his hand so that her gaze was forced to meet his. And then, inexplicably, he bent and brushed his lips lightly against hers. "Don't worry, Addie, this will come right," he whispered, wishing as he did that he could believe it.

She smiled tightly in response, willing nothing of her bafflement to show. *What is he doing?* "I am sure you're right.

Where have Justine and Mr. Mannering got to, do you think?''
she asked, firmly changing the subject.

On the trip home, the other three chatted merrily. ''What
great fun! I vow I am almost completely frozen. Where were
you?'' demanded Justine of Addie. ''We went looking for you,
to tell you the famous news, but honestly, could see no sign
of you anywhere.''

''What news?'' Addie asked.

''It is the most amazing thing!'' Honoria exclaimed, her gaze
pointedly fixed on Addie's face, her words hanging heavy with
meaning. *''The Thames has frozen over!''*

Fitzwilliam choked, Mr. Mannering seemed to be laughing
as he hammered him on the back. And Addie, Justine noticed,
had gone quite pale. Honoria continued. ''Sally was saying that
they are planning a great frost fair on the frozen river! Just
think of the fun!''

And she continued to talk gaily of the upcoming festivities
with Justine and Mr. Mannering for the rest of the ride back
to Curzon Street, which was a good thing as both Addie and
Fitzwilliam seemed to have lost all inclination to join the
chatter.

Chapter 9

When the ladies had received safe escort into the house and the gentleman had taken their leave, Honoria asked if either of the girls wanted to join her for a cup tea and a coze. Justine, who felt too overexcited to sleep, said that she would love to. And they both, clearly, fully expected Addie to do the same.

But for once she could not care what was expected of her. No sooner were they fully in the house, but she was already practically up the stairs, from which position, she turned and said that she was, in fact, vastly, enormously tired from the evening. Leaving her glorious wrap in a puddle on the stairs halfway up and ignoring their surprised faces, she all but fled to her room—to try to make some sense out of what was surely the most confusing night of her entire existence.

Those wondrous kisses and the memory of the way Fitzwilliam had looked at her, with the appreciation of a man looking at a woman—as she had thought only tonight, he never would— ran endlessly, confusingly through her mind. Followed, less felicitously, by what could only be termed the evening's disastrous conclusion.

* * *

Fitzwilliam and Mr. Mannering sat facing each other in the carriage.

"Well?" asked Drew.

Fitzwilliam leaned back against the squabs and crossed one leg negligently over the other, but brushed at his immaculate sleeve in a distracted manner. "They will be happy to receive you, Drew. Although, I did promise, not rashly I trust, that you would wait until tomorrow. And after breakfast, too."

Drew's entire countenance lit up. "Thank you," he said, simply.

"You are most welcome. I think you can be certain that you will be happily accepted."

"And you? How did you fare in your, er, talk with Addie?"

Fitzwilliam pressed the heel of his hand to his left eye to try to stop the throbbing. He wished heartily that he had ridden. A good bruising, mind-clearing gallop was exactly what he needed. "Suffice it to say that I made the most complete mull of it that I've ever made of anything," he admitted.

Drew raised a brow in question. "Addie did not seem particularly overset."

"No," Fitzwilliam said, slowly. "But by rights she should be. The Thames, you know, has frozen over, Drew."

"So, I've heard. Honoria Winstead, in fact, seemed out of reason excited about it."

Fitzwilliam nodded. "And I just may be trapped in the ice," he said gloomily, and decided that since a ride was out of the question, perhaps a good bruising, mind-clearing visit to Bella was in order.

Chapter 10

Apparently not, he thought, much later, as he lay among the warm, scented pillows of her bed. Bella slept beside him, a softly scented pile of luscious curves, barely, but enticingly, concealed by a few scraps of silk. Most nights, at this point, he would have been sleeping a sated, contented sleep. But tonight he was anything but sated and contented. The room felt hot and overly perfumed. His mind felt restless and edgy. And his body felt, well . . . *uninterested*, he decided, was the word. He had assumed that a visit to Bella would exorcise the lingering memories of Addie's sweet response, but to that end, he had been markedly unsuccessful. He had never thought to see the day when they would spend a chaste evening together. But this night, after all, had been comprised of one surprise after another, start to finish.

Piling up more pillows and rolling onto his back, he folded his hands under his head and stared at the ceiling. Why had he told Raymond Walters that Addie was his future wife? If ever there was a case of a man digging his own grave, this was it. But he had no answer for his own behavior. There were probably a dozen other ways he could have told the drunken lout to mind his own business. It was not as though anyone in the polite world would accept Raymond Walters's word over his own. But now, unless he missed his guess, word of this disaster would be all over London by Wednesday. At the very latest. And goodness knew he'd have no choice but to wed her then. In truth, he conceded, if he was to be brutally honest, he had no choice now.

But Addie's sweetly responsive kisses had roused an unexpectedly tender, almost primitive, protectiveness in him. And he had been consumed by a white heat of fury at such insult to her, that those words had simply come tumbling out before he'd had a chance to think. And why ever had he suddenly, after all these years, been moved to kiss Addie Winstead, anyway?

"Not sleeping, Fitz?" Bella's husky voice interrupted his thoughts, as she stretched lazily and, rolling to face him, twined her arms about his neck. "Perhaps, I need to tire you after all," she purred, a hand caressing his chest.

He somehow felt guilty. He hadn't told her anything about his evening's misadventure. And as an engaged man, he had no place here. *But I am* not *engaged,* he reminded himself. *And giving up the freedom to be here, or wherever I desire, is exactly the reason I am not.* He immediately shored up his resolve to set Addie straight on that score as soon as possible tomorrow, and to revel in his freedom for what was left of the night.

"Fitz? Where are you tonight? Did you hear me?"

He smiled lightly, and said, "I did, and I am right here. Thank you, Bella, but no. I think I am tired enough." *That* was certainly not what he had intended to say to her offer, he thought, with a frown.

She pouted a little. "Are you certain?"

"I am," he said gently. "In fact, what I think I most need is a walk." He leaned over and kissed her on the forehead as he made to get out of the bed.

"You are not staying?"

He paused in pulling on his clothes. "Not tonight, Bella. I need some air."

She frowned. "You are tiring of me?"

Fitzwilliam laughed. "As if any man could ever tire of you!" he said, as, fully dressed, he walked back over to the bed. Before she had time to speak further, he dropped another quick kiss, this time on her cheek, and was gone.

Chapter 11

Drew was chuckling to himself the next morning when he made his appearance in Fitzwilliam's breakfast room.

Fitzwilliam was again lost in contemplation of his own odd behavior the previous night. Kissing Addie Winstead on a bench in Vauxhall Gardens. Agreeing to meet Raymond Walters. Declining to bed his own mistress. Really, there seemed no end to the list of oddities. He shook his head and decided to leave off trying to solve that puzzle.

If nothing else, he was at least clearheaded enough in the bright light of morning to realize that he must immediately disabuse Addie of any notion she might have of taking his words of last night to heart. All he need do now was terrify Walters into silence on the cause of their disagreement, which, if he could find the fellow before he had drunk his way through a case of blue ruin, oughtn't be too difficult. And if he felt perhaps a twinge of guilt at the memory of the innocent passion of Addie's kiss, well, he would just have to live with it, since he was once again firm in his resolve to maintain his freedom.

Which pleasingly levelheaded thoughts were followed by the idea that it might be nice to bring Addie a gift. Only, of course, to soften the blow of what he had to say to her. Perhaps something from Messieurs Rundell and Bridge . . . or perhaps those earrings of his mother's—the little diamond drops? He frowned.

Thus, at this point in his musings, the interruption of Drew's entrance was not entirely unwelcome.

"And exactly what is so amusing this morning?" he inquired, eyeing his friend. "I am glad to see that you brought your own *Post*, so you shan't try to usurp mine for once," he added.

"If you weren't still too much on your high ropes to read the boxing column, you would already know what was so amusing," replied Drew equably, as usual.

"I know I have asked this before, but do they, or do they not, serve breakfast at *your* house?"

"Indeed they do. But somehow without the panache that they manage here. And, of course, without your sunny company."

Fitzwilliam smiled. "Since you are determined to run tame in my household, I assume you've seen fit to apprise my staff of your peckish presence?"

Drew nodded. "Saw Simms as I came in. Excellent man, Simms."

"I am gratified that you approve of my choice in staffing. Or, rather, that Simms has chosen me, since that is much closer to the truth. But earn your keep, Drew, by telling me which unfortunate makes an appearance in the boxing column."

"Sandringham. He took on Jackson!"

Fitzwilliam's eyebrows went up. "Jackson? Not as a lesson, but sparring?"

Drew nodded.

"How did he fare?"

"Evinced great game. A glutton of the first mold, apparently."

"What does he say about it?" asked Fitzwilliam, interested despite himself.

"Jackson, as always, was elegant and easy. As usual, it was not possible to hit him while he stood on the defensive. But Sandringham proved himself a perfect trump. Rallying with good spirit. Pluck not taken out of him to the end. But then you *could* read your own paper,'' Drew suggested. ''Certainly for the more amusing bits, the one about about Sandringham bolting out of the Westhavens' ballroom at the thought of a second dance with a certain Miss L. H., quicker than he flinched in the ring from any of Jackson's best. For example.''

''And *you* could eat at your own house. For example''

''Ah, but we've covered that,'' Drew said, looking up as Simms entered, bearing his breakfast. ''Thank you, Simms.''

''So we have,'' replied Fitzwilliam, sounding not unlike a stubborn schoolboy. ''And as I am refusing to read the evil fellow's column altogether, you shall just have to tell me what I need to know to go about in good society these days.''

''Can I not eat first? A man has to keep up his strength, you know.''

''I would expect nothing less.''

''Thank you,'' replied Drew with as much dignity as he could muster, since his mouth was full. He studied Fitzwilliam's face. ''We *did* look for you last night, you know. And I, for one, am fairly certain you were not anywhere near the dance floor. Where were you? And what did you mean anyway that you had made a mull of things? That the Thames had frozen and you were caught in the ice? What did you say to Addie? How did she take it?''

He looked set to continue with more questions, but Fitzwilliam held up his hand, stemming the tide. ''One at a time, Drew. We went for a walk—Now what?'' he exclaimed, cutting off his explanation as Simms entered the room.

''There is a gentleman come to call, sir. A Mr. Thomas Edgerton,'' Simms replied, a certain stiffness to his tone. ''I did not like to disturb you at your meal, but he says it is most urgent that he speak with you.''

''Of course, Simms. Sorry. I suppose you must send the blasted fellow in.''

''Edgerton? Here? What—'' Drew began.

But Fitzwilliam cut him off. ''Hold your questions, Drew, and in a moment much will be answered.''

" 'Morning, Claremont. 'Morning, Mannering," Tom Edgerton said in a pleasant enough manner, when he was shown in and had made his bows.

" 'Morning," said Drew.

Fitzwilliam nodded a greeting. "Coffee?" he asked.

The recent arrival hovered nervously near the door. "Er, no, thank you, my lord, er, Claremont. I, ah—"

"Relax, Edgerton," said Fitzwilliam. "Sit. I know why you're here, and I assure you that I hold no ill feeling toward you. And, please, call me Fitzwilliam. Everyone does."

"Thanks," said the young man, visibly relaxing, but still running a nervous finger around his too-high collar as he crossed the room and took a chair. "P'raps I will have some coffee, after all. Not eager to be here like this, y'know, Clar—er, Fitzwilliam. Seems a dashed rackety business."

"I could not agree more," replied Fitzwilliam, as Drew looked from one to the other with curiosity. "But that is what you get into when you keep rackety company, Edgerton. May I assume you're not here to conciliate, which *is* a second's first obligation, is it not?"

"No, er, yes. That is, it is, but I'm not." He shrugged. "Ray won't have it."

"I'd thought not. What is it to be, then? Swords? Pistols?"

"Er—" began Edgerton.

"You're going to *duel?*" interrupted Drew, his disbelief apparent on his face.

"Hush, Drew." Fitzwilliam leaned forward across the table. "What's it to be, Edgerton?" he repeated.

"But *who? Why?*" burst out Drew, quite unable to contain the questions any longer.

"For goodness' sake, at least allow me to find out *how,* Drew. Rest easy that you will soon know all. Go ahead, Edgerton."

"Raymond, you see, well, he, er, prefers, uh—"

"Yes?" Fitzwilliam prompted in a tone that was beginning to sound impatient.

"To . . . er, to settle your differences in the ring," Edgerton blurted out, as if he were afraid that if he paused again he would lose his nerve altogether.

Fitzwilliam's eyebrows went up. "Boxing?"

"Raymond Walters!" uttered Drew, having figured out the opponent. "But why?"

Edgerton studied the blue-and-gold pattern on the Sèvres cup in his hand with excessive interest. "Boxing," he confirmed in an embarrassed mumble.

Fitzwilliam hoped no trace of his chagrin was visible as he forced his voice to be brisk. "Bit unusual, I suppose, but fair enough. When?" Not taking his gaze from Edgerton, he said, "Do you second me, Drew?"

"Of course."

"Saturday. One month."

Drew nodded. "Where?"

"Jackson's Rooms."

"I shall look forward to it," Fitzwilliam lied.

"Good. Well, glad that's settled." Edgerton put down his cup and rose, giving off a palpable sense of relief. "Again, sorry I had to, old man."

"I understand entirely," Fitzwilliam assured him.

"Well, I bid you good day, then," he said, as he all but scuttled from the room.

No sooner had the fellow cleared the room, than Drew turned on his friend. "What the deuce is going on? You are meeting Raymond Walters in the *ring,* of all places? What on earth for? Answer me, Fitz."

"Give me a chance, would you, Drew? I am meeting Raymond Walters because he took offense when I knocked him down because *I* had taken offense when *he* implied that Addie was a lightskirt."

"Addie *Winstead?*" Drew asked in apparent disbelief. "A *lightskirt?* What on earth? . . ."

"We had gone for a walk, you see," Fitzwilliam explained.

"I **had m**ade your case and so cowhandedly laid my cards on the table."

Drew leaned back in his chair, positively radiating happiness. "Thank you again," he said simply.

"It gave me great pleasure," replied Fitzwilliam with a sincerity that would have surprised many.

"But back to you and Raymond Walters," Drew prompted.

"Right. Well we somehow ended up kissing—"

"Pardon?"

"—on a bench—"

"You were *kissing Raymond Walters on a bench?*" Drew's expression was incredulous.

"Addie. I was kissing Addie." Fitzwilliam leveled a disgusted look at his friend. "Honestly! I begin to think love has addled your brain, Drew."

Drew magnanimously chose to ignore the slight. He continued, his expression only slightly less incredulous than it had been when he'd thought Fitzwilliam had been kissing Raymond Walters. *"You* were kissing *Addie Winstead? On a bench?"*

"Yes. And stop goggling at me, Drew! That was what we were doing when the odious, and incidentally, extremely foxed, Raymond Walters came upon us and implied she was a woman of easy virtue. And now," he said, looking up, "I am not entirely certain, but we may be engaged."

"You and Addie, not you and Raymond Walters, I trust."

"Your quickness of mind is gratifying," mumbled Fitzwilliam.

"Well, I don't know what to say about you and Addie, except that as someone who hopes he is about to become her brother, *I* should probably call you out . . ." Drew began.

"Stow it, Drew," snapped Fitzwilliam.

"But as for Raymond Walters," he continued, "you'd be doing society a service if you *was* to put a bullet through him."

"Apparently, I'm to be denied that chance," replied Fitzwilliam dryly.

"Shame Bridgeton didn't do the job better after that business with his sister."

They both looked at their plates for a minute, and then Fitzwilliam said, "That was just a lucky shot on Walters's part. And even then, if they'd had the sense to have a qualified quack close to hand, Bridgeton would've survived."

Drew nodded. "It was hushed up nicely—what with Walters being hustled away for so long. But still and all"—he shook his head—"I am convinced that even after his time away, Walters remains the same vicious, worthless termite."

Fitzwilliam's brow went up at Drew's unusually vehement expression of dislike. "You like everyone, Drew," he reminded his friend.

"Not Raymond Walters," replied Drew with a frown. "I cannot shake the feeling that he is more than just passing unpleasant. Maybe you *should* kill him."

"I am hardly in the habit. Dislikable as he is, I'd planned just to *crease* his arm or his foot, not put a bullet through him, Drew."

"He could hardly know that though, and since you're about the best shot in England, the thought of meeting over pistols was probably making him nervous. The thought of meeting you in the boxing ring, however . . ." He trailed off and they looked at each other.

Then Fitzwilliam began to laugh. "Would not make *anyone* nervous," he finished. "You can go ahead and say it, Drew. You have to give the fellow credit, though! He chose the one forum in which I've no chance whatsoever of besting him. The only foreseeable outcome is a humiliating public thrashing."

"Deuced cowardly of him, to choose boxing. P'raps, Jackson could take you under his wing. Train you, so to speak. Maybe you are not so hopeless a case as we think," Drew suggested.

They stared at each other across the table for a moment and then, in unison, burst out laughing. "No, really, Drew. What am I to do?"

Drew looked at him. "Flee to the Continent?"

"Not an entirely bad suggestion, especially when one considers that I may have engaged myself to a woman I've no desire to marry. My upbringing, however, requires me to face both like a man,'' Fitzwilliam said on a sigh.

''But Fitz,'' Drew said, frowning, *''why* were you kissing Addie?''

Fitzwilliam smiled, all traces of cynicism gone. ''I wanted to,'' he said simply.

''What suddenly made you want to do that?'' Drew asked, an arrested expression on his face.

''Curiosity, I suppose,'' Fitzwilliam admitted with a grin. The cynicism was back.

Drew was not amused. ''Blast it, Fitz. You can't *do* that,'' he exploded, bringing his hand down on the table so hard the cups jumped.

Fitzwilliam lifted a brow. ''And why not, exactly?'' he inquired.

Drew's anger had subsided. ''Because it's not right to toy with her. She is clearly an innocent. And, besides, she loves you,'' he added.

''Loves me?'' Fitzwilliam stared at him. ''What on earth makes you think that?''

''Just look at her when you are in the room. It's obvious. Surely, you knew that?''

Fitzwilliam shook his head, looking, Drew was pleased to note, troubled. ''The thought had never occurred to me before. I've always assumed that she felt much the same about me as I do about her. Obligated.''

''You've been wrong,'' Drew said bluntly.

''Loves me!'' he said again, shaking his head in disbelief.

''Is that so bad?''

''For her it is.''

''But if you plan to marry her eventually—''

''Well, I can't now.''

''Why?''

''If she loves me, I can only end up bringing her misery,'' he said, as if stating the obvious. ''Surely you can see that. As my father was so fond of pointing out—which he did early and often—''

'' 'Claremont men can't love and can't be faithful to one woman,' '' Drew finished for him, in the tones of one repeating a well-worn adage. '' 'In fact, in the history of the realm, no Claremont man has ever been a good husband.' ''

"Right."

'' 'And a vast number of obliging women will always be available due to the Claremont men's title, fortune, holdings, and, er, legendary prowess at—' '' Drew broke off as a piece of toast hit him square in the mouth. "Hey!" he exclaimed, laughing.

"Enough, Drew," Fitzwilliam said, also laughing. "And although I must point out that you omitted good-looks and polished address—"

"Those were implied, if not stated."

"—you did get the gist of it."

"Loath as I am to disturb this lovely image of generation upon generation of heartless, faithless Claremont men, perhaps you're different, Fitz," Drew suggested.

"I doubt that." Fitzwilliam's face hardened.

"But Addie is not your mother, any more than you are your father," Drew pointed out. "That was their life. This is yours."

"New topic, Drew."

"Very well. How was it? Kissing Addie?"

Fitzwilliam smiled slowly, the hard look gone from his face. "Nice," he said.

"So what are you going to do?"

"I've no idea," Fitzwilliam confessed in amiable tones for one in such a bumblebroth, dropping his napkin and rising. "It's the first time I've thought on it from this direction, you know. That she could love me."

Drew looked as if he was going to say something, but before he could, Fitzwilliam paused at the door and continued, "And not, of course, that I could wish to change the subject, from being raked over the fire by you as to my intentions, but you,

I imagine, are in a pelter to pay a call at the Winstead residence yourself?''

''D'you think it too early?'' asked Drew, who was barely a step behind.

Fitzwilliam looked at him with amusement. ''Just killing time with me, were you? I've already been relegated to second choice?'' He smiled at Drew's guilty flush. ''Goodness no! If Justine's half as far gone as you, I doubt she slept a wink. Go,'' he said, as they headed out, ''end both your agony. And leave me to mine in peace.''

Chapter 12

"Well! How nice to have that settled," sighed Honoria some time later. She sank gracefully into a chair, her half-full champagne glass still in hand. "It's quick, Lord knows, but not scandalously so. And if we have a lengthy engagement, any talk will soon die down. We shall, of course, need to have some type of formal entertainment to celebrate when the announcement goes into the *Post*, but just seeing Justine so happy . . . And what a lovely, a truly, truly, lovely young man! Even if he is a younger son. Pity his brother is so healthy. Ardean always has had the constitution of an ox, and that wife of his, with those *hips* will, of a certainty, provide him a veritable houseful of sons. Oh, well. Some things simply can't be helped, I suppose. And Drew anyway quite puts one in mind of young Arthur Warrington, you know. So it's bound to be all right! Goodness, but he did well for himself in politics—Commons— as you might recall''—sigh—"until he decided that it was far too somber an undertaking. Such a lighthearted young man." She brightened. "But he did come into a title in the end. Unexpectedly. From a cousin, I think it was. But I'm quite certain he did, because I recall that he was in Lords in 'seventy-eight when Chatham—the old Earl—expired on the floor in midspeech, which goodness knows, everyone had quite expected for years, because he was so long-winded. Almost frivolous in his lightheartedness—Warrington, not Chatham, goodness knows—and he looked so well in brown in his salad days. Of course, men powdered then, so who can say how he would have looked with today's styles? And they had all those children, he and his lovely wife—big hips there, too!—although I just cannot seem to recall her name, charming young thing, though, and—'' She looked up at Addie, who was sitting at the writing table, shuffling through documents. ''Addie! You've not attended to a word I've said!'' she accused. ''And you've not so much as *touched* your champagne!''

''I'm sorry, Honny, I did hear you, though—Arthur Warrington and all the somber children in brown,'' replied Addie, hoping she was correct. ''And of course, before that little aside, you were wishing that Lord Ardean would stick his spoon in the wall and his wife turn out to be barren so Drew could inherit and—''

''*Addie!* Enough.'' Honoria held up her hand. ''I must tell you that I am trying excessively hard not to notice that you seem to be *doing that thing* while I am *attempting,* apparently unsuccessfully, to talk to you. Whatever is the problem?''

''It is just that I cannot seem to find my notes on yesterday's bout.'' Addie lifted page after page, scanning them. ''Excellent science on both sides was clearly shown in their defensive attitudes, as I recall. Thomas's style was by far the more graceful and unconstrained, though,'' she murmured, her forehead wrinkled with concentration. ''I hope I can remember the specifics. Amundsun broke ground and got in two light hits, left and right, on the body of Thomas. In this manner, they spun it out for quite a few minutes. Someone wondered aloud why Thomas could not be persuaded to go in and lick him off hand, as every one knew was well within his power—''

''Adelaide,'' shrieked Honoria. ''Stop!''

''Sorry, Honny. But misplacing my notes! It is just not like me." She stood over the desk, flipping over sheets of foolscap and slapping them down with an unusual edge of temper.

Honoria glanced at her niece, at the shadows under her eyes, and wondered, not for the first time, exactly what had transpired at Vauxhall last night. Addie had been tight-lipped, saying only, in a tone that had effectively discouraged further questioning, that they had danced and then gone for a walk to admire the Gardens. No, Fitzwilliam had not come up to scratch, and all in all it had been a pleasant, if uneventful, evening. Honoria, though, felt with certainty that there was bound to be more that could be added to that version of events.

She had just opened her mouth, to voice again a delicate inquiry, when Sprague entered.

He hovered in an uncharacteristically uncertain manner on the threshold of the drawing room.

"Yes, Sprague?" Honny inquired with a regal lift of her brow.

"Er, there is a visitor, madam, and I was not certain whether you were, ah, receiving."

Addie's color, Honoria noted, had heightened considerably at Sprague's words. "Well, that would depend on who it is, of course," she replied, watching her niece out of the corner of her eye.

But before Sprague could have a chance to respond, a medium-size balding man brushed past him to enter the room, saying, "I tell you, there is no need to announce me, man. Why, I am quite practically one of the family! Honoria! Adelaide! You are both a feast for the eyes. Indeed, you are." The new arrival crossed to Honoria and bowed over her hand. "And a crackling fire! Just the thing as it is positively frigid outside!"

"Why, Wallace Raines! I thought you had left Town for the winter," Honoria said, so brightly that her enthusiasm might have been mistaken for pleasure.

"I had, dear lady. Yes. I had, indeed. But then it came to me"—he turned to Addie, making a great show of slapping his sparsely covered head—"and I said to myself, Wallace Raines, I said, just because the lady said 'no' once, does not mean she has not grown in my absence to miss my regard, my caring protection, my doting concern—as would any female with Miss Winstead's delicacy of mind. I am more than ever convinced after this time away that my life needs a woman's touch, Adelaide, some docility and gentleness. And moreover, of considerably more importance than my own humble opinion in the matter, *Mother* now agrees! So I am come back to persuade you to be that woman. Yes, Adelaide, I have returned to renew my suit. Now, then, what have you been writing, my dear?'' he asked, glancing toward the writing table, behind which Addie still stood.

''Some, ah, correspondence.''

Wallace turned to Honoria, his meager chest puffing out slightly. ''That is precisely the reason Adelaide needs a man like myself, to afford her some masculine protection. Never think I am taking you to task, dear lady, but what can you be about, allowing her to overburden her mind by writing letters so early in the day? If we were wed, I should absolutely not allow such a thing. No, no. It is far, *far,* too taxing! Why, at this hour, she should still be abed. Indeed, I should insist upon it.''

''Mr. Raines, Wallace—'' Addie began, a glint in her eye.

''Do join us for a glass of champagne, Wallace,'' Honoria hurried to put in before her niece had a chance to give voice to her thoughts. ''We are celebrating Justine's engagement!''

''Well, it *is* a bit early in the day, not at all regular. But since it *is* such a happy occasion, I don't mind if I do,'' he replied, accepting the glass Honoria offered. ''Never let it be said that Wallace Raines did not know how to celebrate! And just whom, may I be so bold as to inquire, is the fortunate fellow?''

''Drew Mannering,'' replied Addie.

''Mannering!'' Wallace exclaimed, his brow darkening as he placed his untouched glass on a table with a click. ''And I am to assume that you gave your consent to this, Honoria? I cannot say I approve. Not a bit. My, but a man's good sense is needed in this household! From a good family, of course,

Ardean is a title of impeccable origin, but the fellow all but runs wild with Claremont, does he not? It cannot be at all the thing to allow Justine to wed a man with such libertine ways! Why the stories I have heard! Well! They simply don't bear repeating!'' He shook his head.

"Now, just look here—'' began Addie hotly.

"We hardly feel—'' said Honoria at the same moment.

"The stories that don't bear repeating sound vastly interesting. Those, I think you will find, Addie, are usually the best ones!''

All three occupants turned to look at Fitzwilliam, who leaned negligently against the door frame, his amusement clear in his eyes. His color was high from the brisk air and his straight brown hair was windblown. Somehow his presence seemed to fill the room with vitality, and Wallace Raines, in contrast, appeared to collapse in on himself into insignificance.

"Please excuse my bursting in unannounced,'' Fitzwilliam continued, straightening and making his bow to the ladies when no one seemed inclined to reply. "But Sprague told me where you were to be found.''

Wallace looked taken aback, and seemed about to expound on the error of such overfamiliar behavior, but Honoria rose and saluted Fitzwilliam on the cheek. "Of course, my dear boy, there can be no need to stand on points,'' she said.

Addie, her color again noticeably higher than it had been a few moments earlier, didn't greet Fitzwilliam, but also Honoria noticed, did not seem able to tear her eyes away from him as she drained the remainder of her champagne. And then, still not removing her gaze from his grin, she exchanged her empty glass for Wallace's untouched one, and tossed back the second drink, before sprawling inelegantly back in her chair. " 'Morning, Fitzwilliam,'' she said, finally, in what she judged to be gratifyingly steady accents.

Wallace pointedly eyed the empty glasses and Addie's posture, but said nothing, settling instead for hovering protectively by her side.

As though, thought Fitzwilliam, *he expects me to attempt to ravish her here and now.* Amusement still danced in his blue eyes as he reached into the pocket of his greatcoat. " 'Morning, Addie. May I offer you something a touch stronger, perhaps?" he asked, as he pulled out a small silver flask. "You seem prodigiously thirsty today."

"Thank you, Fitzwilliam, but no," Addie replied, striving to sound as though she routinely indulged in spirits before noontime.

"Gracious," he said, replacing the flask, and coming to bow over her hand. "You are resorting to drink at the very thought of the stories that don't bear repeating, I collect. Or is it Drew's *libertine ways?*"

"More a question of the company he keeps while running wild," she replied tartly.

"D'you know," he said, sounding vastly amused, "I don't believe I've ever driven a woman to drink before." He gave her a grin that made her heart crash against her ribs.

Perhaps she was fortunate, thought Addie, that he had never set himself to charming her before, as in this mood he was altogether too dangerous for her peace of mind.

"That, Claremont," exclaimed Wallace, unable to restrain himself any longer, "is no matter for joking. Females, as we know, are completely unsuited to withstand the consumption of strong spirits. Ratafia, Addie, is what you should be drinking. Lemonade and tea are also acceptable for female consumption."

"Oh, hullo, Raines. Thought you were rusticating. What brings you to Town?" Fitzwilliam asked, as if noticing Wallace for the first time.

"Er, business considerations," replied Wallace, nodding coolly at the new arrival.

"Must be pressing indeed to convince you to venture up during such a cold snap. Hard traveling, I should think."

"Most pressing, yes." Wallace compressed his lips into a thin line, and continued. "As you must know, I have a dislike of travel under even the best of conditions."

"And *we* are just celebrating the happy news, Fitzwilliam," said Honoria, waving her glass in his direction.

He looked up, his body suddenly very still. "Happy news?"

"Indeed. The doting couple has gone to pay a call on Drew's sister. And *we* are sitting and finishing our champagne and feeling positively thrilled at our good fortune in welcoming such an exceptional young man to our family," Honoria added, as with a pointed look at Wallace, she handed Fitzwilliam a glass of champagne.

"Of course. Drew and Justine," he said with a laugh, accepting the glass and sitting as Honoria motioned him to do.

Addie shot him an astute look. He had been terrified, she'd wager, that Honny had heard of last evening's adventures.

"Drew is over the moon, obviously," Fitzwilliam continued, smoothly. "Have you set a date?"

"Not until I confer with his mama. I understand she returns to Town shortly."

He nodded and smiled. "So Drew did not prevail upon you, after all, to allow him to get a special license and have the ceremony take place next week?"

"Oh, no!" Honoria gasped. "There is the announcement and the engagement ball and shopping—why the trousseau alone might take months—and the dress . . ."

"To be married in such haste would be *most* unseemly," agreed Wallace.

"I believe Fitzwilliam was joking, Honny," Addie pointed out.

"Of course you were, you dear, silly boy," said Honny with a shaky laugh.

Wallace contented himself with a silent frown at what he clearly deemed unseemly levity.

"Well, I am come, of course, to offer my felicitations," recalled Fitzwilliam. "But also to beg Addie to take a drive with me, despite the cold. And to give her this," he remembered, drawing a small velvet pouch out of his pocket. He rose and crossed to her.

For some reason, he seemed to be feeling a burning need to make sure Wallace Raines witnessed this exchange. Really, for a rejected suitor, the fellow was entirely too proprietarial!

A parting gift! He's come to try to make sure I did not take his words—or deeds—seriously last night, and he's been to the jeweler as though I were a woman of easy virtue! thought Addie, not sure whether to be amused or offended. Still undecided, she opened the pouch. Her breath caught when she saw the tiny diamond drops in their antique settings. At least he had taste. For a minute, despite her misgivings, her throat felt tight. They could not have been more perfectly suited to her.

"Thank you, Fitzwilliam," she said, looking up at him with a smile that reminded him of her unexpectedly sweet response last night. "They are lovely."

"Exploded. But lovely," he murmured, his head bent low over hers.

"Exactly," she murmured back.

And at her look of amused understanding, he felt an odd little tug in his chest. Did, *could,* Addie really love him? And what, anyway, would it mean if she did? He smiled a slow smile in return, that somehow made Addie feel that they were alone in the room. "They suit you, Addie," he said, still quietly.

Honoria's eyes went from one to the other. *She,* anyway, recognized those little earrings of his mother's. Something had happened between these two. And about time it was! She would bet her Almack's vouchers on it.

"Surely, Honoria, my Dear Lady, you cannot intend to allow Adelaide to accept such a gift! Why, it is most improper," Wallace huffed. "And certainly they must be adequately chaperoned if they drive out. Although I am not convinced that Adelaide should leave the house at all today. It is far too cold! Let alone do so in the company of a man with such a—no, I am not afraid to say it to his face!—shocking reputation!"

"Wallace, I am aware that you are trying to protect Addie," Honoria said in firm tones, with as much patience as she could muster. Really, the man was a most extraordinary bore. And pompous, too. Thank goodness Addie had the sense to send him packing the first time and would again! "But she has known Fitzwilliam her entire life, and I cannot think there is even the slightest whiff of impropriety to her accepting a token from him *or* in her driving out with him in broad daylight in Hyde Park! Why, *he* is practically one of the family.''

"And correct me if I am wrong," added Fitzwilliam, a wicked glint in his blue eyes, "but Addie thrives on cold weather. As long as she has a hood on. Do you not?''

"In point of fact, I do," replied Addie, allowing her gaze to meet his for just a second. Her stomach seemed to turn over in response. She was trying very hard not to think of their improper interlude last night, but his teasing kept putting her uncomfortably in mind of it.

"Then *I* shall accompany you. As chaperon," said Wallace, his arms crossed and his feet planted solidly on the ground. "I shall insist."

"We should be glad to have you along," replied Fitzwilliam, "but be forewarned that as Addie and I both so enjoy the cold, I have opened the top on my Cabriolet." And brought the two-seater, in the first place, with the express purpose of discouraging anyone from accompanying them, he neglected to say. He could not resist, however, taking the wind out of Raines's sails. Or putting it in, so to speak, he thought, wishing he could share the little pun with Addie.

"An open carriage! Are your attics to let?" Wallace exclaimed.

"Quite possibly," Fitzwilliam replied with a ghost of a smile.

Addie shot him a glance of complicit amusement. "No, it is excellent thinking, Fitzwilliam!" she said. "To my mind, it is just the day to ride out in an open carriage and really *feel* the elements!"

"Somehow, I just *knew* you would agree," he replied with a grin.

Chapter 13

And so it came about that Addie, Fitzwilliam, and Wallace Raines, ended up squeezed onto a bench built for two, tooling through an oddly deserted Hyde Park in Fitzwilliam's smart little Cabriolet on the coldest day of the year. Even the tiger on the back huddled in his livery and looked as though he would rather be anywhere else. The serpentine glittered coldly beneath a blanket of ice, and the horses steamed the air.

"All of London seems to be talking of nothing other than the weather," remarked Addie, who was having difficulty casting about for polite conversation under the circumstances.

Wallace, seated staunchly between them, shuddered and hunched even further in his overcoats. "You do not plan to go about much, I would hope, my dear. To do so could be disastrous. And this Frost Fair! What folly. For surely the only thing more hazardous to the health than being abroad on a day like today is being abroad at *night* in such frigid conditions!"

"I don't know. I think it sounds like great fun," Addie replied, as she hugged her cloak tighter. "At least, it is out of the ordinary run of things."

"My constitution is simply not strong enough to take such

a risk," said Wallace with a sniff. "Mother, you must know, would never approve such an action."

"My constitution is made of iron," announced Fitzwilliam who had been giving every impression of devoting all of his attention to his driving. "It is second only to Addie's in that regard. *She* has the strongest constitution of any person of my acquaintance. Why, I recall the time in the country, when we were children, that the temperature did not rise above freezing for weeks! The only person in both households who did not take ill was Addie. She not only nursed us all, but when all the staff succumbed, cooked and cleaned and fetched wood for the fire with her own hands. Do you recall, Addie?"

As the story was blatantly and absolutely false, Addie hardly dared glance in his direction. "Indeed, Fitzwilliam," she lied. "But I daresay that I would hardly call your constitution 'iron' considering the excessive whining and sniveling you displayed on that occasion!"

Wallace pulled his greatcoat more tightly about his neck with a cough. "We shall all be fortunate in this instance if we do not take an inflammation of the lungs," he said gloomily, holding a hand to his chest. "Why, I believe my breathing is already becoming labored."

"In that case," replied Fitzwilliam, a glint in his eye, "I cannot imagine that you would wish to accompany us the rest of the way out to Hampstead Heath."

"Hampstead!" squeaked Wallace. "Why I should very likely be dead by then! You are quite mad, Claremont. Adelaide, I am afraid that I must put my foot down and insist that you give up this madness."

"Thank you for your concern, Wallace," Addie said, and smiled—and then kept smiling, because her face had frozen in that position. "But Fitzwilliam is right. I do *so* enjoy this weather! I think I shall continue on."

Wallace glared at her to the best of his ability, which was not all that well as he had swaddled the entire lower half of his face in his muffler and sunk his chin into his greatcoat. "If you are intent on such madness, I can hardly stop you; although

I should point out that I have warned you again and again of the possible adverse consequences of such foolhardy behavior!'' he said.

Or at least that was what Addie thought he had said, but his words were somewhat . . . muffled, she decided, suppressing a giggle.

Fitzwilliam apparently agreed with her translation, as he replied, ''I shall accept the blame for any adverse consequences squarely on my shoulders, Raines.''

''Very well. I suppose the groom is an adequate chaperon, although I cannot like it,'' worried Wallace.

''You may rest easy that it's been an age since I've ravished an innocent in an open carriage in broad daylight, Raines,'' Fitzwilliam, who was fairly convinced that this was indeed the truth, assured him gravely. ''Eventually even the most hardened rake gets too old for that type of thing, you know. And, besides, it's dashed cold out here.''

Wallace looked from one to the other of them, as if unsure whether to believe Fitzwilliam. Eventually he shrugged. ''Take me home, then,'' he said to Fitzwilliam. ''But,'' he continued, pressing a starched white square into Addie's hand, ''if you are determined to continue on in this folly, at least take my handkerchief, as I know that with what I can only characterize as a dangerous, deplorable lack of foresight, you never have one. And you are bound to need it.''

''If you are certain,'' said Fitzwilliam, not giving pause for a reply before wheeling the horses around in the direction of Raines's town house—so that Wallace's icy, ''Quite certain,'' was only a formality.

The remainder of the journey was accomplished more or less in silence, as the noise of the horses' hooves resounded eerily through the quiet, frozen streets. After Wallace had descended the carriage and departed with a final disapproving sniff and a promise to call on Addie on the morrow, provided neither of them was abed with their final illness, Fitzwilliam again turned the horses.

* * *

"You cannot truly mean to continue on, Fitzwilliam," Addie said, as soon as she heard the shiny green door of the Raines townhouse bang closed behind Wallace. "As it is, I shall not be surprised if someone is required to carry me inside. I believe my legs are frozen into this position."

"Of course not. I simply thought we needed to speak with some degree of privacy," he replied, remembering as he did that he had not the least notion of what he was going to say to her. Truly they *were* in a terrible fix, he thought, wondering why he didn't feel more alarmed. It would be just like that fool Walters to blab all over London, and then he would have to marry Addie sooner rather than later, which, he reminded himself, he did not wish to do at all. Even if she, flatteringly enough, did love him, as Drew had suggested. *Especially* if she loved him, he reminded himself. There was, of course, always the possibility that none of this would matter because Walters would kill him in the ring and be done with it.

Addie, who was oblivious to this uncharacteristic emotional turmoil he was experiencing, nodded. "Where shall we go?" she asked.

"I don't know," he admitted, reaching into his pocket and pulling out the flask. "It is too cold to talk here. We cannot go to my house, as it would be excessively improper. At your house, Honoria might join us." He handed it to her.

This time she accepted it and took a drink. "I can tell Honoria that we wish to be private," she replied, choking at the unaccustomed sharpness of the brandy.

"What if the moonstruck Drew and Justine return?"

"I shall send them to gaze dewily at each other in another room," she replied, handing it back. "Just let us go before my *iron constitution* fails me entirely, and I wind up fulfilling Mr. Raines's most dire predictions."

He capped the flask and put it away before skillfully maneuvering the horses. "Should that occur, I for one, should be more than happy to carry you inside, Addie," he teased.

"Oh, I doubt it shall come to that, Fitzwilliam," she assured him dryly.

Once arrived, he helped Addie down, and after pausing to confer with the groom on how to safely attend to the horses in such frigid temperatures, they went indoors.

"Thank you, Sprague, I think I shall keep my wrap for the time being," she said when the butler attempted to relieve her of the garment. "And please, send in tea." She caught sight of herself in the mirror in the hallway and wished she didn't look such a mess. Her hair was coming loose, her eyes were watery and her nose was red from the cold and dangerously close to running in a most inelegant manner.

"And brandy, please. Two glasses," added Fitzwilliam. He, Addie noticed, appeared to have suffered no ill effects from their sojourn. His hair was a trifle windblown, which, naturally, only had the effect of making him look more handsome, and his color was a little high, but his nose was insultingly lacking in redness.

If Sprague was surprised either by their appearances or their behavior, he, imperturbable as usual, did not show it.

"Is Honoria here, Sprague?" Addie asked.

"Miss Winstead departed for a consultation at Madame Boucharde's establishment a short time ago," the butler replied. "She was, I believe, murmuring something about economizing on trousseaus."

"And Justine?"

"She is not returned from her visit to Mr. Mannering's sister as yet. Mrs. Glendower called, however," Sprague continued, producing an elegant—albeit somewhat rumpled—cream-colored square of foolscap. "When she found you from home, she left this."

As Lizbeth Glendower, one of Addie's oldest friends, was decidedly, vociferously not in the habit of leaving her house, let alone her bed, before two of the clock, unless such an action was entirely unavoidable, Addie's heart plummeted. "Thank

you, Sprague," she said, accepting the note and holding it by
the corner as if she could hardly bear to touch it. "Please order
the refreshments and then we wish to remain undisturbed."

Sprague bowed and left them.

"I'll give you a moment," Fitzwilliam said, his eyes meeting
hers with understanding, as he inclined his head toward the
note. They both knew what Lizbeth must have heard. Addie
smiled tightly as he headed into the little drawing room.

With shaking hands, she unfolded the missive, and almost
laughed, despite her distress. Her friend wrote much the way
Honny talked. In fact, during the summer months, which Lizbeth and her husband spent in Scotland, unraveling her frequent
and highly enjoyable letters had often provided Addie the better
part of an afternoon's entertainment. And, of course, this note
having been scrawled in a hurry, not only had Lizbeth apparently omitted the blotting step, she was in rare form.

My Dearest, Dearest Addie,
    Dearest! Oh! Addie! And to think you never thought!
I never thought. Well, truly! No one ever thought. Well,
to be sure, Honny thought. A Momentous Event, surely.
Simply Momentous! Was it the cloak? Mere felicitations
do not, cannot, I think, suffice on this occasion. My heart
is full for you. Did you wear the white wool dress? But
why, my love, did you tell Raymond Walters before me,
your dearest friend? Glendower and I would like to be
the first to fête you on the occasion of this most thrilling
event.
    I do, I trust, despite my affront, remain ever Your
Dearest Lizbeth.

Addie re-folded the note. Truly, she could not bear to look
upon it a moment longer.

She had not truly believed that Raymond Walters would
keep Fitzwilliam's announcement to himself, but still a tiny
corner of her had hoped. But if Lizbeth had heard, everyone
would have. Although she loved her friend dearly, no one had

ever accused her of discretion. Now Fitzwilliam truly had no choice but to marry her and she just could not bear it. She had meant every word when she had told Justine that she couldn't tolerate being married to him against his wishes. And it was not, if she were really to examine the matter, entirely a reluctance borne of altruism. There were some things she just knew she could never live with, and watching Fitzwilliam scamper blithely in and out of her life—and her bed—between entertainments and dalliances was one of them. But it seemed that now her only choice was that or ruin.

On that melodramatic thought—almost worthy of Lizbeth, she decided—Addie sneezed. And then sneezed again. *How perfect. Now I get to go in, with my nose running in a most inelegant manner, to tell Fitzwilliam that he has no choice but to follow through and marry me,* she thought, as she pulled Wallace's handkerchief, accepted so reluctantly, out of the pocket of her pelisse. She stared at it, an idea glimmering. *I could accept Wallace,* she thought. It would answer. Goodness knew, he seemed eager. And certainly an engagement to such a proper, upstanding citizen—some would say downright priggish—would quell any gossip. There was after all no reason that anyone would accept Raymond Walters's word on what had happened against a chorus of her own, Fitzwilliam's, and Wallace Raines's.

Inside the drawing room, Fitzwilliam stood by the fire, warming his hands.

He knew what Lizbeth Glendower had heard. And he knew exactly, to a letter, where that left him. Well and truly trapped in the ice, as he had told Drew.

But, well, in that case, perhaps it was fruitless to struggle.

The surprising thing about it all, was that he could not seem to mind as much as he knew he should. In fact, with the knowledge had come something perilously like . . . well, relief that the matter was settled for him.

To be sure, he had not wished to get shackled. *Did* not wish to be shackled. But to have the tree with no bark on it, he *was* going to have to do it sometime. With someone. And it might as well be Addie.

She was turning out to be a remarkably entertaining companion, he thought. And then there was that odd tug somewhere in the region of his chest, that he got when he thought about Drew's assertion that she loved him. The idea that this woman who had known him for her entire four-and-twenty years on earth, and knew him for himself, might actually love him, well, it felt strange, to say the least.

Strange, certainly, but not altogether unpleasant.

In fact, he was beginning to think that being married to Addie might be relatively pleasant, even. And pleasant, he decided, could be good.

If it was not exactly what he would wish, it certainly would not be the worst fate that could befall him. *Her,* maybe, he thought with some guilt, but not him.

But what a tangled web. And life with Wallace Raines? the other side of Addie's mind cried. It essentially amounted to making a sacrifice of herself, she knew. But then she pictured Bella Carstairs spilling out of that gown and remembered Fitzwilliam's expression as he had gazed at her. It had been well, *wolfish,* was the word that came to mind. And she understood that she would never know a peaceful moment in a marriage with him. That there would always be something, someone, between them. *With Wallace, at least, I would know where I stood*, she thought. *And he would lack the power to destroy me.*

So with a deep breath, she pasted on a smile and walked through the drawing room doorway.

Chapter 14

What is he thinking about? Addie wondered as she came into the room and Fitzwilliam turned from the fire to look at her. The very sight of him, the expression on his face, part amused, part quizzical, part rueful, made her heart turn over with longing as she joined him and stretched her own hands toward the warmth of the flames.

But before either could speak, the door opened again, and, expecting a maid with the refreshments, they both turned. Instead, Nellie entered, knitting basket in hand. "I heard you were in need of a chaperon, Miss Addie," she said, making her curtsy and heading for a chair in the corner. "And seeing as Miss Honoria and Miss Justine are both in the way of being out, I thought I would step in."

"In point of fact, we are not. In need of a chaperon, that is," retorted Addie. "We have been trying to rid ourselves of one all morning, actually, and wish to be private."

"I don't know," Nellie clucked. "Whatever would Miss Honoria say if she heard that I had left you alone with a gentleman?"

"She would no doubt say, 'Good. Perhaps Fitzwilliam will

be compromised beyond endurance and at long last brought to his knees'," retorted Addie, her tongue unguarded by cold and confusion and perhaps the unprecedented amount of spirits she had consumed that morning. "And Fitzwilliam is hardly a gentleman, anyway."

Fitzwilliam stifled a laugh.

"Very well, Miss Addie," replied Nellie stiffly before curtsying again and retreating.

Addie subsided to a chair with a sigh. "I suppose I shall be apologizing for that for the rest of my natural life. Perhaps, I shall be fortunate if Mr. Raines's gloomy prognosis comes to pass and I am carried off to my untimely end. At least my penance will be shortened." *And I won't have to marry him,* she thought.

Whatever Fitzwilliam would have replied was lost as there was a brief knock followed by Cook herself thrusting her ample body through the door. Freshly changed into a sparkling apron and lacy cap, she struggled under the weight of a tray loaded with tea things: sandwiches, cakes, brandy, and glasses. Fitzwilliam crossed the room and relieved her of the tray. She stood in the doorway, arms crossed over her bosom, and surveyed the two of them. "Wish to be private, do you?" she said in a disapproving voice. "Waste of good seed cakes, if you ask me," she added, inexplicably, before departing and closing the door firmly in her wake.

On her departure, Addie shook her head as Fitzwilliam, looking somewhat bemused, set down the tray on a little table. She poured tea with stiff fingers, and they sat, facing each other.

"Are you warmer?" he asked as he began to recover some feeling in his fingers.

"I am beginning to be," Addie replied, as she put down the cup she had clutched in both hands and divested herself of her wrap.

"It was the only way I could think of to rid us of Mr. Raines's company. Sorry to have put you through that," he apologized.

"Don't give it another thought. Really. I am fine," Addie

replied. But the fact that she was still shivering gave the lie to her statement.

"Have some brandy," Fitzwilliam recommended, pouring them both glasses.

"I hardly think I need more—"

"Trust me, Addie, have some."

"This is three times now in one day you have driven me to drink, Fitzwilliam," Addie teased as she accepted it. She sipped at it, actually enjoying the tendrils of warmth it sent through her. Emboldened to have done with this, now that she had made up her mind, she leaned forward and took a steadying breath, before beginning. "We are both agreed that we need to speak, and we might not have much time before we are again interrupted."

All Fitzwilliam could think was that he was experiencing the strongest desire to return to where they had been last night before the interruption. "Well, I, ah," he began, his mouth suddenly dry. "I—"

She broke into his meandering. "It's not necessary, you know, for you to—"

"It is," he replied, his tone harsh.

They both subsided awkwardly.

He knows that Lizbeth knows, and he thinks he has no choice but to honor his promise to my father, even though that's the last thing he wants to do, Addie thought, trying to read his impassive face. *How humiliating.*

It was time to unburden his mind.

And then, as luck would have it, she sneezed again. She reached into the pocket of her wrap. "How fortunate that Mr. Raines foresaw just such a thing coming to pass and lent me a handkerchief," she said, withdrawing it.

"What a bore Wallace Raines is," commented Fitzwilliam, glad of having time to stall. "Why do you put up with him?"

She directed a reproving stare at him. "I put up with him because I have accepted his offer to become his wife," she heard her own voice replying in frosty accents. There, she had made herself say it.

Thank God! he thought. "Really?" he heard himself asking, his voice sharpened by surprise, and maybe something else in its wake. "Have you?"

"Yes."

"And exactly when did you do that?" he asked, his eyes searching hers.

"What is the difference?"

Take this reprieve and run, he suggested to himself. *Stand, offer your heartfelt felicitations, and leave.* To his surprise, his body did not obey. "Only that Honoria, notably, failed to mention it when she was cataloging happy news this morning, and, of course, that you all but accepted my offer last night," he pointed out instead.

"I did no such thing," Addie snapped. *"You,* without my approval, told Raymond Walters that I was your fiancée. I simply did not correct you."

"It is the same thing," he insisted, knowing himself to have completely taken leave of all reason, but goaded by the same mysterious fury he had felt when Walters had insulted her.

"It certainly is not."

"It is!"

"Is not!"

"Is! Besides. You cannot marry him. He's a bore and a fool! And a prig," he added for good measure. *"And* he suffers from a paltry constitution."

"I can and I will," snapped Addie, all too aware that she was firmly cutting off her escape from a future that was bleak, to say the least. *Better that, though, than being wed to a resentful and unwilling Fitzwilliam,* she reminded herself. *At least, Wallace will dote on me, and will not keep a virtual harem of mistresses.* It seemed not much consolation. "You told me to accept someone else," she pointed out. "And I'd rather have a prig for a husband any day than a libertine!"

"Your heart is engaged then?" he asked, with as much sarcasm as he could muster.

Her gray eyes were clear. "Absolutely. Why would you ask that?"

"You kissed me last night, Addie," he said softly, leaning closer, his blue eyes glittering dangerously. "Or have you forgot?"

She flushed. "Is that a reminder or an accusation?" she asked. "Because in either case it is monstrous ungentlemanly of you!"

His lips were even closer. "Ah, but as you pointed out, I am no gentleman. One with my *libertine tendencies,* you see, must delight in throwing your indecorous behavior in your face."

"In that case I would point out that again, *you* kissed *me*. I merely, foolishly, did not stop you," she retorted. *It must be all those strong spirits,* she told herself, *that are making me so bold. And so tingling with warmth. Wallace was undoubtedly right. I should have confined myself to ratafia.*

Fitzwilliam stood and walked lightly to where she sat. He took her almost empty brandy glass out of her hand and set it down on a table. His fingers brushed hers. "Would you stop me now?" he asked, his voice a husky whisper, his gaze holding hers.

Every nerve in Addie's body suddenly seemed centered in her fingers, where their hands touched. She looked away from his hypnotic eyes, which seemed to grow darker by the second. "Yes," she forced herself to say.

"Because you would truly desire me to stop?" he asked, gently turning her head so that her eyes again looked into his.

"Yes." Her words were barely audible.

He shook his head. "I don't think you would," he whispered, sinking to his knees beside her chair.

Her breath caught.

He reached up and took her face between his hands. "I can barely stop myself," he murmured, seemingly as much to himself as to her.

His hands were infinitely gentle. They exerted no pressure, but she seemed unaccountably to be leaning closer. "Tell me to stop, Addie," he breathed, his mouth a fraction of an inch away from hers.

All she could think about was eliminating that fraction of an inch. "Stop." She gasped.

"No," he whispered, as his mouth closed in on hers.

Fitzwilliam had simply intended to demonstrate that he held a power over her that Wallace Raines never could. But the instant their lips met, he forgot why he had started. He kissed her hungrily.

And Addie knew that this was a whirlpool of sensation in which she would happily drown. She leaned in, every inch of her body feeling a scorching need to be pressed against him, and kissed back with equal hunger.

A deep black wave of desire seemed to crash over Fitzwilliam. He had expected that gentle sweetness again that he would kiss her slowly and lingeringly, sweetly, as befitted her innocence—and well enough to banish thoughts of the ridiculous Wallace Raines from her mind. But this time her mouth and her touch ignited a storm of fire and need. Within a second, he had lost any idea of kissing her gently in his sudden overwhelming need to kiss her into the same state of feverish insensibility, to pull her to the floor and feel her body burning and willing in his arms. "Do you still want me to stop, Addie?" he breathed.

"Please don't" she whispered urgently against his mouth. Only their lips and Fitzwilliam's shaking hands where they still held her face, touched. It was not enough—nowhere near enough. She wrapped her arms around his neck, and he made a noise of pleasure. She sighed against his lips.

And Fitzwilliam was on the point of abandoning his conscience entirely and pulling her down to the Aubusson in fact, when he thought he heard a noise in the hall.

Chapter 15

"Addie! Fitzwilliam! There you are," came Justine's voice from the hall as the door swung open. "Sprague was not certain you were still here!" She entered, followed by a positively beaming Drew.

"We were just having some tea and, um, brandy," explained Addie, as she dabbed at a spill on her skirt. "Do join us."

"Brandy?" asked Justine, looking from one to the other, obviously puzzled.

"We had a drive in an open carriage," Fitzwilliam explained. "And I prescribed it to thaw out your sister. Felicitations, I understand, are in order," he added, removing his arm from the mantel, and walking to Justine. He took her hands and kissed her briefly on the cheek. "I'm so happy for both of you."

"Thank you, Fitzwilliam," Justine replied very properly, while trying to figure out why the atmosphere in the room felt just slightly off. Fitzwilliam wore his usual expression of slightly amused boredom, but her sister seemed flustered and a little breathless. Her color was unusually high. And come to think of it, upon closer examination, Fitzwilliam's legendary blue eyes possessed an unusual depth. And was he a touch breathless, also? Or was that her imagination? *Surely,* they had not interrupted an embrace between Addie and Fitzwilliam?

"Ah, you had a drive in an open carriage? Today?" Justine asked, clearly not sure what to think.

Addie nodded. "Fitzwilliam remembered how much I enjoy the cold," she explained.

"He did?" Drew asked, looking surprised, at the same moment that Justine said, "You do?"

At Addie's look, Justine said, "I mean, you do! Of course."

"Well, we were coming to see if you two wanted to join us for a trip to the theater this evening," Drew ventured. Apparently unsure what to make of any undercurrents in the room, he went back to gazing besottedly at Justine as he said it.

"No!" said Addie and Fitzwilliam at the same time, each privately feeling the need to sort through the events of the last two days.

At this Drew did manage to tear his gaze away from Justine long enough to aim a frown at Fitzwilliam.

"I have the headache," Addie offered by way of explanation.

"And I have, er, plans," Fitzwilliam said.

Plans with Bella Carstairs, no doubt, Addie thought tartly, as he went on. "In fact, I, regrettably, really must take my leave this very moment. Thank you, Addie, for your company on such a pleasant drive, and for the . . . tea."

"You are most welcome, Fitzwilliam," she replied stiffly. "Shall I see you to the door?"

He bowed. "That would be lovely."

He offered his arm in a formal manner, and Addie took it. Justine's eyes followed them. She frowned to herself.

"Every time things get interesting we are interrupted," Fitzwilliam remarked in very low tones, as they walked into the hall.

"Thank you, Sprague, but I will see Lord Claremont to the door," Addie said, by way of dismissing the hovering butler, her face flaming anew at Fitzwilliam's words. "And a good thing it is, too," she collected herself to reply in equally hushed tones. "Besides, you flatter yourself, Fitzwilliam. Things were not all that interesting."

He raised a brow. "Really?"

"Really. In fact, Mr. Raines is *much* better at that," she said.

The brow went up farther. "Is he!" he said.

"Indeed."

"What about this, Addie?" he asked softly, backing her against the elegantly blue-and-white-striped wall. Without even so much as looking about to make certain they were unobserved, he tipped her chin up and rubbed a gentle thumb across her lips. "Is Raines better than this?"

She opened her mouth to reply, but before she could do so, Fitzwilliam bent his head and closed it with his own. His lips were hot and skillful, and, for good measure, his hands took a most improper possession of her waist. And he kissed her until they were both dizzy.

Oh, my, he thought blankly as that same black wave of desire tossed him to the bottom. *Oh, my.* "Is he?" he demanded in an urgent whisper, his lips still against hers.

"No," she gasped. If Sprague and Honoria and, come to think of it, all the patronesses of Almack's, had walked into the hall at that moment, she doubted she would have had the strength to stop him. "No."

"I didn't think so."

He let her go, as suddenly as he had begun. And Addie remained against the wall. Truthfully, she doubted her legs would hold her on their own. "Although what he would have to say about this hardly bears consideration," she managed to say, congratulating herself for her presence of mind, but wishing all the same that she was not breathing quite so heavily.

"Actually, I prefer not to consider what Mr. Raines has to say on almost any topic, Addie," Fitzwilliam said, as he shrugged into his greatcoat. "And especially not this one."

"There is no reason to concern him with our trifling, albeit shocking, lapse of judgment, Fitzwilliam," Addie said as sternly as she could.

"Trifling!" Fitzwilliam said. "Well I like that. Need I prove myself yet again?"

"No!" Addie yelped.

"Good." He smiled as he bent in her direction. "I should kill another man, you know, Addie, if my future wife even *thought* about kissing him in the way you were kissing me," he said lightly.

"Well, Wallace need never know," Addie replied firmly.

"Ah, but *you* will," he pointed out.

She shrugged. "It was of no moment, Fitzwilliam. What is a kiss—to you, of all people?"

"Oh, Addie." He smiled, so sweetly that her knees felt like to buckle again. "Sometimes a kiss is not just a kiss." He bent closer, and Addie would have fled if she were able. "Perhaps you should just tell Honoria that I was compromised beyond endurance and at long last brought to my knees," he whispered, his lips almost brushing her ear, as he opened the door.

What on earth does the infuriating man mean by that? Addie wondered, as she closed the door behind him with as hard a thump as her shaking hands could manage.

Now what on earth, Fitzwilliam wondered, as he stood atop the front steps, his back to the recently thumped door, *did I mean by that?*

Chapter 16

"Addie?" Justine ventured, when, a short time later, she poked her head around the door of her sister's bedchamber and found her there, curled into a ball on the bed in the midst of a mound of pillows. "Is something amiss? Why did you not return to the drawing room? I had thought you would come back after you had seen Fitzwilliam to the door—and, by the way," she added with a tilt of her head, "the two of you seem to be getting on rather well."

Addie sat up, rubbing her eyes. "I am sorry, Justine. Please apologize to Drew for my abominable rag-manners."

Justine smiled, and crossing to the bed, sat down beside Addie, who had propped herself against the pillows. "Drew left for home a short time ago. So we can have a coze. Is something amiss, love? You do not seem quite yourself. Not since last night, in fact," she added pointedly.

"No, no. Nothing. I had a note to write to Wallace Raines is all, and then I decided to rest for a spell."

Justine looked at her sister. "Wallace Raines? I thought he had departed for the country after you refused him. Surely, to listen to him talk, and talk he does, his constitution is far too delicate to have ventured back in such inclement weather?''

"Mr. Raines is returned to Town," Addie replied. "He came to call this morning. In fact, he drove out with us."

"Wallace Raines agreed to go in an open carriage *today?*" Justine asked, her surprise visible. "Surely, he is not hoping to renew his suit? And anyway, why did you need to send him a note?" she demanded suspiciously.

Addie looked down and toyed with a cashmere throw.

"Addie?"

Still Addie did not reply.

"Surely you didn't!" her sister cried.

Addie kept her head down. "You may wish *me* happy also, Justine."

"Wallace Raines? *Wallace Raines?*" Justine repeated. "You are going to marry *Wallace Raines?*"

"For heaven's sake, Justine, stop repeating yourself! You heard what I said. Yes." She forced her head higher. "I am."

"I am sorry, Addie, it is just that I can't believe that—I am surprised that you would—that you are"—she stopped and took a deep breath—"that you would accept Wallace Raines when you are so obviously head over ears for Fitzwilliam," she said quickly.

"Well, Fitzwilliam is *not* head over ears for me. So, yes, I am—going to marry Wallace, that is." Addie held up her head and forced her backbone straighter. She met Justine's gaze. "I have, in fact, just this past hour had a note delivered accepting the kind renewal of his flattering offer of marriage. The correct response, as I believe I have already pointed out, would be to wish me happy."

"I only wish I could. But how can I?" exclaimed Justine, her eyes filling with tears. "You know you will never be happy with him. Why, you can barely tolerate him! So don't go all reproving on me, Addie."

Addie took her hand. "I am sorry, Justine. Truly. Don't pay any attention to me. I guess I'm just a little out of sorts today."

"*That* is exactly my point. You should not be out of sorts

on the day you accept a marriage proposal. You should be, well, over the moon."

"No, Justine. *You* are over the moon. *I* am content. I will be happier with Wallace than with a miserable and faithless Fitzwilliam. Trust me on that."

"Addie," Justine began, looking uncomfortable. "I know this is a bit awkward, but I got the impression—I thought that, er, when we came into the drawing room that you and Fitzwilliam might have been, um, that we might have interrupted—"

At which point Addie saved her from having to say more by burying her face in her pillow and beginning to sob.

"What on earth has happened, love? *Something* must have to make you accept Wallace," said Justine, reaching for a handkerchief, but stopping as Addie pulled one out. "Don't cry," she said, beginning gently to pat Addie's back.

In reply, Addie sniffled into the handkerchief in what Honny would have deemed a most unladylike manner.

"Is that Fitzwilliam's?" Justine asked, eyeing the sadly damp and rumpled white square.

"No," Addie sniffled. "It is Wallace's. Fitzwilliam is not," she said, beginning to sob again, "a handkerchief type of man. Wallace is. Which," she bawled from amidst her pillows, "is exactly why I am crying."

Justine continued to pat her back. "I know exactly what you mean," she said, and oddly, she did.

"But handkerchief men make infinitely better husbands than nonhandkerchief men. Everybody knows that," Addie sobbed. *"They*, you can be sure, do not keep dozens of mistresses."

Justine thought on this. "Well I am not convinced of that. And I'm not certain that handkerchief men are of all that much use anyway, except when you sneeze," she said. "And besides, it is not as though you do not possess plenty of your own."

"But I never remember to take one when I leave the house, so if I were to marry Fitzwilliam, neither of us would ever have a handkerchief when we needed one. And that, anyway, is not at all what I meant," Addie wailed.

"I know, Ad, I was teasing. Trying to get you out of the dismals."

"Oh, what a mess," Addie said, still sobbing.

"Tell me, love. It won't seem so bad when somebody else knows. You need not carry all burdens by yourself, you know, Addie."

"Well, it all started at Vauxhall last night. No. Actually, when I was on my way to Jackson's the other day and was accosted and almost assaulted by that odious Raymond Walters," Addie explained, sniffling, but sounding slightly improved. She dried her eyes on the counterpane rather than resorting to Wallace's handkerchief again.

"You were what?" demanded Justine. "How dare he! Why did you not—"

"If you are going to interrupt—"

"Sorry. Go on."

"Well, all I had been thinking were vain thoughts about my new cloak," Addie continued. "And shocking ones about Fitzwilliam's naked torso—"

"Pardon?" Justine exclaimed, unable to restrain herself from interruption in this instance.

"At Jackson's. When he was in the ring," chided Addie. "I am making a sad mull of this telling, am I not?"

"An uncharacteristic mull," Justine confirmed. "Why don't you start again, at the beginning?"

Addie desisted sniffling, and throwing the offending handkerchief into the corner of the room, took a deep breath, and spilled the entire tale from start to finish.

When she had finished, Justine, who had shown remarkable restraint in not interrupting even once said, "I am still not entirely certain that I understand in all this what prompted your acceptance of Wallace's offer, Addie."

"Isn't it obvious? Raymond Walters told people. Lizbeth had heard already."

"Well goodness knows, if Lizbeth has heard, so have a lot of others."

"Exactly."

''But I still don't understand how being engaged to Wallace takes care of that.''

Addie frowned at her. ''If I am engaged to Wallace, Raymond Walters will have nothing credible to spread about, because no one would believe that the fiancée of such a prig—er, fine and upstanding gentleman, would behave with anything but the utmost propriety! And moreover it means that Fitzwilliam doesn't have to face marrying me or else knowing that he has destroyed my reputation.''

Justine stared back at Addie. ''Forgive me for saying this, love, but that is the most ridiculously addled thinking I have ever run across! No. Don't say anything. If you are using Wallace to protect your reputation—which incidentally, I did not know you cared so much for—why not use Fitzwilliam? Who could say anything about you kissing your own intended husband? Goodness knows there is nothing shocking in *that*.'' Here, she had the grace to look down as color flooded her face.

''But don't you see? I can't marry Fitzwilliam! I *love* him,'' wailed Addie, wiping her tears away with the back of her hand and wishing that she had not been so quick to throw away Wallace's handkerchief after all. ''I'll be miserable. We'll both be miserable.''

''But that is exactly why—''

''No!'' Addie sat up and gripped Justine's hand. ''I simply won't do it. So save yourself the trouble of a lecture on misplaced pride.''

''Addie . . .'' Justine began, and then threw up her hands. ''I give up. I can see there is no talking sense into you today. But have you thought of what Honoria will say to this?''

Addie, still sniffling, shook her head dumbly.

''Let me prepare you, then, because she had not given up hope of bringing Fitzwilliam to the sticking point; you can be certain!''

At these words, Addie, again remembering Fitzwilliam's whispered good-bye and the events that had led up to it, gave vent to a renewed burst of sobs. Justine, who could not remember having seen her sister cry above twice in her entire existence, sat helplessly by, patting her shoulder and murmuring soothing words.

Until they both jumped at the knock at the door.

"Enter," called Justine, since Addie was in no fit state.

"Miss Addie? Miss Justine?" said Nellie, sticking her head around the edge of the door. "Mr. Wallace Raines is below stairs ordering Sprague to fetch the best champagne, and Miss Honoria has just arrived home. And is looking fit to blow an artery. I think you'd best come down!"

Chapter 17

"Ah, champagne again," Honoria said, just a shade too cheerily, putting down her glass. Untouched, Addie noted. "Two happy events in one day. Who would have thought it?" *Just wait,* she thought, *until I get Addie alone.*

"Just a sip, now, Adelaide," cautioned Wallace. "I realize we are celebrating, but it could have hazardous repercussions to the innards to overindulge twice in the same day. Mother, I know, always recommends allowing the liver a full week to cleanse itself between small glasses of sherry. Most prudent, I think."

"Most prudent, indeed," agreed Justine.

Addie smiled vaguely. *What have I done?* she wondered. *I've saved myself from one awful fate, but is this one worth it?*

"The intestinal workings of the fair sex are not equal to ours," Wallace confided to Drew—who, unable to be parted from Justine for any significant length of time, had returned—in serious tones.

"I, er, I had not heard that," Drew replied, looking at Justine out of the corner of his eye. "We must have a care for your intestinal workings then, my love."

Justine choked, and Wallace radiated approval at Drew.

"My dear lady—may I call you Aunt?" he said, turning to Honoria, not waiting for her somewhat reluctant nod, before continuing. "Now that Adelaide has agreed to make me the happiest of men, I hope you will see your way clear to making your home with us. It will be a relief, I should think, dear Aunt, to finally have a man in charge. And Mother, I know, will so enjoy having a contemporary along on the wedding journey."

This time Drew choked.

"On the wedding journey!" Honoria said, faintly.

"And once we are safely settled in the country, away from this pit of infectious humors, Adelaide will, naturally, wish you to bear her company."

Settled in the country? "I, um, *like* London," Addie ventured.

Wallace looked scornful. "That, my dear, is because you do not know what is best for you. No, no. We shall eschew the city altogether. You shall soon come thank me, I am sure, when you realize how much more healthful country air is." He smiled thinly.

And so it went, until Wallace, at long last, pleading fatigue from the excitement of the day—and the desire to pen a long epistle to his mama—took his leave. But before he departed, Honoria gaily pulled Justine and Drew out of the room to allow the happy couple a *moment,* as she put it.

"I do think we shall rub along tolerably, Adelaide," Wallace said, pressing her hand between his two clammy ones, "so long as you learn to have a care for your health and sensibilities. Do not worry, my dear. Between us, Mother and I shall help you to curb this recklessness of yours. And now, Addie," he said, gazing at her, still clutching her hand, "I realize as a gently reared female you might find this offensive, but a fellow really is entitled to a betrothal kiss."

She smiled, she hoped encouragingly. "I understand that, Wallace." Oh, how true that was.

He ignored her upturned face and pressed a brief kiss upon her cheek. "I shan't chance endangering both our health or offending your delicate sensibilities with a kiss on the lips, Adelaide. Most imprudent during winter months, you must know.

No sooner had he accomplished this notably unloverlike speech and taken himself off, but Honoria, who Addie would have bet had been all but plastered to the other side of the door, practically burst in. "And what exactly have you done, my girl?" she demanded in awful tones.

Addie raised her chin. "I have accepted Wallace. I should think that would be obvious, Honny. I should also think that you would be pleased. I'm saved from a life of spinsterhood, and certainly," she added glumly, "from being reduced to what you can only consider the odious task of writing about boxing to keep the creditors at bay. Certainly there's no question of me sneaking off to Jackson's under Wallace's watch. No. He's eligible, he's from an excellent family, and he's extremely wealthy. I'd think you'd be in alt."

"Well, all I can say is that *this*," Honny retorted, looking thoughtful, "is not a case, Addie, at all like Simon and Maribelle. No. No, indeed. It is, in fact, if one looks at it objectively, much more of an ilk with that of Lord Keswick and Miss Hartshal. And one does grant that this is some time past, but still, from that perspective the similarities are quite striking! And when the Dowager, that would be Lord Keswick's mama, of course, decided to change the wall hangings in the dining room—French, don't you know—and they'd been in the family, well, *positively* forever! But one hardly needs point that out! That would have been the summer of, oh, let me see—"

"Honny," Addie interrupted. She was tired and heartsick and not at all up to deciphering her aunt's conversation this evening. "What does this mean?"

"It means, of course, Addie, that whatever has passed between you and Fitzwilliam in the past two days—and I'd wager it's been quite a bit—he gave you his mother's earrings this very afternoon, and now you, my foolish little headstrong niece, have gone and accepted another man! And a pompous, priggish one at that,'' Honoria said, quite succinctly, before sweeping out of the room.

Addie put her head in her hands. How to make any sense of this? Last night—goodness, had it been only last night?—Fitzwilliam had told her, straight out, that he had absolutely no interest in marrying her. And *then* he had kissed her. And called her his fiancée. And agreed to meet Raymond Walters over her. And today, Justine had gotten engaged to his best friend. And Fitzwilliam had given her his mother's earrings! And then he had all but tumbled her on the floor. And she had let him. Wanted him to, in fact. And now she was engaged to Wallace Raines, and Fitzwilliam was no doubt tangled in the sheets doing goodness only knows what to his mistress, with that very expert mouth, at that very moment—completely and utterly oblivious to the sacrifice she was making of herself, and of Wallace, too, she was beginning to realize.

Chapter 18

Had she but known it, Addie was not far wrong in her guess as to Fitzwilliam's whereabouts. As to his activities, however, she might have found herself surprisingly off in her guess. He had, in the end, found himself distinctly disinclined to do goodness only knows what to his mistress, after all. Although that had been his original intent, certainly. And he was at that moment, lying next to her feeling intensely irritated by, well, *everything*.

Well, not everything, exactly. Just most things.

It had seemed to him, upon departing the Winstead household, a capital idea to purge this entire extremely confusing two days by paying a visit to Bella. And so he had. But now, here he was. Having, once again declined to take her up on what she was paid for, lying wide awake, his hands behind his head, staring moodily at the ceiling, with Bella pouting, even in her sleep, next to him.

She, as usual, had been set to work him over with that knowing, voluptuous touch. And he had inexplicably declined. She was beautiful. She was his. She was well paid for. And she wanted him.

Hell, *he* had been shocked to hear his own voice saying that really all he wanted was dinner, a decent bottle of port, and sleep. But now that drowsy, sated state was once again eluding him. Which, he had to admit, considering that he had gone from being contentedly single to possibly engaged and then once again back to firmly single, all in the space of four-and-twenty hours, was also not all that surprising. Oddly, though, he was not anywhere near as relieved as he ought to be, considering his narrow escape. Not that he was fully escaped—there was still his upcoming bout with Raymond Walters to be got through. But at least with Addie firmly engaged to Wallace Raines there would be no question of anyone believing any tittle-tattle that Walters might try to spread.

Addie. He sighed. She apparently was the crux of his current problem. Bella was there, available, disappointed even. And he hadn't wanted her, with her vast repertoire of sensuous expertise, even a fraction as much as he had wanted to pull Addie Winstead onto the floor in her own drawing room and, well, what?

Fitzwilliam shook his head. What on earth was coming over him? It was entirely unsuitable even to *think* that way about a gently bred young lady. Most of the men of his acquaintance wouldn't. Didn't about their own wives, in fact.

Bella sighed in her sleep and moved closer. He edged away, thinking irritably that perhaps what he needed was a new mistress. And to think, just a few days ago he had thought his affaire with Bella the most satisfying liaison he had ever had. Now he cast his mind speculatively over the eligible widows of his acquaintance. Rejecting all of them, he thought of all the dashing young matrons who had indicated that they would not object to sharing a few hours in a bedchamber. No, he decided, not in his style to cuckold. And none of them would contrive to hold his interest, anyway.

Damn. The irritating, inexplicable fact was that he couldn't stop thinking about Addie—and puzzling over his own response to her. Even now, just the thought of how she had felt pushed up against the wall of the hallway made his blood surge. He glanced over at the delectable Bella. But not for her.

He rolled irritably onto his side, facing away from Bella. When he had handed Addie up into his Cabriolet that morning, he had been unable to help but notice that she was possessed of an extremely well turned ankle and shapely calf. And at the same time that he was thinking how much he would have enjoyed a glimpse of the rest of those legs, he had noted that Wallace Raines was pointedly *not* observing the same thing.

What a waste, he thought. Wallace Raines was definitely a man upon whom a well-turned ankle would be squandered, or he missed his guess. *Now, as something of a connoisseur, I would appreciate them properly,* he decided. Enticing visions of starting at her ankles and kissing upward filled his mind. Lord, she would be shocked, he guessed, with a little smile. Not that any of it mattered, since Addie and her ankles were betrothed to the unappreciative Wallace, and he, Fitzwilliam, had absolutely no desire anyway to bracket himself to Addie. And certainly there could be no question of kissing *those* legs without the blessing of a man of the cloth.

He inched a foot out of the suffocating warmth of the satin duvet and shifted, trying to get comfortable in the overly soft goose-down mattress, and thought again of his parents' marriage.

His father, also, had been quite a connoisseur. And had spent the majority of his time openly pursuing his hobby, while his mother had wilted ever more miserably, year by year. Until, of course, that jolly Christmas Eve during which the old man had finally put an end to his miserable existence by expiring in the arms—and not coincidentally, the bed—of a parlormaid while the rest of the family had been hanging decorations.

All in all, it had been no better and no worse than any other Claremont family Christmas, he thought grimly. Except that afterward he had had to resign himself to spending the rest of his life as Earl Claremont—a title that made his skin crawl to this day, since it was a name inextricably bound, in his mind, with his father. A man without, Fitzwilliam had to admit if he was being honest, *any* redeeming qualities. None whatsoever.

Claremont men, he reminded himself, as if he really needed reminding, *possess impermeable hearts and a distinct disinclination toward monogamy.* And even believing that, practicing that, hell, making it the family motto, as he did, the hideous old libertine had chosen the daughter of one of his best friends as a match for his presumably equally faithless son.

Which was why, God, the thought of any woman, of Addie, loving him all but made his knees knock. Addie, of course, had known his parents, but in truth he doubted that she knew the specifics of what a truly miserable union it had been. But goodness knew, he did.

He sighed again and decided, much to Bella's displeasure, that it was past time to take himself off. And so he found himself retrieving his clothing to once again go home from his mistress's bed. Unfulfilled and unsettled.

Chapter 19

"Bloody hell!" screamed Fitzwilliam, the next morning, as he collapsed to the floor holding his nose.

"Are you all right? I hadn't meant to hit you so hard. It's just that I thought you would surely deflect the blow before it—"

"No." Fitzwilliam looked up and held out his hand. "I know you only meant to pink me, not punish me so severely, John. Let us talk a moment. I could use the rest, anyway."

John "Gentleman" Jackson extended his hand and helped Fitzwilliam to his feet. "Shall we sit a spell, Lord Claremont? Give you a moment to regain your equilibrium," he suggested, leading the way to some chairs.

"*Please,* call me Fitzwilliam. Everyone does," Fitzwilliam said.

Jackson smiled levelly. "Certainly. If that's what you prefer."

They took seats opposite each other, and Fitzwilliam mopped his face and glistening torso with a towel. Jackson, who had not even broken a sweat, looked at him, clearly with some degree of curiosity, but held his peace.

Fitzwilliam felt, rather than saw Jackson's gaze. "I suppose you are wondering why I have suddenly requested private lessons," he said, his face still in the towel. "And specified that they were to take place before the instructors and attendants arrived."

"I had assumed that when and if you wanted to tell me, you would do so," replied Jackson, ever the soul of discretion, in neutral tones. "But yes, I confess that I had not thought to see you take up the sport."

Fitzwilliam lifted his face from the towel and looked at his companion. About Jackson, it had once been said that it was impossible to gaze upon his form without thinking that nature had sent him to earth as a model. Nature, however, had not been as kind to his face as to his physique. His forehead was low, and the brushed-forward style in which he affected his hair made it seem even more peculiarly so, his nose and mouth were coarse, and his ears projected overly from his head. But his eyes were said to form a large portion of his power as a pugilist. And indeed, Fitzwilliam thought, they were somehow riveting. Under this compelling gaze, in fact, he felt the urge to spill the entire tale.

"Not much for sparring," he began, somewhat unnecessarily, since every one of his five previous private lessons had ended in more or less the same way as today's. If Jackson had to bite back a grin at this understatement, it was not apparent on his face. He only nodded with a sympathetic look. "Frankly, after Truesdale," Fitzwilliam continued with a shudder, "I had vowed never to find myself on this side of the ropes again. But now. . ." He trailed off, studying his boxing shoes.

"You find yourself overcome by a love for the sport," Jackson suggested with a grin.

"Oh, I've always had a love for the sport," replied Fitzwilliam with a grin in return, "as long as it is you, rather than me practicing it. Not that it isn't a signal honor to be knocked down by you. I swear it, John, I've never seen a man more elegant and easy on his feet—"

"However . . ." Jackson prompted, effectively cutting off what promised to become a paean to his own skills.

"However"—Fitzwilliam paused, looking uncomfortable as he recalled his own predicament—"I, er, find I have been issued a challenge in the ring. One I have no choice but to accept."

Jackson looked at him consideringly. "Are you certain about having no choice?" he asked.

Fitzwilliam threw back his head and laughed. "Is that your kindhearted way of telling me that I've no chance?" he asked.

"No, no," Jackson assured him. "But having seen you shoot and fence, my lord, I can well understand why your opponent chose as he did. Do you mind if I ask who issued the challenge?"

"Raymond Walters," Fitzwilliam replied. "Where does that leave me?"

Jackson's response was unsatisfyingly prompt. "Needing quite a bit of work."

Fitzwilliam frowned. "I'd guessed as much. Can you help me, do you think?"

"I'm not certain," Jackson admitted.

"Be candid," Fitzwilliam said. "No need to mince your words."

"Well . . ." Jackson hesitated, and then, seeing only interest in Fitzwilliam's expression, continued with candor. "I actually find myself somewhat surprised even now by what a poor pupil you show yourself. You have an excellent physique—one of the best I've seen—and a grace and quickness in everything else, that makes your showing in the ring all the more surprising. It may simply be that you lack the patience to learn the science of the sport. As I've pointed out time and again, you are too easily hurried and all too often can be pushed to rush in instead of waiting on your guard, and your distances are frequently ill-judged. But beyond that"—he shook his head—"well, I'm at a loss to explain it."

"And Raymond Walters? Again, honestly."

"What I say shall remain between us?"

"Absolutely."

"He is good, but brutish. He relies on a violent attack that overwhelms and eventually exhausts his opponent. And he prefers to go without gloves, which allows him to inflict more damage, especially about the face. I'm sure you realize that there are very few gentlemen, certainly among my customers, who prefer their sparring bare-handed. As to your chances, a man with a good, patient, defensive attitude could probably keep him from being able to connect many effectual hits. But your style stands almost no chance against him. You don't hit or lunge as well as he does, and as things stand now, you won't be able to keep him at bay."

"You paint a grim picture. Should I despair?"

"Never despair," replied Jackson with a smile. "We shall keep working at it. The problem, though, from my way of seeing it"—here his smile turned to a frown—"is that you need more intensive training than I am able to give you. A few morning lessons will not accomplish what needs to be done. It seems to me that what you really need is someone who can go away to the country with you for a sennight or two and really concentrate on working with you."

"Could you not do that?"

Jackson shook his head. "I honestly don't see that I can leave my responsibilities here so suddenly." He motioned around them. "And may I ask where this match is to take place?"

"Here."

"Under those circumstances it would be considered, and rightly so, unfair tactics were I to work too much with you."

"I can see your point. But who, then?"

"I've several instructors who should do handily."

"You don't suppose," began Fitzwilliam, leaning forward in his excitement at his sudden idea, "that the fellow who writes the column in the *Post* would consent to do it, do you?" he asked, deciding he might as well swallow his pride altogether.

"That's hard for me to answer," replied Jackson smoothly, "as I've no idea who he is."

"I am not altogether certain I believe that," replied Fitzwilliam with what he trusted was a shrewd look, or as shrewd as could be expected from a man who had just been soundly beaten. "But at any rate, I'd not ask you to be a go-between. I was thinking I could write to him in the care of the *Post* and see if he would consent to observe me."

Jackson hated to cast a pall over such hopefulness. "I agree it might help. I've rarely run across such an excellent eye for the sport," he said. "I vow, he even catches things I miss. But he seems most intent on remaining anonymous, and he's somehow cagey enough to find his way in here in secret day after day," he shook his head in perplexity. "So I'm not optimistic that you'll be able to lure him out."

"I would pay him whatever he asks, if that might make a difference," offered Fitzwilliam, carefully. "This match means a great deal to my honor."

"I am certain any man would take that offer into account when formulating his decision," replied Jackson, equally carefully. Fitzwilliam knew that was as close as Jackson was going to come to admitting he knew the wretched fellow. "I cannot see that it could harm anything to try contacting him," Jackson continued. "Through the newspaper, of course."

"Of course. And so I shall, as soon as I get home. Assuming that I am able to walk out of here," Fitzwilliam replied with a rueful smile. "In the meantime, shall I see you tomorrow for more punishment?"

"Same time, same place," Jackson confirmed, wondering if there was, in fact, any way he could convince Addie to help. It might just answer on any number of points.

Chapter 20

Addie attempted to suppress a yawn. Her inability to keep her eyes open was surely a result of there having been so much excitement of late, she assured herself. And not, as she might otherwise have been inclined to think, a response to Wallace's company. He had this day, as had become his custom since she had accepted him, dropped round for a morning call.

Funny, really, to refer to them as morning calls, Addie decided, since they in actuality began in the afternoon, and in his case, at least, stretched interminably onward into evening. This was in direct contrast to Fitzwilliam's calls, which had been, since he had pushed her up against the wall and kissed her shamelessly and then disappeared, presumably to go to his mistress, some five days ago, nonexistent. She blushed just thinking about their last parting. Really, it was altogether for the best not to think about how long Wallace's visits felt, she decided, as she suppressed another yawn.

She had seen Fitzwilliam since, though, being put through his paces by Jackson on a fairly regular basis of late. Which was surprising, considering that those rooms were a place she would have thought he'd have been avoiding under any and all circumstances. But every time she'd been there this week, there he'd been, in the ring with Jackson himself, the rooms otherwise deserted. And if he'd improved so much as a hair, she certainly hadn't been able to detect it. And she rather prided herself on a good eye for such things.

The judgment displayed by Jackson, even in his instructing mode, had foiled Fitzwilliam at almost every hit. He hadn't, Addie thought, connected more than two that morning. And Jackson managed time after time to put in rallies of blows in quick succession, fibbing him easily. And if the man even knew there was such a thing as sparring with judgment to gain time, he showed no sign of it.

And Jackson was never too fast with his pupils, Addie knew, so he was holding back a considerable amount—likely more than he was giving. She shook her head. And he had a good six-and-ten years on Fitzwilliam.

Wallace paused—expecting a reply?—and Addie realized that she had no idea on what topic he had been conversing. He slurped his tea noisily, having made his apologies before the fact, with the announcement that obstructed nasal passages frequently rendered quiet sipping all but impossible between the months of November and May. But it was, in this instance, a relatively small inconvenience to bear, he had added, considering that their jaunt in Fitzwilliam's open Cabriolet should have in all likelihood resulted in his untimely demise.

Addie ignored the voice in her head reminding her that she had deemed listening to this man sip his tea for the rest of her life very definitely the lesser of two evils.

She pasted a resolute smile to her lips. Thusly encouraged, Wallace began another monologue, and she allowed her thoughts to drift back to what she had seen during her morning at Jackson's.

Raymond Walters had faced Tom Edgerton not long after Fitzwilliam had departed without so much as a rubdown. Lord, he was going to be stiff, she thought. At first Addie had almost beaten a hasty retreat in her terror that she would be recognized. It had not taken long, however, for her to realize that he wouldn't have noticed her presence had she been in the ring next to him, so intent was he on the brutish beating he was inflicting on poor Edgerton. That Raymond Walters was in training for a Very Important Fight was a fact being whispered about amongst the onlookers. Whoever his eventual opponent might be, Addie could not help but feel for him. Walters's style was effective enough; there was no disputing that fact. But it embodied none of the grace or science that made the sport such a pleasure to behold, she thought with disdain. He had relied instead on simply giving Edgerton such a relentless battering, and bare-fisted, too, that the fellow was eventually beaten into a state of exhausted submission. And today was friendly sparring. She hated even to dignify such unsporting behavior by writing about it, which could only serve to further decrease the honor of the sport in the estimation of the general public. But, at least, by doing so she might be able to give his opponent some idea of what he was going to come up against, she reasoned. Although likely the fellow already knew.

"Adelaide!"

From Wallace's querulous tone, which had been increasingly entering their exchanges these last few days, she realized he was saying her name not for the first time. She truly had been engrossed in her own thoughts. "Yes, Wallace," she replied, resolving with a trace of guilt, that she really would try harder in the future to attend to what he was saying.

"You were not attending!" he accused.

"I'm so sorry, Wallace." She smiled in apology. "I must confess that I was woolgathering."

He frowned. "When we are wed, Adelaide . . ." he began.

Addie had to swallow a sigh, her guilt rapidly vanishing. This was becoming tiresome already.

"Yes?" she replied, an edge to her voice.

He took another noisy sip of tea, and said kindly, which of course, made her feel guilty for her uncharitable thoughts, "Your head will not be so cluttered, my dear, and I'm certain you'll be able to attend me better."

Addie closed her eyes momentarily, the guilt gone.

"It will be easier then, of course," Wallace continued, still not unkindly. "Having a man, once again in charge, I think you shall find, will relieve you of what can only have been the odious burdens that females were never meant to carry. And Mother, of course, can serve as an exemplar in that arena."

Addie opened her mouth to formulate a reply that felt satisfactory while not giving vent to her true thoughts, but was effectively saved from having to do so by Honoria's appearance.

"Addie, Wallace," her aunt trilled as she swept through the double doors, trailing none other than John "Gentleman" Jackson himself, and adding unnecessarily, "we have another visitor, my dears!"

"John!" Addie said, with genuine pleasure, standing to welcome him as he made his bows.

"You are looking uncommonly well, Addie," he said, straightening and embracing her fondly. "Almost as well as your aunt, who incidentally, only appears to grow younger with each passing year."

Honoria, indeed sounding almost like the debutante Jackson was painting her, blushed and giggled at this transparent bit of flattery.

Addie stared at her aunt. "Mr. John Jackson, may I present Wallace Raines?" she said, having given up on Honoria to recover her wits from the compliment and do her duty. "My, er, fiancé," she added, almost as an afterthought.

Jackson's dark brow went up, but he refrained from comment, and Addie had to assume that he had already been made privy to an earful from Honny on the topic. "Honored to make your acquaintance, sir," he said, and Addie knew he was taking note of Wallace's paltry grip as they shook hands. "And my"— he slid a quick glance in Addie's direction—"felicitations, of course, to both of you."

"Well, well. This *is* unusual. *Most* unusual. Indeed," Wallace said, his excitement at being in drawing-room company with the world's most celebrated pugilist warring with the conflicting feeling that such a presence could not be at all the thing in a household of women. Not to mention his conviction that boxing as a sport was almost entirely the domain of ruffians, libertines, and characters of lesser moral caliber in general. He finally settled for standing close to Addie and smiling at the newcomer in what he deemed a friendly but not *encouraging* manner. He did, after all, see no reason not to boast at his club in a casual manner of having taken tea with Jackson *en famille*.

I wish Wallace would stop hovering, Addie thought with irritation as she poured tea for the newcomer. *And what is he doing with that ridiculous grin on his face? Why does he not realize that he has overstayed his welcome and leave us?*

"Wallace, Mr. Jackson was one of Papa's closest friends," she explained, aware that his sense of propriety was no doubt quivering.

He smiled tightly in response to this information, but still did not yield his place.

Jackson's friendship with her father had indeed been close enough that his presence for a call would hardly occasion comment. But Addie knew that with both of them so reluctant to call attention to their association at the moment, he would not have come unless he had something of import to discuss. Goodness knew, they saw each other almost every day, but certainly did not speak.

Honoria who had been surveying the selection of cakes with a deal of interest, picked up a seed cake. "Addie and I had been discussing the wording for puffing the news off to the *Post,* Wallace," she said before pausing to take a dainty bite. She finished chewing, swallowed, dabbed her lips with a napkin, and then continued with a frown, "We simply cannot seem to agree on the exact details. Especially since no date has been set. But of a certainty, we cannot even consider doing so until Drew's mama returns. So worrying. It quite brings to mind that *debacle* back in 'ninety when Antonia Spencer got the wording confused and positively *all* of London was convinced she was marrying Corbett Smythe, Viscount Ackerly, but she was in actuality marrying Corbin Asterly, Viscount Smythe! Truly! *I* never did understand the ruckus myself, as it was apparent for anyone to see that Ackerly was *Completely Unsuitable* on account of the fact that he was practically in his dotage, already married, and had seven children to boot, not to mention *at least* that many mistresses—which, I suppose, does account for everyone's willingness to believe that poor Catriona, his wife, was agreeable to letting him wed again. Although, to be honest, considering the circumstances *that* would have been *most*—"

Wallace, aghast was on his feet. "My dear lady! Of course you cannot expect to pen this yourselves!" he burst out. "That is exactly the type of thing of which I was speaking earlier to Adelaide. That type of burden you gentle ladies should not even *dream* of having to undertake! Wording an announcement requires writing, and writing requires a type of thought process of which females are simply not capable." Having apparently forgotten his concern for the proprieties in his indignation, he directed a conspiratorial smile in Jackson's direction, while saying, "I shall assist you, Honoria. I shall just need a quiet place in which to compose my thoughts. If our visitor can make do with Adelaide's company, perhaps we should excuse ourselves and I shall show you how it is done," he suggested.

"Addie's company, as always, will be a complete pleasure," replied Jackson, ever the gentleman.

"But to have no one with whom to discuss the masculine pleasures of your chosen sport—"

"I will endeavor in any case to speak of something more suitable to a female's ears," Jackson assured him gravely.

And apparently satisfied with that, Wallace allowed himself to be led out by Honoria.

" 'To have no one able to discuss the masculine pleasures of my chosen sport!' " Jackson said, no sooner had Wallace and Honoria cleared the room. "There are a few points of intelligence regarding your interests that your, ah, fiancé has apparently not been apprised of, Addie."

Addie sighed. "Can you not even wait until they are out of earshot before you upbraid me?"

"Upbraid you? I am doing no such thing, my dear. It is just that he seems somewhat, er, well, *staid*. And it *was* a surprise, a not entirely welcome one, to be introduced out of hand to your fiancé, when I had no idea such a person existed." He looked at her intently. "When I had thought, in fact, ah, been under the impression that—"

"I'll spare you the trouble of trying to phrase it delicately." Addie took a deep breath. "As events with Fitzwilliam were not coming to pass, I thought it prudent to accept Wallace."

Jackson trained his gaze directly at her, and Addie too felt the power of those piercing eyes. "But will you be happy with him, Addie?" he asked softly. "Forgive me for asking so plainly. But as your father's closest friend, I consider it my province to assure myself of your happiness as he would have. And in this case, I am not entirely convinced."

Addie fidgeted with her cup and looked down at it so he would not see her eyes fill with tears. "We shall go on tolerably enough. And anyway, there is no reason," she continued bracingly, "to think that I would have been happy with Fitzwilliam. Wallace *means* well."

He still gazed at her intently. "I am not certain that is enough, but I will let it rest. I am come, actually, to request your help, and I beg that you will consider carefully before giving your answer."

"Well, I am certainly intrigued now," Addie said, and smiled at him, relieved to be moving away from the subject of Wallace. "And, it goes without saying, would welcome an opportunity to help *you* for a change."

"I've a pupil who needs your assistance and is prepared to pay handsomely for it."

Addie's eyes opened wide. "Exactly what kind of pupil?" she asked.

"What kind do I have?" He grinned roguishly.

"You intrigue me further," Addie said carefully. "Go on, John."

"Actually, although to be honest, I'm not certain if this

makes things harder or easier, it is, well, ah, Fitzwilliam,'' he said in a casual tone.

"Fitzwilliam!" Addie replied. And Jackson could not help but note that she had gone extremely pale. "Did he put you up to this?" she demanded. "He did! Didn't he? That . . . that . . . Wallace was right! He *is* a *libertine!* I may have behaved shockingly with him, but—"

"Behaved shockingly with him?" Jackson interrupted, entertaining the thought that perhaps he had not hit the fellow hard enough, after all.

"Well, yes. No. Yes. But that doesn't give him license to— Oh! How *dare* he—''

"Addie," Jackson interrupted gently. "Hold your punches a moment, my dear, and explain yourself. Rest assured that Fitzwilliam did not put me up to anything, but I am now thinking about laying the fellow out myself, instead of assisting him! What do you mean you have behaved shockingly with him? He merely came to me for more assistance than I can offer at the moment. He is to spar against Raymond Walters, you see, and needs—''

"*He* is to spar against Raymond Walters?" Addie demanded. Having now gone from frighteningly pale to alarmingly flushed, she got up and began to pace the little sitting room. "Are you telling me that it is *Fitzwilliam* who is to meet Raymond Walters?" she asked again. "That's who Walters was practicing for? *That's* who Fitzwilliam has been practicing for?"

"Yes, but—''

"Boxing? Oh my, and this is *all* my fault," she wailed, throwing herself back into her chair. "How could Mr. Walters be so odious?"

"Addie?" Jackson frowned. Addie was usually so very sensible—not at all subject to this type of baffling unpredictability. "How on earth can it be your fault? And for the last time, what do you mean you have behaved shockingly with him?"

So, for the second time in a week, Addie found herself sobbing out the tale. This time, on the comfortingly solid chest of a very bewildered John Jackson.

"Goodness," he said, when she had finished. He patted her back and frowned over her head, as she still leaned against his substantial chest. He wished he had time to think. True, her behavior with Fitzwilliam was, as she had described it, scandalous. But it was not like Addie to be so driven by her emotions. Nor did it seem in character for Fitzwilliam, he had to admit, to toy with a lady. He didn't know him all that well, to be sure, but what he did know he couldn't help but like.

And in honesty, he could not be comfortable with the advent of this Wallace Raines. And Honoria, to judge by the surprisingly succinct earful she'd given him on the way in, wasn't any better pleased. Perhaps it would serve even better than he had thought to throw Addie and Fitzwilliam together. It just might, in fact, be the answer to everyone's problems.

"So, you do see why I cannot possibly help him?" Addie demanded, sniffling, as she straightened and looked at him.

Jackson, who well knew the advantages of sparring for wind, ignored his wet shirtfront and stirred his already well-stirred tea. Still silent, he drained the dregs from his cup. When he did speak, his tones were thoughtful. "Mm. Actually, no," he said. "Considering what you've just told me, it seems you are almost obligated, Adelaide, to help him."

Addie sniffed, wishing for once that one of Wallace's handkerchiefs was close by, as she, as usual, had forgotten hers and none seemed to be forthcoming from Jackson, further proving her point about why she needed to marry a handkerchief man. "Obligated? To Fitzwilliam?" She sniffled. "I don't understand, John. How could that be?"

"Well, you've just told me that it was in defending your honor that he got into this in the first place, *and*," Jackson pointed out in reasonable tones, "Walters no doubt got the idea issue the challenge for the ring based on the piece *you* wrote about Fitzwilliam and Truesdale! Goodness knows you did a good job of making him sound an easy mark, which, I grant you, he is. It seems to me that as such, you actually *owe* him your assistance."

At his words, Addie got up and began to pace again, as

she did, twisting a small gold bracelet that she wore. Jackson observed, but allowed her to pace uninterrupted with her thoughts, until she stopped abruptly, and, turning to him, said, *"If* I were to say yes, and that is a monumental *if,* how would I even go about it? I can't simply mention it at Almack's, you know. *Thank you for the lovely country dance, Fitzwilliam. The lemonade here seems even weaker than usual tonight, does it not? Surely puce is not Miss Thomaston's color, and by the way, have I mentioned that I am* Anonymous?" She shook her head at the improbability of that scenario. "He'd think me unhinged, to say the least."

Jackson laughed. "You only need say 'yes,' Addie, and leave the rest to me," he said.

Addie resumed her pacing. It was tempting. She was, after all, as Jackson had pointed out, partially to blame. And it would be a challenge, to be sure. But if one was to be honest, and she could not afford not to be, well, there were other temptations. Ones that filled her with both dread and longing. "I don't know," she said, finally. "How would we manage it? Wallace, you know, would not . . ." She held up her hands.

Jackson let out a breath of relief. He knew he had her hooked. "Come tomorrow to the rooms in your usual outfit at your usual time, Addie, and as I said, leave the rest to me," he said, firmly squelching any ideas she might have of protesting further. She sat again, and he covered her hand with his. "Trust me," he said. "You won't regret it."

She looked at him, and this time he felt the power of her steady gray gaze. "Won't I?" she asked.

"No," he responded, considerably, truth be told, more emphatically than he felt. "You won't."

Chapter 21

"Have you taken leave of your senses?" Justine demanded when Addie found her in the little conservatory where she was tinkering with her roses despite the fact that given the season, there was not a bloom in sight. "You have, haven't you?"

Addie sighed. "Likely yes."

"Well, you must have." Justine peeled off the gloves she used when gardening. "How on earth do you propose to manage to teach Fitzwilliam to box?" she asked, setting them down on a table.

"What will these be?" Addie asked, ignoring Justine's question and nodding toward the bush Justine had just mulched.

"Portlands," Justine replied. "They're new. A damask crossed, I think, with a crimson China."

Addie sighed again. "Perhaps I should take up gardening or something ladylike, work on my embroidery skills or some such."

Despite her horror, Justine had to laugh at her sister's woebegone expression. "Well, Wallace would approve, certainly. And may even have a list of more ladylike pursuits he has deemed suitable. But as you do have that tendency to kill plants, more or less by being in the same room with them,'' she pointed out, ''I shouldn't choose gardening. In fact, I'm about to suggest that we quit the conservatory altogether in the name of the well-being of my roses. And as for embroidery, well, yours is . . .'' She shrugged eloquently.

''My ladylike accomplishments do not, it is true, amount to much.''

''No. All in all, you would do much better to try to persuade Wallace to see milling in a new and *ladylike* light,'' Justine suggested, and they both laughed. ''Or, of course,'' Justine added, sobering, ''Find yourself a less conventional husband.''

''Justine.'' Addie's tone was quiet but the cautionary note was clear.

''Very well. I shall restrain myself, albeit with difficulty, from going down that road for now. I will say instead that I think you must be dicked in the nob to even be considering this scheme.''

Addie laughed and raised a brow.

Her sister smiled back at her. ''Drew taught it to me. Do you think I should use it on Honny?''

''Well it certainly is all the go, and makes you sound awake on all suits when you use it to the cow's thumb, but I shouldn't raise that breeze unless you desire to be subjected to a bear jaw,'' Addie replied.

''I give up.'' Justine gave a theatrical sigh. ''Your cant will always be better than mine. Perhaps Wallace will consider *that* a ladylike achievement.''

''Almost certainly he will,'' Addie agreed.

''Come, love, let's go have some tea,'' Justine suggested, and sparing one last concerned glance at her roses, she led the way into the hall. ''We can tally more of your ladylike accomplishments on the way,'' she suggested. ''Singing?''

''God, no.''

''Ah, pianoforte?''

''*You* be the judge,'' Addie suggested. ''Goodness knows you've heard me play.''

"Hmm. How about learning to lard your conversation with French, à la mode? Arranging flowers? Watercoloring?"

"No. No. And no. Even thinking about those things bores me witless," Addie said as they entered the drawing room. "There is no help for it, Justine, I shall simply have to stick with facers and drawn corks."

When they were comfortably settled, with Addie pouring, she said, "Well what exactly did John have in mind?"

"John Jackson or John Fitzwilliam?" Addie queried.

"Jackson. I always forget that Fitzwilliam even has a first name."

"Well, he does, and he pointed it out to me just the other night." Addie handed her sister a cup.

"Really?" Justine asked with interest, taking a sip.

"Mm." Addie swallowed her mouthful. "But I told him it would give Honoria fits to hear that from my lips."

"And it would. Unless of course it was in the way of a wedding vow," Justine shot back.

"Well it won't be that." Addie examined a sandwich and then took a bite. She swallowed and then giggled. "It's much more likely to be in the way of, *Not much of a rib-roaster, John. Now aim for the nob.*"

Justine laughed at this. "And *that* I am certain would not give Honny fits!"

"Not at all," Addie agreed, still laughing herself.

And then Justine sobered. "But surely you cannot mean to do it, Addie, to help him with his boxing. I mean, it sounds impossible to help him, anyway, and how would you even—"

"John, John *Jackson*, said to leave it all to him. That he would take care of the details." Addie shook her head at her own folly in even considering the scheme.

Justine was apparently of the same mind. "But why would you even consider such a thing?" she asked, a line between her brows.

"To help him."

"No, Addie." Justine shook her head with conviction. "You may be fooling yourself, but that won't fool me. I do believe you want to help him, but that's not enough. It just won't wash.''

"I did, I mean, it is, after all, my fault that he got into this in the first place and—"

"Addie."

Addie looked at her sister and was the first to drop her eyes. She put her sandwich back onto the plate and looked up again. "To be with him. Just a little longer," she said quietly, her gaze meeting Justine's once more.

"Then why—"

"No!" Addie stood and realized she was shaking. "I've heard it all before, Justine, every word. It's his obligation. It's my obligation. It doesn't matter if he doesn't love me. I'm the most stubborn person alive. Well it doesn't matter. None of it matters." She looked at her sister. "I won't marry him."

And then she fled the room, leaving Justine looking thoughtful as she picked up another sandwich.

Chapter 22

Jackson thought of Fitzwilliam giving Addie cause for regrets as he forced himself to place a well-aimed but light right-hander beneath the fellow's ribs, which was almost disconcertingly easy.

"Oof. Enough," pleaded Fitzwilliam from the floor.

"Already?" asked Jackson as Fitzwilliam picked himself up and leaned back, panting against the ropes.

"Wind knocked out of me," he gasped in reply. He stood for a moment and then, his breath returning, shook his head. "Might as well just stand there and let Walters do his worst," he said in glum tones.

From the corner where she was unobtrusively mopping the same spot for at least the tenth time, Addie could easily hear their conversation. She slid a quick glance over at the two men. Even at this unholy hour, winded, sweating, and gloomy, Fitzwilliam was the most glorious man she had ever seen.

"Well," she heard Jackson say, in casual tones, "I might have a solution." And it was all she could do to keep from disgracing herself by casting up her accounts in panic.

Fitzwilliam managed a grim chuckle. "Then you're even more a miracle worker than I'd credited you, John."

"You are still interested in pursuing assistance from *Anonymous,* then?" Jackson asked, leaning casually against the ropes and unlacing his gloves.

"As I see it, the fellow's my only hope of salvation. Found out the name of the publisher yesterday. A Mr. Snedens. I'd planned on going round this afternoon to ask him, no, make that beg him, to contact *Anonymous* on my behalf."

Jackson removed his gloves and put them down. "No need, he said, without looking up. "The, er, *fellow* has already agreed to help you."

"You spoke to Mr. Snedens?"

"No." Jackson crossed his arms and pinned Fitzwilliam again with that gaze, before continuing. "I spoke to *Anonymous.*"

"And? Will he help?"

"Yes. But there are conditions."

"I cannot imagine that under the circumstances they could possibly be enough to make me refuse his help," Fitzwilliam assured him grimly.

"These conditions have been imposed by me, not *Anonymous,* mind you." Jackson's tone and his expression defied Fitzwilliam to refuse them.

Fitzwilliam inclined his head. "Of course."

"You will behave at all times as a gentleman toward *Anonymous,* whatever that might entail. You will also obey any prescribed training regimen as though it came from me."

"Done," Fitzwilliam said, with alacrity.

"And you will work out the monetary arrangements directly between yourselves."

"Agreed."

"Excellent. I think we've a deal, then," Jackson said, loudly.

"That was all?"

"Yes."

"I had expected more conditions somehow."

And so had she, Addie thought in alarm. *What was Jackson about? Where was, don't reveal her identity? Where was, don't*

walk away when you see who it is? Behave at all times as a
gentleman! What the hell does that mean?

"Those, in the end, if there are more, will be up to *Anonymous.*"

"Of course." Fitzwilliam laughed. "You *are* cagey, John.
I vow, you had me completely convinced you didn't know
him."

"Well, in truth, I don't know *him,*" Jackson said, a grin
crossing his face. He motioned toward a corner.

There was a maid there. And the girl, who Fitzwilliam had
not even noticed, put down her dust rag and started in their
direction. Before Fitzwilliam had time to wonder at this, Jackson continued. "I do, however, know *her.*"

And then, to Fitzwilliam's surprise, he began to laugh.

From his pale face, and look of horrified recognition, there
could be no doubt that Fitzwilliam did not find the situation
nearly so amusing. He and Addie stared at each other.

Her gray eyes, he registered, were huge in her pale face as
she slowly pulled off her mobcap.

She was terrified, and Fitzwilliam's silence was not helping
matters.

Just when the quiet threatened to stretch on longer than was
bearable, he said, "*Jesus!*" in the most stricken tone she had
ever heard him use.

Addie was too terrified to even remark on his blasphemy.
She was shaking so, in fact, that she doubted she could even
get the words out. "Fitzwilliam, I—"

"*Jesus!*" he said again, in an equally shaking voice, and
then, "*Addie!*"

Jackson lounged against the ropes, arms still crossed, watching them.

"Is this some kind of joke?" Fitzwilliam demanded in
choked tones, looking from Addie to Jackson and back again.
When Addie shook her head in silence, he began to unlace his
gloves. Finished, he tossed them onto the floor and stepped out
of the ring, breaking the stillness. "This *is* a joke, right? It had
bloody well better be. But surely I don't deserve it? I'd thought

better of both of you." He was about to stalk from the room, in high dudgeon, when Addie's words stopped him in his tracks.

"You will end up on the receiving end of a winding blow to the torso every time you try to mill on the retreat the way you did this morning, you know, Fitzwilliam," she said, and this time her voice was clear and sure. "You provide the easiest mark imaginable for a cross-body blow. And, indeed, you would do well to consider that what you have received from John are the merest sparring-school taps in contrast to the hits Walters will deal you."

At her quiet but authoritative words, Fitzwilliam, despite his pique, turned to face her. "It really is you, then, Addie? *You* are *Anonymous?*" he asked, almost in a whisper.

She nodded.

Fitzwilliam sat down shakily in a chair and rested his head in his hands. "Jesus," he said again, this time with less venom. "You knew about facers and rib-roasters? And facers and drawn corks, and blacked peepers, and, Jesus! Covent Garden opera dancers? Bella!" He truly looked as though he were in shock.

She nodded, forcing herself to meet his gaze levelly.

He shook his head slowly. "But why?" he asked, still holding her gaze. "Why would you do that?"

Jackson handed Fitzwilliam a towel, and he mopped his face with it before distractedly picking up his discarded shirt and shrugging into it.

Addie was relieved to be freed from the intensity of his expression. "Money, mostly," she said bluntly as she sat down opposite him. "At the beginning, anyway."

Seeing that they were fully engaged with each other, Jackson took the opportunity to slip into the other room, leaving them, most improperly, alone. But under the circumstances, *that* impropriety seemed the very least of it.

"Money!" he heard Fitzwilliam repeat, blankly, as if that was the last thing he had expected to hear. "You needed money?" And then Jackson discreetly closed the door behind himself.

"Yes, money," Addie replied. "You have heard of it? 'Tis vulgar to need it, Honny tells me, but—"

"But why did you not come to me? Surely you must have known that I would never have allowed ..." he began to demand, but trailed off as he caught sight of her face.

"What would you have done?" she asked, her voice almost a whisper.

"Married you," he practically snapped in his anger at himself for having only seen what he had wanted to see.

"That," Addie said, calmly, "is why I did not come to you."

"Of course," he mused, almost to himself, "that is why."

Addie looked at the hollows under the high cheekbones and the shadows in his eyes. She firmed her chin. "I did not wish you to marry me, you see."

"I do see." So much for the fantasy of Addie loving him. Not only had she not come to him in what must have been a dire hour of need, but she had lied outright to him about their circumstances when he had asked at Vauxhall. The idea of marrying him, in fact, was so distasteful to her that she had resorted to writing about boxing and then pledged herself to share the name and the bed of Wallace Raines. In spite of his aversion to marriage, he truly felt wounded that she would go to such lengths.

All of which somehow combined to make him no better than his father had been. Callously pursuing his own pleasure with no eye to his responsibilities to such an extent that she would choose that dull stick Wallace Raines. He shook his head at this thought. And he had judged himself better than that.

But he forced himself to smile, and said, carefully, "No, it would appear that you did not. I am sorry that the idea was so repugnant to you."

"Oh, no, never that, Fitzwilliam," Addie hastened to assure him. "It is only that I had, ah, well, already formed a *tendre* for Wallace, you see."

Fitzwilliam raised a brow. "Ah, yes. I'd forgotten." Now, that, he just knew, was a clanker. He could well believe that the mere thought of bracketing herself to a Claremont man revolted her down to her very toes, and goodness knew, he could sympathize. But that she loved Wallace Raines? Never.

He recalled the heat that seemed to have flared between them, remembered how sweet she had felt under his lips and under his hands. And then he thought of her throwing herself away on such a cold fish as Raines because of his own careless disregard. And was, suddenly, so blindingly furious that he had to catch his breath. *She may not want me, but she'll let me do my duty by her and she'll like it, or I'll be damned,* he promised himself savagely, declining to examine his sudden volte-face on the subject. And he knew just how he'd do it.

He smiled again, tentatively. And she smiled back. The same way.

And so they sat, smiling uneasily uneasily at one another for a moment, each wondering what the other's next move would be.

And then, "I do not guess Honoria has seen this, ah, charming costume," Fitzwilliam said, lounging back, seeming from Addie's perspective, perfectly at his ease now, and crossing one leg over the other.

"No."

Fitzwilliam smiled again and allowed his eyes to roam boldly over her, making her flush. Really, what was it about this revolting outfit? she wondered. First Raymond Walters and now Fitzwilliam. Honoria, with her attention to the defects in Addie's mode of dress, would surely die if she knew that it was in fact their kitchen maid's grubby castoff that was bringing men flocking with a predatory look in their eyes.

"I'm finding it rather fetching, myself," he said, sitting forward again and fingering the sleeve, as if confirming Addie's suspicion, "but I can easily see that Honoria would not, indeed. In fact, I should guess that she'd rather starve than allow you to go about like this."

"You are right, I am certain," Addie allowed, with a quick intake of breath at his touch, an answering smile beginning to tug at her own mouth. "Which is why she has not seen it."

Now that he had gotten over the shock, Fitzwilliam, the infuriating man, seemed to think the entire thing vastly amusing. He let go of her arm and, lounging back again, started to laugh, while she stared at him in amazement.

"Oh, Addie," he said, laughter overtaking him. "You asked me about my eye at Vauxhall, and all the time, you knew. It was you! *You* wrote that about me," he finally gasped.

She nodded again, unsure what to make of this change in his mood.

"Of all the rotten, ill-using, despicable things to do," he said, still laughing. "To think it was *you*, of all people. And all this time I'd thought——" He shook his head.

"Well, you were, ah, in need of improvement," she replied carefully.

"I should say so. But still, what a trick to have served me, the man——" He stopped and looked at her.

Addie looked at her feet, refusing to meet his gaze, and remained silent.

"I agreed to Jackson's conditions, Addie, but then you already know that," he said, suddenly serious. "So let us discuss payment."

"You will not pay me, Fitzwilliam," she said firmly. "Indeed, the family fortunes have changed. Justine will be well taken care of, and Wallace is a very wealthy man."

"I most certainly will pay you, Addie," he said, equally firmly.

"There is no need for that. And I cannot accept your money, Fitzwilliam."

"I'd never miss it, you know."

"I still cannot accept it."

He smiled. "Well then, it seems we are at *point non plus*, Addie, because I cannot accept your help without payment. And, as I am certain John Jackson has pointed out, you cannot, in good conscience, withdraw your help, due to the simple fact that you got me into this in the first place with that absurd column." He smiled. Slowly.

And she felt her breath catch.

''So, what, then, shall we do?'' he continued in tones that left her absolutely no doubt that he had already decided.

Addie knew she was the mouse in the cat's paw, but that smile had addled her. ''I don't know, Fitzwilliam. What?'' she asked, swallowing.

He leaned closer, resting his elbows on his thighs, still smiling. ''I promised Jackson, as I am certain you heard, lurking about as you were, that I would behave at all times as a gentleman with you. So let us agree on the gentleman's payment, Addie. A wager.''

''I do not gamble, Fitzwilliam,'' she said, repressively, and sat straighter in her chair to put more distance between them. ''Nor do I, for that matter, *lurk*.''

''Hardly gambling! And the lurking, well, I suppose that is open to interpretation. But what I am proposing is a simple little wager between, er, friends, Addie.'' He had somehow closed the distance again. ''We *are* friends, are we not?''

She eyed him warily and sighed. ''And exactly what are the stakes you are proposing?''

''Nothing much.'' He smiled again. Slowly. Again.

And her insides curled.

''If you train me, and I win—''

''Unlikely,'' she said, dryly. ''I should aim for survival were I you.''

He ignored her. ''—you marry me,'' he said lightly.

She gasped. ''No!''

''As our fathers agreed.''

''No!''

''And, if I lose—''

''More likely.''

''—I shall release you from their agreement and settle enough blunt on you that you will have no need to marry Raines. Or, for that matter anyone where your heart is not engaged.''

''No!''

''Yes,'' he answered quietly.

"You forget that I am betrothed to Wallace. The announcement has already been sent."

"*You* forget that *I* hold a prior claim, Addie. Get unbetrothed."

"People do not simply get unbetrothed, Fitzwilliam. Not and live to hold up their heads in society. The announcement has been sent. And you, anyway, released me, specifically to accept someone else, in case you've forgotten."

"I've changed my mind," he said airily, and Addie thought, entirely too arrogantly. "And believe me, as my wife you'd have no problem holding up your head. Announcement or no."

"But if you lose, and I get unbetrothed, which quite frankly I don't think is even a word, from Wallace, Raymond Walters will still have the means to damage both our reputations."

Fitzwilliam gestured dismissively. "Hang Raymond Walters. Who else knows that you are *Anonymous*, Addie?" His voice was suddenly, disarmingly, soft.

She blinked at his change of topic.

"Honoria? I realize she hasn't seen the little maid costume, but does she know?"

Addie nodded.

"And Justine?"

Addie nodded again, wondering where they were headed with this.

"Who else? Oh Lord! Drew! What a laugh he must be having at my expense."

This time Addie shook her head. "I know that Justine won't have told. I doubt she'll keep it from him when they are husband and wife, though."

"Of course not. And rightly so. Do you intend to share this little lark with Wallace when you become as one, Addie?" he asked, so casually that she wondered she hadn't seen it coming.

"You must know I do not, Fitzwilliam," she replied.

He smiled and lifted a brow. "I rather thought not."

"Blackmail, Fitzwilliam?" Addie said, raising a brow in return. "Hardly the *gentlemanly* thing to do."

"Well that, Addie, is a most *unladylike* accusation. I am, in fact, deeply wounded. I had no intention of blackmailing you. No, indeed. I prefer to think of it as . . . persuasion, offering you options. But however you choose to phrase it''—he looked at her meaningfully—"it certainly *would* be a shame for Wallace to hear of this.''

She looked back at him, the hurt so apparent in her expression that he had to remind himself it was for her own good. "And you, Fitzwilliam? What is there for you in this?'' she asked quietly.

His face shadowed. He looked, just for a moment, as serious as she had ever seen him.

Then he grinned, and said lightly, "I do right by you, Addie, as I told your father I would, and as I should have done some time ago.''

"Oh.'' She sighed, wishing there could have been just a trace of something else there.

"You would do this to me? For the sake of doing your duty? Truly?''

"Oh, yes,'' he said without missing a beat. "And *you* would lampoon me in the *Post* for all the world to read?''

She could not help but smile. "Touché, Fitzwilliam.''

He grinned in return.

"So I've no choice.''

"Not much, I'm afraid.''

"Agreed, then,'' she said, and then added, "but with reluctance,'' as she put out her hand.

Fitzwilliam let out the breath he had not realized he'd been holding. "Your reluctance is noted,'' he said, clasping her hand in a firm shake. His gaze though, was disconcertingly soft as he lifted the hand to his lips. Not at all the manner, truth to be told, in which he generally sealed his gentlemanly wagers.

And as the heat curled through her body from that ever so slight brush of his lips, Addie vowed that she would elope with Wallace to Gretna Green, if need be, rather than allow Fitzwilliam to sacrifice himself to duty. Thankfully, she told herself, he stood no chance of winning against Raymond Walters.

Chapter 23

Drew's fork almost stilled in the air. "Addie Winstead is *Anonymous*. That's very droll, Fitz," he said. "You almost had me believing that for a moment. It's something of a shame you ain't much for gaming, you know, because a fellow really can't tell when you mean . . ." His voice trailed off, as he saw the serious expression on his friend's face.

"Surely you don't mean it," he continued. "It simply can't be . . ." He trailed off yet again.

And so it went for some time.

Until, after many explanations on Fitzwilliam's part, and exclamations along the lines of *you cannot mean it,* and *surely this cannot be true,* on Drew's part, Drew finally said, actually going so far as to push his plate away, as he did, "I trust you will excuse me, then, when I ask if you have lost your mind? To be accepting Addie's help, having compromised her at Vauxhall is bad enough, but forcing her to wager on her engagement, well, it truly is above all things, Fitz."

"Never tell me that you are so incensed that you have lost your appetite?" Fitzwilliam replied coolly.

Drew retorted with all the heat Fitzwilliam's words were lacking. "I dashed well am, and I dashed well have."

"I see." Fitzwilliam waited.

And then Drew allowed, "Well, perhaps I haven't lost it *entirely,*" as he pulled back his plate. "A fellow does need breakfast. But that don't mean I'm not still incensed, Fitz."

"I'd trust not. And your anger, believe me, does you credit, Drew."

"But how can this be?" Drew asked, which, to be honest, was not the first time in the course of this conversation that such a sentiment had crossed his lips.

"How can what be?"

"Any of it. That she's *Anonymous,* that you are meeting Raymond Walters, that she's training you, that you've wagered to get her to break her engagement. Any of it!"

"Well, you can believe me, Drew, I had much the same reaction. Worse in fact."

"Indeed, I can." Drew nodded wisely. And then a thought hit him. "Does Justine—"

Fitzwilliam was nodding before the question was even out. "—know? She does."

Drew gazed at Fitzwilliam, and then began to laugh. "The little minx. Justine, not Addie, but Addie, too, I suppose. Well, you must admit it is rather funny, Fitz. I mean, she did skewer you over a flame, but well, and here you were the whole time thinking her so ladylike and refined."

"Yes, Drew," Fitzwilliam agreed with an air of great patience. "I *have* thought on that. And I did, believe it or not, see *some* humor in the situation."

"But to wager on the outcome of the mill with Walters . . . Well I don't know if it is all the go."

"I don't either, to be honest, but it was the only way I could think of to stop her from marrying him. I *was* a little taken aback, at the moment, what with her shedding her little maid disguise, and believe it or not, perhaps not thinking at my best."

Drew looked amused. "Lost your savoir faire for once, had you?"

"You could say that," Fitzwilliam conceded.

"Does it matter so much? Her marrying Raines?"

"Certainly. He's a pathetic rasher of wind. He'd forever be trying to turn her into something she's not—and shouldn't be."

Drew knew he was pushing. "Do you love her?"

"Of course not." Fitzwilliam looked impatient. "But I think we'll deal tolerably together, and letting her marry Raines is hardly what her father would have expected when he asked me to do right by her."

"Hmm. Suppose you're right." Drew looked at him so intently Fitzwilliam couldn't help but feeling that his thoughts were farther away than his words. "But a house party! Where she will *train* you! I mean, the mind positively boggles at the idea of a *female* . . . Well, never mind. But, truly, how do you propose this could work?"

"Jackson's figured it all out. In addition to being the finest boxer in the land, he's a dab hand at intrigue, apparently." Fitzwilliam raised a brow. "We will be celebrating the alliance between you and Justine. With your mother away, it is only fitting that someone does something along those lines. We shall invite Ardean and Suzanne and Madeleine and Freddie, so your siblings will be there, and Justine and Addie and Honoria. A cozy family party, really. I thought Kenston. I've always liked it and don't get to spend much time there."

"I don't know," Drew said slowly. "What about the boxing? How will you manage that?"

"There's that silly little ornamental dairy at Kenston. It's a fair distance from the house, and I'd thought it would do rather well for the construction of the ring."

"And she agreed? Actually said *yes,* to this ridiculous scheme?"

Fitzwilliam nodded, uncomfortably aware that she hadn't been given much choice.

"And, let me surmise. I, I would hazard a guess, am to spar with you as a part of this, ah, *training?*"

Fitzwilliam nodded again.

"Oh, lord. But what if I kill you?" Drew wondered aloud. "Strictly by accident, of course. I mean, I'm not exactly

Belcher, not all that good in fact, but, hell, it's not as if a fellow has to be—Never mind. When do we go?''

Fitzwilliam smiled. ''What do you have planned for tomorrow?'' he asked.

And Drew groaned.

Chapter 24

"I confess, I *am* looking forward to it," Madeleine Barrist said, smiling over her teacup at the Winstead ladies. "It's actually rather capital of Fitzwilliam to do this. We are all thrilled, needless to say, that Drew has actually managed to engage the affections of such a lovely young lady of excellent sense—which is much more than we'd dared hope for. And a house party will be just the thing to make it clear that the match is to the liking of both families." Here Justine blushed prettily, and her future sister-in-law continued. "Not, mind you, that as his older sister I am not in possession of any number of tales, the telling of which could not but send you running, Justine, my dear, but I like you so well that I think I shall not!"

Amidst the laughter that followed this remark, Addie studied their guest.

Mrs. Barrist, she decided, looked a good deal more like Drew than one would notice at a casual glance. They were built along the same lines, but where he was somewhat stocky, it translated into a pleasing roundness on his sister. Her blond hair was fashionably dressed, but with enough simplicity that Addie could see nothing of which to disapprove, and her willow green dress, although also in the first stare of fashion, was deceptively understated. Her brown eyes, like Drew's, were good-humored and direct, as was the lady herself. In short, she was almost impossible to dislike, and Addie could not feel the least discomfort at the prospect of her sister joining this family.

"I agree entirely," Honoria said. "Although one cannot but regret—and I know I've said it before—that your dear mama will not be returned from her travels. So much planning. So many decisions." She sighed with the weight of it all.

"True." Madeleine turned amused eyes toward Justine. "But I will be happy to assist in any way possible. And the house party, at least, should offer a respite from the planning."

Addie smiled and shook her head at Honny who was offering her the plate of cakes, as Justine said, "I must confess a little trepidation at the idea of meeting Lord and Lady Ardean. Drew, though, assures me that they are not so intimidating."

In response to which Madeleine waved an airy hand.

"What an utter piece of nonsense, to have any fears on that score. William is the most amiable of brothers and not at all grand, and Suzanne is of much the same disposition."

"Her cousin, Mathilda, was a sad romp as I recall," Honoria said darkly. "I remember her from her come-out year, and if ever there was a gel up to some maggoty piece of work at every turn, it was she."

"To be sure," Madeleine agreed. "And although I think you would find that marriage has settled Mathilda to a pleasing degree, I can assure you that Suzanne is not in the least like her. No, in fact, if anything, the two of them, William and Suzanne, are dull as ditch water these days. All they think of between them is tenants and responsibilities, and—Good Lord!—farming. As if I ever thought to see the day when William would prefer a discussion on crop rotation to a new waistcoat or a bet on which of two turtles would cross Green Park faster!"

"Now that you have relieved my mind, I have to think the house party an excellent idea, also," Justine said with a smile.

And Addie had to think what a ridiculous idea *she* thought

it—not, mind you, that anyone seemed to care for *her* opinion. Although not two days ago, Justine had been of similar mind. Exactly when, she wondered, eyes narrowing, had her sister come around on this plan? As last *she'd* heard from Justine on that score, her thoughts on Addie training Fitzwilliam had included the words *impossible, insane,* and unless memory failed, *dicked in the nob.*

Wallace, in fact, had almost managed to put paid to the entire scheme. Being adamantly against the ladies visiting the home of a bachelor—*especially this bachelor!*—he had appealed to Honoria to put a stop to the journey. But Honoria, whose suspicions that there was more here than met the eye had been quietly confirmed by Jackson's note, had refused. And eventually, Fitzwilliam had been prevailed upon, by way of Drew, by way of Justine, to issue, albeit grudgingly, a proper invitation to both Raines *and* his mother.

"To provide countenance, you understand," Wallace had explained to Honoria, adding hurriedly, "Not, of course, that *you,* dear lady, are not countenance enough. But with Mother present, there can be no question of there being the least impropriety."

To which, Honoria, who was hoping for a little impropriety in certain quarters, had held her peace.

For once, Addie had been in sympathy with Wallace's opinion, although admittedly for different reasons. But then, the day after she had met with Fitzwilliam at Jackson's, the notice of her engagement to Wallace was in the *Post.* Her sudden betrothal, following as it did, so closely on the heels of Justine's precipitous engagement, the Winstead girls had become something of a nine-days wonder, with seemingly the whole of London converging on the house to offer their congratulations and, perhaps, collect a snippet of gossip. Thankfully, the time of year being what it was, Town was thin of company. Even so, by the third day of sitting stiffly in the drawing room, Wallace at her side, receiving callers, Addie felt she would have walked to Kenston.

Today, at least, Wallace, had pleaded pressing business and

was absent from the little drawing room on Curzon Street. For which circumstance Addie could not help being relieved, and especially so, considering what happened next:

Addie's cup was halfway to her lips.

And Madeleine was saying, "We shan't stay above two sennights. Freddie is bound to be sullen and fidgety. Feels there is no point in being from Town if he can't hunt," she had gone on to explain apologetically, before adding, "And to be truthful, I find it difficult to be parted from the children for any great length of time."

When there was a commotion at that door.

"How could you, Addie?" a distraught voice had wailed.

At this, all four of the room's occupants had turned from the little table near the fire around which they were gathered, to see a small figure in such a state that she could only have been either one of the Furies, or Lizbeth in a taking.

"I am from Town for four days. *Four days* only! And I return to *this!*" she had cried, waving a copy of her *Post*.

"Lizbeth!" Addie had said in calm accents, while rising. "How nice that you are returned." And then, pointedly, "You *do* know Mrs. Barrist, do you not?"

Addie had paused, and Madeleine and Lizbeth had exchanged somewhat distracted, but nonetheless cordial, acknowledgments.

"Tea?" Addie had asked, giving Lizbeth a brief hug by the way of greeting.

"Tea? You are offering me *tea* at a time like this? A vinaigrette I should think would be much more to the point," Lizbeth had wailed, before detaching herself tearfully from Addie and throwing herself into the chair she had just vacated.

Justine had laughed gently. "Lizbeth," she had said, her eyes alight, "if you've ever fainted in your life, well, then I'm a . . . an—I don't know. But I'm a something I'm not."

"There is a first time for everything, you must know, and this! It is beyond all reason," Lizbeth had then retorted.

But her dramatics were beginning to subside, Addie had noted, shooting Justine a grateful glance and resumed her seat.

And then, seeming more composed, Lizbeth had sat up out of her elegant sprawl and removed her gloves, then her stunning *douillette à la Russiene,* followed by her modish little Kutosoff hat. Setting them aside with a care that had belied her avowals of agitation, she had straightened her glossy dark curls and, her bosom still heaving charmingly over the neckline of her blush-colored gown, said, "Some tea, I suppose, would not go amiss. But please, sweet. The shock, you must know." She waved a languid hand.

"Good girl," Honoria had said managing to positively radiate approval at Lizbeth's approximation of delicate sensibility while simultaneously giving Addie a dark look, and adding, "The vinaigrette, you can believe me, Lizbeth, has been put to excellent use by me this week."

"I should think so," Lizbeth had responded in deeply commiserating tones as she accepted a cup from Justine. And Addie had wondered why the two of them, Lizbeth and Honoria, did not just throw rocks at her and have done with it, when Lizbeth once again waved the paper accusingly in Addie's direction—if ever a paper could have been waved accusingly—as her cup rattled dangerously in its saucer. "When I left," Lizbeth had cried, "you were last seen kissing Fitzwilliam—"

Later, Addie could swear there had been a gasp, but she did recall clearly that Madeleine Barrist had suddenly realized she had sadly overstayed the proper amount of time for a morning call, and begun to gather up her things.

"And now—" Lizbeth had waved the paper again.

"That is not this morning's, I collect?" Addie had said dryly, and she thought quite calmly, under the circumstances, which had included Madeleine Barrist still being present, Justine's stifling something—Addie was not sure what behind her hand, and Honoria raising an elegant brow most eloquently.

"Indeed not. Four days old, in fact." Lizbeth had glared at her. "And it contains the most *interesting* and indeed *positively unexpected* announcement," she had said.

Addie had sighed. Subtlety had never been Lizbeth's forte. Justine and Honoria had both developed a very sudden urge to see Madeleine Barrist to the door, and the three of them had abandoned the room with an alacrity not generally seen at number Thirty-four Curzon Street. And so, Addie, abandoned entirely to Lizbeth's wrath, had endured a lengthy and, she was forced to point out, somewhat less than objective, diatribe on the character flaws of Wallace Raines (many and varied), and the vastly superior nature of Fitzwilliam (all the go, top of the trees, an out-and-outer, and bone-meltingly handsome). Lizbeth had followed these pronouncements by expressing her considered and vociferous opinion on exactly what kind of pudding headed chuckle-brain would accept the paltry one when the vastly superior other was there for the taking. Especially when *the person doing the accepting in question*—although due to her great delicacy and restraint, she had pointed out, she was not in fact naming names—had been spotted at Vauxhall sneaking off down Lover's Walk to behave in a deliciously scandalous manner with the infinitely preferable specimen. . . . Well!

Eventually Lizbeth had halted her invective, a condition which she could not like, but was forced to accept due to the necessity of drawing breath, and Addie had been able to slide a word in edgewise. But instead of the heated defense of her actions and disavowals of her behavior at Vauxhall, what came out was yet another watery confession. *Gracious, but I'm turning into a watering pot,* she had thought as she dried her eyes on Lizabeth's surprisingly comforting handkerchief.

"Thank you. You know I never have one of these," she had sniffled.

To which Lizbeth had replied carelessly, "Oh, it's not mine; it's Glendower's." Which response had been the catalyst for yet another bout of tears. And Lizbeth, puzzled, had said, "Don't worry, love, he'll never miss it."

In reply to which, Addie had to laugh, albeit in a somewhat sodden manner, and explain the handkerchief story.

"It'll be all right, Ad," Lizbeth had said, coming over to the edge of the chair where Addie had perched, and taking her hand. "I've been hasty. It's the shock, you must know. Forgive me?"

Addie had nodded through her tears. "Of course."

At Addie's nod, Lizbeth had said bracingly, but looking, it was true, highly doubtful. "Perhaps you and Wallace are better suited than I'd thought. After all," she had said, brightening, "remember how we were used to call Glendower Glen*dour?* And look how happy we've been!"

Which had the unfortunate effect of setting Addie off again.

Chapter 25

And now, a mere two days later, Addie sighed and stretched her legs, trying to get comfortable, as she watched the frozen landscape fly past. Fitzwilliam's carriage was luxuriously equipped and sprung, to be sure, but still the journey northward was long and tedious.

Although Fitzwilliam and Drew had gone on ahead, Fitzwilliam had insisted not only on supplying the luxurious traveling coach, but, as Honoria was happy to point out at every conceivable opportunity—which, Addie thought dryly, seemed to arise at steady ten-minute intervals—had arranged for their every comfort along the way. At each stop, he had left a fresh team, and they were met with downright obsequious service, sustaining food, and hot bricks. Still, as the journey stretched on, all the occupants were heartily sick of traveling, and Addie could not help but be thankful that today was to be the last day of it.

And Wallace, across from Addie and next to Honoria, seating as he had insisted was only proper, was worried. "I am most concerned that these heated bricks are beginning to cool," he fretted. "I should dislike excessively to once again fall victim to a chilblain."

"My brick is still warm and my feet are not the least bit cold. Shall we exchange?" offered Justine from next to Addie.

"Oh, no! Thank you, dear girl," Wallace exclaimed, turning a horrified expression upon their side of the coach. "No, no, no. As a female *you* surely are in more need of it than *I*! Indeed! Much more at the mercy of chilblains, ladies are, you know."

"Take mine, Wallace," said Addie, wanting only to stop him from fussing, and irritated beyond reason by the sight of him swaddled in traveling robes and blankets like an aging duenna. "I am not using it anyway."

"You should be, Adelaide," he reproved. "As I just warned Justine, you, as a female—"

"I think I know whether my own feet are cold," Addie snapped. And then was instantly contrite. It was not Wallace's fault that she was using him so abominably and was so heartsick over the infuriating Fitzwilliam and his equally infuriating wager. "I am sorry," she said, at his hurt expression. "Please, Wallace, accept my apologies. I never have been much of a hand at being cooped up in a carriage for long stretches of time." She smiled weakly.

"Think nothing of it, Adelaide," Wallace replied with the air of one making great allowances. "No female of gentle birth can be expected to withstand the rigors of travel with grace. In fact, Mother is wont to say . . ."

What Mother was wont to say, Addie could not have said, as her attention immediately drifted back to the window. Fitzwilliam's infuriating wager, as she could not help but think of it, was becoming more tempting by the second. Either way, win or lose, it offered her a chance to end this ill-conceived engagement.

Her head ached, and she leaned it back against the squabs. She had not been sleeping well, which, she decided, was hardly surprising. She had walked into this thinking to save both Fitzwilliam and herself from an unhappy union, one which could only be repugnant to him, and heartbreaking for her. But she had not, in truth, taken Wallace's feelings much into account. It cried out against every sensibility to have used him so ill, she thought, and then decided for at least the hundredth time, that having dragged him unwittingly into this, she would just have to do her best to make him a good wife.

Once again resolved in this direction, she smiled tentatively across the carriage at Wallace. And, encouraged, he continued. ". . . one of her dictums that I think you might want to take to heart, Adelaide, as—and here I speak as one with your best interests in mind—adherence to it would display a prudence not heretofore seen in your conduct." He paused to blow his nose vociferously, and then, as she had learned was his habit, examined the handkerchief for signs of an unhealthy mucus. Having apparently made the judgment that all was well with his lungs, he smiled benignly around at his traveling companions.

And Addie, who was strenuously avoiding Justine's wayward elbow next to her, could not summon even a ghost of a return smile.

As they finally swept through the gates of Kenston House near dusk that afternoon, Addie became aware, forcefully, of what an advantageous marriage her father must have thought he'd arranged for her. The carriage swept up a lengthy avenue bordered by what Honoria identified as imported lime trees. To their right there lay a large wood, and on their left, what were presumably formal gardens beneath their blankets of snow, bordered by a river. Ten minutes later, they passed a series of frozen ponds. Justine exclaimed at the winding rhododendron walks, and then the carriage started up a hill, overhung by trees, finally arriving in a pool of golden light cast by the setting sun before an impressive three-storied entrance portico flanked by four columns. The house itself was a Robert Adam masterpiece, a stunning confection of white stucco, flanked by two symmetrical wings of arched Palladian-style windows. And this was one of Fitzwilliam's lesser holdings. Perhaps she should have taken his blunt after all.

But then all thoughts of money were gone, as he and Drew came out to meet them. Drew, in his anxiousness to see Justine—having been parted from her for all of five days, hurried down the steps to the carriage. And Fitzwilliam strode along behind, his appearance jolting Addie, as she looked out the window, with the force of a blow. He looked different from the Fitzwilliam she had come to know in Town, and more, somehow, like the boy she had grown up with. He was still almost painfully handsome, to be sure, but he seemed to have lost some edge, some polish, Addie thought. He was wearing boots and breeches and was, despite the cold weather, in his shirtsleeves. Swirling around his ankles, in what seemed to be a pack, but on closer inspection when they, at his laughing command, sat, were four dogs. He stepped over them and waved the footman away indicating that he would help the visitors down himself. Drew already had Justine out and was asking her innocuous questions about their journey, but looking as if he'd like to devour her.

Giving up on Drew to do the civil, Fitzwilliam handed Honoria down and kissed her fondly on the cheek. As she stretched and declared how good it felt to be on her feet again, he reached up to assist Addie. But instead, found himself face to face with Wallace Raines, who was struggling to free himself from the selection of several blankets in which he had wrapped himself, mummy-style. "If you would just, oof, give me an, argh, assist, Claremont," he grunted, "in disentangling, ug, myself, I could, OUCH!" he shrieked as an arm suddenly came free and his elbow crashed against the side of the coach. "Thank you. No need for assistance, after all," he continued as though nothing unusual had taken place. He clambered down, very much on his dignity, and reached up for Addie, who was carefully, Fitzwilliam noted, not meeting anyone's gaze. "Do hurry, Adelaide," he urged. "We must get inside. I trust you *do* have ample fires going, Claremont? The ladies are like to become victims to a chilblain if we do not hurry them inside. What is Mannering thinking to keep the younger Miss Winstead standing about? Does he not realize the dire consequences should the cold of the ground seep through her boots?"

I'd wager what he's thinking has absolutely nothing to do

with the cold seeping through her boots, Fitzwilliam thought with a strictly inward grin, as Wallace again urged Addie inside.

"Come, Adelaide," he said, taking her arm. "I hope I am not so foolish as to let *my* fiancée put herself at risk for a chilblain! Indeed!"

"No, Addie!" Fitzwilliam ground out. "Don't move a step." Everyone halted to see what was amiss. He went to her swiftly, and, ignoring Wallace's horrified gasp, swung her up into his arms so that he held her easily against his broad chest. "Don't want the cold to seep through her slippers," he explained cheerfully over his shoulder as he headed toward the house. The dogs followed.

"Put me down, you odious man!" she objected, although, she did not, he noted, struggle.

"Sorry, Addie," he responded so that only she could hear. "Can't have you becoming, ah, *victim to a chilblain,* now, can we?"

She stifled a laugh and said repressively, "No. That would never do." In truth, cold was the last thing she was feeling. Even through the numerous and heavy layers of her traveling apparel, she could feel the firmness and heat of him. Lord, how her heart was racing. She devoutly hoped he couldn't feel it.

Fitzwilliam looked down at her face and was surprised by the surge of tenderness mixed with lust that jolted through him. He wondered, just for an instant, what it would feel like to carry her over the threshold for real. *Through the door and straight up the stairs to my bedroom.* And almost sighed at the impossibility of *that.* In truth, he had found that he had missed her out of reason these past few days, for a woman who until recently had barely figured as part of his day-to-day existence.

"Put me down, Fitzwilliam," she said again, still more breathless than she would have cared to admit. And then remembered to add, "You odious man."

He ignored her. "We've got a nice little ring set up, Addie," he said, still for her ears only, as he mounted the steps.

Her face lit up. "Really?" she asked in tones that another

woman might have reserved for a particularly elegant gown or perhaps an exceedingly fetching bauble.

"I think you'll like it," he replied, his lips so close to her ear that his breath lifted a tendril of hair, sending ripples down her back.

"Claremont!"

Wallace Raines's tone stopped him in his tracks. He looked back, still holding Addie. God, she felt good, he thought, restraining himself, with difficulty, from putting his hand on her bottom, which, he told himself firmly, would not do at all.

"Surely you do not intend to allow these . . . these . . . *mangy mutts* inside!" Wallace demanded.

Fitzwilliam's hand slid up just a fraction of an inch beneath Addie. He looked at the dogs already trotting through the doors ahead of them and shrugged. "Hardly a matter of allowing. They pretty much seem to do as they please. And *mangy mutts* is hardly any way to refer to hounds sired by the Duke of Rutland's dogs, I shouldn't think."

Wallace was clearly almost beside himself. Whether because of Fitzwilliam's high-handed mauling of his fiancée or over the issue of dogs, the onlookers were not quite sure. "But the hair!" he gasped. "The dust. The dirt."

It was the dogs.

Honoria sighed.

"My respiration, which is never *good* this time of year, mind you, will become *constricted!*" Wallace wailed.

"Not to worry, Raines. I specifically heard Mrs. Jeffcott, the housekeeper, instructing the maids not to let them into the Blue Chamber to sleep—as they generally are wont to do—while you are *in situ,*" Fitzwilliam replied cheerfully. He couldn't help himself; his hand moved again, ever so slightly.

"Put me down, Fitzwilliam, or you'll find yourself the recipient of a cross-arm that will make Jackson's look amateurish," Addie whispered.

"You forgot *you odious man,*" he whispered back.

"You odious man," she replied with dispatch.

He choked back a laugh, but did as she had asked, setting her gently on her feet in the entry hall.

His eyes, however, held a dangerous look, and Addie did her best to ignore the sensation that her heart was going to hammer through her chest. Really, Fitzwilliam's behavior, amusing though it admittedly was, was outside of enough!

"These dogs have slept in my room?" Wallace asked in tones generally reserved for discovering a murderer on the premises.

Addie crossed the hall and took Wallace's arm, saying comfortingly, "Don't mind Fitzwilliam, Wallace, he is no doubt teasing you." She directed a scowl at their host. "You *are* teasing, are you not, my lord?"

The *my lord* was clearly intended to put him in his place, but Fitzwilliam somehow couldn't feel truly chastened. Addie had enjoyed being in his arms as much as he had enjoyed having her there, he was certain. He admitted that he was teasing, and Wallace breathed a sigh of relief.

"Well, then," he said. "I do so wish that Mother had already arrived with my bed linens—it simply does not do, she often says, to sleep on bed linens that have been used by others. Nonetheless, I do think—and here I speak as one about to assume the grave, although indeed not entirely unwelcome, mantle of responsibility for the health and welfare of two of these estimable ladies; indeed, I trust I do so without complaint—that we should immediately retire. The ladies, especially, are no doubt desirous of a lengthy restorative interval in their beds."

And so apparently am I, thought Fitzwilliam, not trusting himself to look at Addie without laughing, *desirous of a lengthy restorative interval in Addie's bed.* But he only said, blandly, "Of course. How rude of me to keep you standing here—"

"In a drafty hall!" Wallace interjected.

"—when you must be weary from your travel. I shall have Mrs. Jeffcott show you to your chambers directly. Unless," he added, intercepting the look Honoria was bestowing on an oblivious Wallace, "you would prefer some refreshment first?"

"Thank you, Fitzwilliam, some refreshment would be most welcome," Honoria said firmly.

"I really think, although I would not, of course, presume to contradict you, Dear Lady," Wallace began, "that the wisest course of action—"

"Then don't," Honoria said. "Contradict me, that is, Wallace. I am parched, not weary, and some tea would be all the restorative I need."

"Then tea it shall be," Fitzwilliam said, leading them into a small, comfortably furnished salon and crossing to the bell. "Unless, Addie," he could not resist adding, "would prefer something stronger, as seems to be her wont these days. Brandy, perhaps, or champagne, Addie?"

"Tea, thank you, would be just the thing, Fitzwilliam," Addie said in a voice that let him know exactly what it was costing her not to add *you odious man.*

"Ah. You are mending your ways. Quite commendable," he replied, trying not to laugh as he pulled the bell rope. "Mr. Raines has convinced you to adopt a policy of moderation, I collect." He ordered tea from the footman who had appeared on the instant. "And you, Mr. Raines, do you in fact prefer a rest? Or do you join us for refreshment?"

Wallace folded his arms. "I shall stay, thank you," he said stiffly.

"Has the weather improved in Town since our departure?" Drew asked, having solicitously settled Justine on a rather lovely scrolled-arm Grecian sofa.

"No," she replied. "In fact, if anything it has grown colder. The Frost Fair has been a great success, I understand."

"Indeed it is all anyone talks of," Addie added.

"Except for the Winstead girls' engagements," Justine reminded her dryly, and the little company laughed.

"People will, and do, *talk,*" Wallace chimed in. "Indeed yes. They do. But Mother says—and says it often—that such a sad tendency to attend to others' business is the sign of a small mind. Oh! No, no, no. Sorry. A small mind is accountable for people's unwillingness to pay proper attention to the liver!

Talk is due to an excess of spleen due to digestive distur-
bances!'' He looked around triumphantly. *Goodness, what a
scintillating conversation this is!* Addie thought in the silence
that followed this pronuncement. *If the entire house party is
to be like this, we will all likely expire from boredom.*

Indeed, Fitzwilliam, although he sat, every inch the proper
host, listening and smiling politely as they awaited the tea tray,
had developed a glazed look in his eye. As though his expiration
might as well come sooner rather than later, as far as he was
concerned, she decided.

She might, however, have been surprised to know the reason
for the glazed look. As Wallace expounded on the little understood *link* between an excess of spleen and unwarranted gossip,
Fitzwilliam was, in fact, thinking that ever since Addie had put
one of those nicely turned ankles out of the carriage in his
driveway, he had been unable to stop thinking of her in a way
that was distinctly less than proper.

''Sugar?'' Honoria asked him, and it took him a moment to
realize that she was pouring out the tea.

''Ah, no, just milk, please,'' he replied, trying to figure out
what on earth had come over him. He looked over at Addie,
still dainty and ladylike, sipping her tea. But then her gaze met
his over the edge of her cup, and he went right back to wanting
her in a most improper manner. *Good Lord.* He shook himself
out of his reverie. This would never do. Perhaps he should get
Bella up here. And with all haste. She had been less than happy,
certainly, both with his abrupt departure, and with his decision
to take his leave of her by letter. Her return missive, in fact,
had alternately consisted of tearstained protestations of devotion
and blisteringly dismissive animadversions on his masculinity
these past few weeks. Although, considering that he doubted
he'd been this aroused in company since he was fifteen—
and by the sight of Addie Winstead sipping tea, no less—his
masculinity was the least of his concerns at the moment.

No, Bella clearly would not answer as the remedy to what
ailed him. But what, he wondered as he set himself to being
an attentive host, would?

Chapter 26

How much luggage could possibly fit into one carriage? Addie wondered, looking out from her vantage point at the window of her bedroom. She held the luxurious gold silk of the draperies to the side and tallied what she had seen. Already eight trunks, six valises, ten traveling cases, seven portmanteaus, and a seemingly unending selection of hatboxes, bandboxes, reticules, and baskets had been unloaded. All of it, or at least the vast majority, if she was not mistaken, containing a selection of tonics, nostrums, and health-preserving outerwear. And now the footmen were bringing out yet another trunk, and her future husband, alongside her future mother-in-law, was directing them as to which items went where.

Her future mother-in-law, Addie thought, was as daunting a figure as she remembered. Her serviceable bonnet was crammed down on top of what Addie knew from previous experience was a no-nonsense knot of steel-colored hair pulled uncompromisingly back from her face. Her outer garments were buttoned to her chin. And somehow, Addie got the feeling that she was not as much resigned to this match as Wallace made out.

At this moment, she was, unless Addie missed her guess, in

the midst of reading Wallace a thundering scold over his lack of a hat and gloves. Poor Wallace. Already possessed of a dragon of a mother and about to be shackled to a terrible wife. Addie leaned her head against the cool glass of the windowpane and thought about their predicament. Not, of course, that she thought about much else these days, and especially had not on the journey north. She closed her eyes. And it was all the worse because the situation was entirely of her own making. But there could not possibly, it was being borne in on her second by second, be a more ill-suited couple than Wallace and herself.

Opening her eyes again, Addie watched Wallace return to the house and disappear from her view, presumably through the front door, only to reappear a moment later, garbed in hat and gloves. His mama smiled her approval.

Somehow, no matter how hard she tried, she just could not imagine feeling more than a moderate amount of affection for Wallace. At least with Fitzwilliam there were some vestiges of their old friendship, which seemed of late to have been reappearing. And certainly it seemed there was heat between them, something of an understatement considering that she seemed in danger of igniting every time he touched her.

But wed to Fitzwilliam, she told herself brutally, she'd better be damned well prepared to share that heat with whomever took his fancy of the moment. Goodness knows his mother had where his father was concerned. And it certainly seemed, if his past was anything to go by, that there was heat between Fitzwilliam and any number of people.

Perhaps the thing to do, she mused, was to get Wallace to kiss her. A proper kiss this time. Maybe she would practically ignite in his arms after all.

A tap on the door interrupted her observations and, turning from the window, she bade the person enter. "Good morning, Sally. Thank you for the breakfast tray this morning. I suppose I was a little more tired from yesterday's travel than I had realized," she said by way of greeting the maid who had been assigned her during their stay.

"Begging your pardon, miss," Sally said with a little curtsy.

"But if you don't mind, I'll just have these set down in here."
She gestured behind her, and Addie became aware of two
footmen attempting not to struggle under the weight of the two
trunks, one balanced atop the other, that they held between
them. "And one of the housemaids will be up in a trice to take
care of things."

Addie smiled. "Thank you Sally, but that won't be necessary.
I think there is some misunderstanding. These are not my
trunks."

"Begging your pardon, miss," Sally said again, and Addie
eyed the trunks with mistrust. "But Mr. Raines said as how
we was to bring them up to you and send someone immediately
to make up your bed with new linens."

"But I've slept in it only one night. And the linens, I trust,
were clean before my arrival?"

"Of course, miss." Sally looked shocked that anyone could
suspect otherwise. "Why, Mrs. Jeffcott would never countenance anything less."

"Well then, you see? I am sure they are fine until such a
time as Mrs. Jeffcott deems new ones necessary."

"But, miss—"

"Very well, you may put them down in here," Addie said
with a distinct lack of graciousness, but having taken some
measure of pity on the poor footmen balancing the trunks
between them. She watched as they did so and then sped off
with a palpable air of relief. "However, I hardly think I need
to have the bed changed when I've slept in it but one night.
We'll just leave them, and Mr. Raines never need know."

"But Mr. Raines said, miss, as how the linens on the beds
here, being of silk and linen and the like, presented a danger
to the lungs. Most explicit, he was, that you were at no cost
to sleep another night on them," the maid explained, looking
terrified. "Said as how your lungs were excessively delicate
and you could breathe in harmful vapors from the silk and do
yourself damage! And that my job was as good as gone if I
let you. I'd no idea, miss, I swear, or I—"

"Sally!" Addie stemmed the flow of chatter. "I assure you. Your job is quite safe. My lungs are fine—"

"I'll say they are," said Fitzwilliam, stepping lightly into the room. "I can hear you bellowing halfway across the house! You may leave us, Sally."

"Yes, milord." Sally gave him a brief curtsy before fleeing, looking, Addie decided, almost as relieved as the footmen had.

"I was not, Fitzwilliam, bellowing," Addie said.

"Turning my household upside down already, are you, Addie?" he asked, looking amused.

"I was simply pointing out, Fitzwilliam, that the linens hardly need to be changed after but one night."

"But what about the harmful vapors?" he asked as he closed the door. "Are you not concerned?"

"I am confident I can withstand their effects—Open that door, Fitzwilliam. On the instant," she snapped. "This cannot be at all the thing."

"But we do need to talk. Do we not, ah, *Anonymous?*"

Addie flushed. "Don't call me that." This was the first time she had been alone, really alone, in his presence since he had pushed her up against that wall—a memory that had haunted her far more than it should have, since it was an episode best forgotten. And his nearness inside her bedchamber, no less, was unsettling.

"I *do* need your help, as you may recall." He was leaning, negligently, and quite safely, as far as her virtue was concerned, against the closed door. "If Raymond Walters is not to kill me, after all. And this seemed a good opportunity to discuss our plans."

"Oh, I recall well enough, Fitzwilliam," she said, crossing to the writing desk and producing a sheet of paper. "Although I hardly agree that this is the appropriate time or place for such a discussion."

He raised an eyebrow. "Shall we have it instead in the drawing room over tea, Addie?" he asked, taking the sheet of paper from her hand. "Perhaps Mrs. Raines would like to participate. After she finishes overseeing the unloading and inspects her son for signs of ill health, of course." He studied the page in silence for a moment, and then looked up, frowning. "What the devil?"

"Just a little program of training I've jotted down, Fitzwilliam," Addie replied with a grin that he could hardly credit coming from the same Addie Winstead he knew from the ballrooms of London, so full of the devil was it. "A regimen that I think you will find vastly improves your performance in the ring. Jackson did assure me, you know, before I agreed to take you on, that you would follow any regimen I gave you."

"Yes, but Addie—"

She held up a hand to stop him. "I realize, Fitzwilliam, that this may seem drastic. But Captain Robert Barclay, who is the acknowledged master of ritual training, always prescribes it to the letter."

"But I had assumed that we would work on my hitting, some footwork, perhaps, to start."

"And we shall, but you get ahead of yourself, I'm afraid. We need to start with conditioning. You must first attend to your stamina and physique."

"I hardly think," he said, softly, pushing himself off of the closed door where he had been leaning and beginning to advance on her with such feral grace that Addie backed up a step, "that my stamina—"

Addie backed up another step.

"or my physique—"

Another step. God, his eyes were mesmerizing.

"are any cause—"

Another step.

"for concern."

She stopped backing up, only because she felt the backs of her calves brush up against the edge of the bed. Really, he was *far* too close. "Do you, Addie, think my physique is any cause for concern?"

She made her tone dry. "Indeed it is hard to tell what, if anything, is really you under those painted-on jackets, Fitzwil-

liam. Although I understand they are all the crack for a Bond
Street beau.''

He stopped in his tracks. ''A Bond Street beau! Are you
implying, Addie,'' he asked, still looking far more amused than
he'd any right to, she decided, ''that I am padded under these
jackets? Because I assure you, this is all me. Do you care to
check?''

God, how he wished she would. He could hardly believe
how much he wanted her little hand, both hands, on his chest,
sliding over his shoulders, down his arms. . . . He took a steadying breath.

Addie shook her head, her throat suddenly too dry to respond.
Unfortunately for her peace of mind, she already knew far too
well what lay under Fitzwilliam's jackets. And it was the last
thing she wanted to think about.

''Of course,'' he said, with the air of one deep in thought,
''if I win this little boxing match, you'll be marrying me, Addie,
as we promised our fathers you would, and—''

''I'll be doing no such thing, Fitzwilliam,'' she replied. ''I
have every intention of completely ignoring this ridiculous
wager. And anyway, unless you start following this regimen''—she tapped the sheet he held—''there's not much point
in discussing what will happen in the event that you win.''

''So you still insist on this absurd course of action, do you?''

''One must take the first step first when it comes to training,''
she replied, her voice prim.

''I meant marrying Wallace Raines.''

''One generally marries one's fiancé, Fitzwilliam.''

''Generally,'' he replied, equably. ''But, Addie?''

''Yes?''

''Have you given any thought to what is under those baggy
sacks he calls jackets?''

''No!'' she said in repressive accents. ''Certainly I have
not.''

''Well I should were I you. If there is one thing a husband
wants, it is an interest from his wife's direction in what lies
under his jacket.''

"This conversation cannot be considered at all proper, Fitz-william."

He grinned. "I know. Shall we have it again?"

"Get out," she advised through clenched teeth.

"Very well," he said, with a smile, and Addie breathed a sigh of relief at his easy capitulation.

He backed up a few steps and sauntered toward the door, allowing her to put some distance between herself and the bed. Just as he was about to reach for the door handle, however, there was a tap on it.

Addie looked around wildly and then at him. "Addie?" came Justine's voice through the door. "Addie, are you in there?"

"J-just a minute, Justine," she forced herself to say, looking accusingly at Fitzwilliam.

"I'll go into the dressing room," he whispered.

"It's locked," she whispered back.

"Locked? Why?"

"Sally hadn't got the key last night, and she was going to get one from Mrs. Jeffcott this morning, but I guess she forgot what with the trunks—"

"Addie?" Justine called again.

"Just a second."

"Blast!" Fitzwilliam swore under his breath.

"Go! Get under the bed," Addie ordered him.

"Are you insane?"

"Ad-die? Are you all right?" Justine was starting to sound concerned.

"Just get under," Addie hissed, crossing the room. "You can't be found here. Justine! I didn't think to see you up and about so early," she said, brightly, as she opened the door immediately had Fitzwilliam's feet disappeared beneath the bed draperies.

Justine actually blushed at this innocuous comment, and then Addie said, before she recalled Fitzwilliam's presence and blushed herself, "You and Drew, I collect, have been stealing a few before-breakfast kisses behind the, ah, snow-covered skeletons of the rosebushes, Justine?''

"Drew wanted to, ah, show me the grounds this morning. He said that they are especially lovely early in the day.''

Addie grinned at her sister. "And are they?''

"Are they what?''

"Lovely?''

"Oh, yes!'' Justine replied fervently, and then they both laughed.

"I'd wager you barely remember a thing you saw, my love.''

Justine blushed anew at this and drew her sister to sit down on the brocaded armchairs in front of the fire. "Enough about me, Addie. We've barely had a chance to talk in days with such hectic preparations and then the traveling. But it is such heaven to be here at last. And this is the most beautiful house, is it not?'' She paused and Addie nodded.

"Honny came in last night before I went to sleep and lectured me for a good five-and-thirty minutes on Editha Proctor and how she gave up a chance to marry the Marquis of Standish who had a beautiful estate in the Lake District and was eventually forced—Editha, I think, not the Marquis of Standish—to wear a most unattractive shade of yellow, which even at it's best is *not* a color for everyone, you do know—that part is a direct quotation—at the Enderfields' boating party in 'oh-two.''

Addie laughed. "Oh, dear.''

"Just so.'' Justine nodded sagely. "It was something of a confusing nonsequitur, even for Honoria, and I am not sure where exactly, but I feel certain there is a lesson for you in there somewhere, Addie. Does Mr. Raines have a fondness for unattractive shades of yellow, perhaps? Surely Fitzwilliam does not—''

"I am sorry to interrupt these fascinating musings, Justine,'' said Addie, once again forcefully reminded of that gentleman's most unnerving position at the moment. "But I am positively starving. So hungry, in fact, that I don't think I can sit here another moment.''

Justine frowned. "But I thought you'd had a tray up here.''

"I did, but I find myself hungry still. Ravenous, actually. Come down to the breakfast room with me, love," she said, standing and bustling Justine toward the door. "Let us see if there is any food left."

Justine allowed herself to be edged toward the door, but frowned at Addie. "Is everything all right, Ad?" she asked. "You *are* behaving rather, well, oddly."

"Everything is fine, Justine," Addie said, but before going out the door, could not resist saying, "And do you know, the only yellow I've ever seen on Fitzwilliam was in the fading bruises from his bout with Truesdale. So *that*, anyway, cannot have been Honny's point."

Chapter 27

"Look at this, will you, Drew," Fitzwilliam said a few minutes later. He was in the library with Drew, shaking the piece of paper that Addie had handed him under his friend's nose, and feeling only slightly the worse for his most undignified foray under the bed.

He tipped a dozing dog off of his favorite chair and took a seat. The dog looked at him reproachfully before laying his head on his master's immaculately shined boot and going back to sleep.

Drew took the sheet, a grin spreading over his face as he read.

"I don't know how you can possibly think she loves me, when, in fact, it is completely clear that she is trying to kill me."

"You think that?"

"I do think that, yes. Not only does she not want to marry me—prefers in fact, to marry that old woman she's engaged to—she wants me out of the way entirely."

"Hmm. Rather a black motive to attribute to such an amiable sort, don't you think?" Drew was still scanning the sheet.

"Nice penmanship! The mark of a true lady, my nanny always said."

"Drew!"

"Sorry. Well, the first three days don't sound so bad, Fitzwilliam. All you need do is take two ounces of Glauber Salts—whatever they are! Reasonable enough.

"And then?"

"Well I do concede that the part where she has you starting your 'regular exercise' does sound rather, ah, harsh. You are to rise at five in the morning and run half a mile at top speed, I collect. Uphill. And then walk six miles at a moderate pace, coming in about seven to breakfast, which should consist of beefsteaks or muttonchops underdone, with stale bread and old beer."

Fitzwilliam groaned. "Please continue. Antoine, by the way, will no doubt resign, be on the first boat back to Paris, when he hears of this new regimen I am about to adopt. Do be sure to enjoy your next few meals, Drew. For within the week he'll be gone. Bound to be."

"Well, let's see what comes after that delectable-sounding repast. Ah, yes. After breakfast you are again to walk six miles at a moderate pace, and at twelve, lie down in bed for half an hour. On getting up, you are to walk four miles and return by four to dinner—"

"Dinner at four? That will definitely be the last straw for Antoine. He barely considers eight to be a civilized hour."

Drew smirked. "The hour may be the least of your problems. Did you see what dinner is to consist of? No? More beefsteaks or muttonchops with bread and beer. And then immediately after, you are to resume your exercise by running half a mile at top speed and walking six miles at a moderate pace. But good news!" He held up his hand to stop Fitzwilliam from speaking. "You are to take no more exercise that day. Ah, but more bad news, I'm afraid."

This last was said to Fitzwilliam's back, as he had risen, and, shaking the dog off his foot, gone over to the floor-to-ceiling window overlooking the south lawn, where he appeared to be muttering darkly to himself.

"It seems that after following this course of activity every day for a week, you must then take a four-mile sweat, which is produced by running four miles, in flannel, at the top of your speed. Immediately upon returning, a hot liquor will be prescribed. It is termed the sweating liquor, and is composed of the following ingredients: one ounce of caraway seed; half an ounce of coriander seed; one ounce of root liquorice; and half an ounce of sugar candy; mixed with two bottles of cider, and boiled down to one-half. After ingesting that delectable-sounding brew, you are then to be put to bed in your flannels, and covered with six or eight pairs of blankets and a duvet, where you are to remain for twenty-five to thirty minutes before walking gently for two miles. You are then to have your usual breakfast—shouldn't think you'd have much appetite at that point—and continue with your regular exercise. Whew! Perhaps she is trying to kill you, after all."

"She said—she, *actually* said—" Fitzwilliam broke off, looking so indignant that Drew was hard-pressed not to laugh.

"She said what?"

"She said that my stamina and physique needed work!"

"Well, goodness knows she's the first woman ever to say that! And to a Claremont, no less!"

"Indeed." Fitzwilliam fixed him with a glare. "And then I had to hide under the bed and—"

"Ah, Fitzwilliam? What—"

"No, Drew, don't ask. We'll all be happier. Since it appears I'm about to be tortured and starved," Fitzwilliam muttered, "before being killed in the boxing ring defending the honor of a fiancée who is not even mine, and whom I don't want, I might as well have a good breakfast. I don't suppose you left anything for me?"

"An egg or two," Drew replied amiably, "but now that you mention it, I *could* use another go-round myself. And, Fitzwilliam?" he added, handing back the offending sheet of paper.

"Mm?"

"Are you so certain you don't want the fiancée?"

"Don't be ridiculous, Drew," Fitzwilliam replied. "Now, shall we go and investigate my table?"

But before they could move, there was the unmistakable sound of a throat being discreetly cleared from the direction of the doorway.

"Yes, Hedges?" Fitzwilliam inquired, turning round to face the door and hastily putting down the sheet of paper.

"The first of the other guests, sir, they have arrived."

"Thank you, Hedges," Fitzwilliam responded, squinting at his butler. "But something more than that must have occurred. You look completely out of countenance, man. Not like you."

"Well, sir." The butler looked at his feet. "It is just that Mr. and Mrs. Barrist have arrived—"

"Surely that can't be what's put you in the fidgets, Hedges? After all, part of the point of this entire fiasco, ah, I mean house party, was to give the Winstead ladies and Drew's family a chance to get better acquainted."

"Well, the Barrists, are, ah, *accompanied,* my lord, by unexpected guests."

"I see. And who would that be?" Fitzwilliam inquired with a grin. "Who could possibly merit that expression, Hedges? Bonaparte, after all, is otherwise engaged. Byron would never leave the accolades of London's literary salons to journey to such a decidedly unfashionable locale. Prinny is safely in London, and my father," he added, flatly, his grin gone, "is, thankfully, still dead." He looked at his butler. "Worse?" At his nod, Fitzwilliam's eyebrow went up, but his tone was still flat. "Than that lot?"

"Miss Lavinia Haverford and her, ah, mother, my lord," Hedges choked out.

"Good Lord!" Drew burst out.

"I see, Hedges. In fact, I think I see very well, indeed. And Drew summed up my thoughts exactly."

"But why on earth would Madeleine and Freddie have brought them here? Why would they want to come?"

"I'd guess that as last year's attempt in which the wheel fell off of their carriage just down the lane from Claremont House was unsuccessful, they're having another go. And since you are spoken for, Drew, it would seem that I must be the object of their, ah, interest. And your sister, you know, has ever had a soft heart. They likely imposed themselves, and she was unable to rid herself of them. But whatever the reason, they're here now, and since, unfortunately, I have ample room to accomodate them, I suppose we've no choice but to go and greet them.

"Ah, sir?" Hedges shifted uncomfortably.

"Surely there cannot be more?" Fitzwilliam raised his brow.

"Actually, sir, there is something of an, of a . . . an *incident* taking place in the kitchens. Antoine''—here the butler looked to the frescoed ceiling with a great show of one gathering his patience—"is in yet another rage, and has been ever since Miss Addie Winstead stuck her head into the kitchen to request that a dose of Glauber Salts be served with your breakfast. When he heard that his food had made you dyspeptic, he—"

"Dyspeptic? That is what she said?"

"Yes, sir. Said at your age it is not uncommon."

"She did, did she?" Despite everything, Fitzwilliam was hard-pressed not to grin. "I'll tell you what, Hedges. Can Mrs. Jeffcott and some of the kitchen maids contrive to get us the rest of the way through breakfast?" At the butler's nod, he continued. "Good. Give Antoine a bottle of my best Claret and tell him to take the afternoon off. I'll get him sorted out later. Now, Drew, let us go welcome our new arrivals." He headed for the door. "And, Hedges?"

"Yes, my lord?"

"If you're as smart a man as I credit you, you'll take a bottle of that Claret for yourself, and come to think of it, stow a decanter in my bedchamber. As this, you can believe me, is only the beginning."

Chapter 28

There were enough people milling about inside the doorway to make a fellow feel that he had stepped into the lobby of Grillon's Hotel rather than his own front hall, Fitzwilliam reflected a moment later. Maids, grooms, footmen, and, naturally, dogs, scurried this way and that, to the extent that Fitzwilliam was not entirely certain which were actually attached to his household and which were new arrivals.

"Ah, Claremont," trilled a rather stentorian voice. Not much meant for trilling, he decided as he winced, and only partially from the use of his title. "I *knew,* just knew, you would not mind having us along. In fact, as I told *dear* Madeleine, when I heard this was a family party, I made sure we must have been intended to have been included, especially as we missed the chance to have that nice visit last year at Claremont House! But I quite understand that you might have forgot, as it was on rather short notice that this party was assembled, was it not? Not everyone, after all, remembers that the Haverfords, on my late husband's papa's side," she said, pronouncing 'papa' in a rather affected French manner, Fitzwilliam noted, "are, after all, connected to the house of Ardean. My dear departed

Edward's papa''—English, this time—*"was,* in fact, third cousin to Drew and Lord Ardean's maternal grandfather, you know. No!'' she motioned Fitzwilliam stop when he would have replied. ''There is no need, dear boy, to apologize. We are here, after all. No damage has been done.''

''Had I but known, Drew, of the connexion when we met at Eton,'' Fitzwilliam said, sotto voce, ''I doubtless should have declined your acquaintance altogether.''

Drew smiled. ''Since we were eleven at the time, even one as perspicacious as yourself cannot have been expected to anticipate the future hardship our friendship would bring.''

Madeleine looked apologetic, as well she should, Fitzwilliam thought, as he assured the Haverfords that he was excessively pleased to have them, during which Lavinia Haverford somehow managed to attach herself to his arm.

''It really is too kind of you, Lord Claremont,'' she said, in an admirably forthright manner, as she gazed up at him, her eyes, twin pools of violet, ''to accept unexpected guests with such equanimity.''

The girl looked remarkably fresh for having just arrived, he could not help but note, and smelled rather delectably floral. ''We didn't want to impose ourselves on you last evening, so we just stayed in town at the Coach and Four,'' she explained as if reading his thoughts.

And then began the inevitable conversation on the vagaries of travel. Seeing that the Hon. Freddie Barrist had moved away from the group and stood at the window, hands clasped behind his back, muttering under his breath, Fitzwilliam detached himself from Miss Haverford's not entirely unpleasant grip, and joined him.

'' 'Morning, Fitzwilliam. Pinch of snuff?'' Barrist offered, unclasping his hands, and withdrawing an enamel box from his pocket. ''Spanish bran, y'know,'' he added, expertly flicking open the top. ''And a pinch of this, a pinch of that. Secret blend. Got Lumley begging me for the receipt, you must know.''

''I'm certain you have, but lord, no, Freddie, not in the

habit,'' Fitzwilliam replied. ''I've enough vices, goodness knows. But that isn't one of them.''

''A vice!'' Freddie looked so horrified that Fitzwilliam laughed. ''Never say that, man. Only a vice if the stuff's drenched in vinagrillo.''

''Well, welcome, anyway,'' Fitzwilliam replied, laughing. ''But what, may I ask, has you in such a brown study? You've just arrived, and you're already staring out the window and muttering. Not, mind you, that I'll begrudge you some staring and muttering once you've been here a few days, certainly. I'd guess, in fact, that we're all headed in that direction. But this, well, frankly, Freddie, it seems a bit premature.''

''Hunting,'' Freddie Barrist mumbled.

Fitzwilliam leveled him a humorous glance.

''Look at it out there.'' Freddie motioned out the window, his disgust apparent. ''Frozen solid! Hounds all over the place, sired, I am given to understand, by no less than Rutland's dogs. Top of the crop of hunters eating their heads off in your stables, too. And ground too frozen to take a run, doncha know. Even *these* hounds'll never be able to track the scent. Blasted waste, if you ask me.'' He looked at Fitzwilliam. ''Ground ain't too frozen for the Haverford hounds to track the scent, though. I'd watch it if I was you, m'boy. Take care not to draw the covert. No flirting or sheep's eyes in *that* direction unless you want to end up in the parson's mousetrap so fast you won't know what day it is. Enough said. Consider yourself warned, m'boy.''

Fitzwilliam assured him that he considered himself amply warned. In return he was rewarded with a quick version of how the Haverford women had more or less invited themselves along, and how Madeleine, as he had guessed, had been too soft-hearted—downright hen-hearted her husband would have it—to say no. In exchange for which information, Fitzwilliam promised Freddie that he would do his best to provide sport, frozen ground notwithstanding, and Freddie then asked if it was too much to suppose a perishing fellow could get some sustenance, or did one have to stand about all day listening to the demmed females twitter? At which point Fitzwilliam assured him breakfast was ready and waiting, that he had been headed that way himself, in fact.

He did have to admit, as he led them, chattering, toward the breakfast room—incidentally, putting Hedges's nose entirely out of joint by doing this himself—that Lavinia Haverford *was* a taking thing. She had been on the Town two seasons, he thought, and recalled having danced with her several times at various assemblies. The gossip, if he remembered aright, had it that although she had received more than her share of offers, she, or at least her mama, was dangling for a better title than had come her way thus far. As well she might, since she was rumored to have six thousand a year and was possessed of an uncommonly pleasing face and figure. As she commented on the beauty of his house, once again leaning on his arm, he smiled down at her and begged that she desist calling him Claremont, to which she agreed very prettily.

At the door to the breakfast room, Fitzwilliam commanded the two dogs who had managed to attach themselves to him to sit and stay. Blithely ignoring him, they trotted ahead through the door, and he had to suppress a laugh at Wallace's look of dismay.

Justine gave a little squeal of pleasure at Madeleine's arrival, and ran to hug her. There then followed a general flurry of greetings, as footmen pulled out chairs and all the new guests were seated. As he took his seat, next to Lavinia Haverford, Fitzwilliam tried to catch Addie's eye. She, however, had hers fixed resolutely on her aunt.

Honoria looked up from the toast and coffee that sat in front of her, and she and Mrs. Haverford stared at each other—for all the world like two fighters in the prize ring summing up each other's strength while circling each other, Fitzwilliam thought, although he could not, to be honest, much like the analogy at the moment.

"Hello, Honoria," said Mrs. Haverford, her words more or less dripping ice. "Hello, Gretchen," she said, in slightly warmer tones, to Mrs. Raines.

"Hello, Millicent," returned Honoria, hers equally cold. "How, ah, *unexpected,* it is to see you here!"

Millicent Haverford bared her teeth in a rather grim estimation of a smile. "A family connexion, don't you know."

"Not on *your* side, I trust," Honoria replied succinctly, managing to convey in her expression that the whiff of the shop still clung to Millicent Haverford's excessively stylish vandyked walking dress.

And thus, the battle lines were drawn.

"And how nice to see your nieces again. Congratulations to both, I understand, are in order. How happy we are to be present to help the families celebrate this momentous occasion!" Millicent Haverford replied. "And *dearest* Addie does look well, of course. How forward thinking of you, to be sure, my dear, not to have taken to wearing caps just yet, since you did, in the end, manage to bring *dear* Mr. Raines up to scratch! Does she not look well, Lavinia, dearest?"

Lavinia's expression managed to convey otherwise as she replied, "Very well, indeed."

Mrs. Raines, who had a bowl of what looked to be gruel in front of her, and was busily directing her son to partake of another helping to fortify himself, joined the conversation on this point. "Well, she should, goodness knows, take up caps! My son may have saved her from spinsterhood, but one would be foolish indeed to overlook the warmth and protection a cap can afford the head!"

And Honoria took the opportunity to say, "I must say that *dear* Lavinia is also looking well. Especially for one once again on the hunt, er, I mean, one who has so recently endured such a *grueling* journey."

As Mrs. Haverford sputtered, Lavinia replied very prettily, with thanks for such a lovely compliment. "For I am sure *you* understand," she confided to a bemused Addie, "how difficult it is to look fresh while traveling." Lavinia then managed just a suggestion of a blush as Fitzwilliam's left arm accidentally brushed against her right one as he took up his fork.

Addie stared at his arm. He had brushed Lavinia Haverford.

With his *left* arm, while taking up his fork. He was *left*-handed? As she watched, he put his fork down and stirred his coffee. With his right hand. Addie stared, transfixed, as he picked up his knife, and holding it in his left hand, cut his ham. He then laid it down and picked up his fork, right handed this time. And then, at Drew's request, he passed the marmalade and then, for no apparent reason whatsoever, transferred his fork to his left hand and resumed eating. Was the blasted fellow right handed or left handed, Addie wondered, still staring as he changed hands several more time, or seemingly, both? In either case, he had no doubt had been trained to box as a right-hander—a technique some espoused, but which her father had always decried. *That* could explain quite a lot.

Could he be ambidextrous? If he was, it was fully possible that his left hand was dominant. Struck by her discovery, she looked up, only to find him watching her back, a brow raised in question. Embarrassment at having been caught out at watching him so closely made the color thud into her face, and he gave her a knowing little smile. Then her eyes narrowed as she examined the other part of the equation. He had brushed Lavinia Haverford, perilously close to her right breast, in fact, and she had blushed. What on earth, she wondered, were the Haverfords doing here, anyway? Not, of course, that it could be any of her concern who Fitzwilliam did and did not choose to invite to his home, but a single gentleman did not generally invite young misses of quality to his home unless his interest lay in an honorable direction.

Was all this talk about unengaging herself from Wallace just that? she wondered. Had this been his intention all along? To be free of his obligation to her so that he could make the beautiful Lavinia his wife? Had Fitzwilliam somewhere along the line fallen in love? And had his heart already been engaged that night at Vauxhall? And if so, what was he playing at with her? The thought almost squeezed the breath out of her.

Fitzwilliam, who was in fact, not at all refining on the attractions of Miss Haverford, but rather recalling his sojourn under the bed with amusement, grinned to himself. "Hedges," he said to the still-simmering butler, "Please, have the footmen serve the elder Miss Winstead another helping. I want to be sure she has enough, as it is my understanding that she is uncommonly hungry this morning, ravenous, in fact, I do believe she said."

"Ah, no, thank you. I've quite enough already," Addie retorted.

"Oh, no. I insist, Hedges." Fitzwilliam waved expansively. "If you are sharp-set, Addie, I shall do without if need be. More bacon, eggs, kidneys, ham, and toast for Miss Winstead, please."

She did not object, although, Fitzwilliam reflected, she did look rather green as a footman piled her plate. *Serves her right,* he thought. *Glauber Salts! Six mile runs! Sweating liquor!* He grinned again as she resolutely forked up more food.

"Do you know, Fitzwilliam," she said, her fork hovering, "I do believe that what this breakfast is missing are muttonchops! Perhaps tomorrow?" and had the satisfaction of seeing his grin disappear.

"I vow, I've rarely seen you eat so much, Addie," Honoria said, squinting at her niece's plate. "It must be the country air."

"You'd best have a care, my dear," Mrs. Haverford warned, still smiling stiffly. "Even though you have wrapped up *dear* Mr. Raines! After a certain age one cannot be too careful, you know."

"True! Demmed true," agreed Freddie Barrist. "Make a point of it m'self. Never have more than a dozen eggs." He sighed regretfully. "Here, boys, sit. Excellent fellows!" he said to the dogs, who had rightly pegged the person in the room most likely to tip them table scraps on the sly, and were now begging for a second round of creamed kidneys.

Mrs. Raines looked as if she would say something about dogs in the breakfast room, but just then Madeleine Barrist spoke.

"Well, Addie—unlike you, my darling husband," she said,

eyeing Freddie's middle somewhat pointedly, "does not need to worry about that. *She* looks as slim as a post."

"Penelope Woolway, you know, puts on quite a bit of excess girth every time they go to Kent. Or is it Northamptonshire, I wonder?" Honoria mused. "Says the sea air, or is it the farm air—not that farm air, particularly sheep-farm air, is all that appetizing, one must say, with odors here and there that one had rather not mention at all—gives her an appetite. No, it must be Kent because surely only sea air could have that effect?" She paused and looked around for confirmation. "Say!" she said, as if just thinking of this. "Is she not a connexion of yours, Millicent? One hopes Lavinia did not inherit her unfortunate propensity toward excess girth!"

Justine smiled at Drew. "Definitely Kent," she said, clearly to Honoria, but without removing her gaze from his.

"I *love* Kent," he replied, with what Fitzwilliam could not help but feel was an unnecessary amount of enthusiasm.

She smiled again. "I do love Northamptonshire, also."

"As do I," he agreed, smiling, in his best friend's opinion, for all the world like a simpleton. "As do I!"

"Well, I," said Mrs. Raines between spoons full of gruel, "find it most indelicate for a female to be possessed of a hearty appetite!"

"I would agree, Mother," Wallace said. "Especially when breaking the fast. It overloads the system to eat heavily so early in the day. Besides, a restful night, I always think, should be followed by a light appetite in the morning." He looked reprovingly at the large forkful of eggs Addie had halfway to her mouth.

If I were engaged to Addie, I, unlike you, you mutton-head, would be thinking of about fifteen ways to ensure that she'd be starving in the morning, hang the restful night, Fitzwilliam thought, shifting in his chair. "I don't know. I like a female with a healthy appetite," he said with a grin.

"Have another serving of eggs, my dear," said Millicent Haverford promptly, to her daughter.

"Thank you, Mama, but I don't care for any more, just now," Lavinia replied.

"I *said,* 'have some more eggs,' " her mother said in tones that would brook no opposition.

Lavinia gulped. "Yes, Mama."

"She is incorrigible at the breakfast table," her mother confided to the company at large, as Lavinia pushed her eggs around on her plate. "Why, sometimes, at home she eats an entire *platter* of beefsteak and eggs!" She looked around at the assembled company with an air of triumph. "An entire platter! I tell you! Why, the girl eats like a veritable stablehand."

"You don't say!" said Justine, since no one else seemed much inclined to say anything.

"Oh, yes, I do. I do, indeed," replied Mrs. Haverford.

Lavinia somehow managed to look flirtatiously out from under her eyelashes at Fitzwilliam and simultaneously at Addie's gluttonous portion of food. "Well, I suppose I am fortunate in not yet having reached the age where excess girth creeps on." She peeped at Addie. "One, however, does not like to be thought indelicate in company, you do understand," she said.

Mrs. Raines frowned at the exchange. "You really should not force the girl to eat, you know Millicent. Especially eggs." She sniffed. "They overload the digestive tract. It's a known fact!"

Addie looked at Fitzwilliam and quirked a brow at his full plate. "I've heard that," she replied, to her future mama-in-law. "In fact, do you know, I even read somewhere recently that some gentleman who trains, I believe it is *boxers,* of all things"—she frowned, feigning concentration, and Honoria flashed her a look, eyes narrowed, and Justine, looking suspiciously like she was laughing, raised her napkin to her mouth. "Captain Robert Barclay! That's it. Well, *he* permits his boxers to eat only the *yolks* of eggs. Raw!"

Gretchen Raines looked at her with something approaching approval. "Very sensible! Although"—she shuddered—"I cannot like the boxing part."

Mrs. Haverford could not agree fast enough. "Heavens, no!"

"Meynell, I understand, always feeds his hounds an egg. For a glossy coat, y'know," Freddie contributed. "D'you feed these fellows eggs, Fitzwilliam?" he wanted to know. "Beautiful coats. Demmed fine fellows!"

Fitzwilliam looked around his table. Wallace Raines and Addie now had their heads together—Addie was no doubt being treated to a discourse on the merits of gruel, or possibly the dangers of eggs, he thought, but together, nonetheless. Drew was watching Justine eat a buttered muffin with rapt concentration, as if he were witnessing the most fascinating spectacle he'd ever seen. From next to him, two pairs of eyes, one brown, one violet, belonging to the Haverfords, mother and daughter, bored into him with frightening intent. Even the dogs had forsaken him, and were sleeping contentedly with their heads on Freddie Barrist's boots. And for the price of a few table scraps.

Fitzwilliam was the only person at the table with nothing to show for his past and nothing planned for his future. Looking at Addie as she nodded in reply to something Wallace said, he felt suddenly bereft. As lonely as he could ever remember. As if he, somehow, unintentionally, had truly taken the first step toward becoming his father.

And then Addie's eyes met his, and he raised his glass, almost imperceptibly, in a toast, his gaze never leaving hers. Then he tossed back his first dose of Glauber Salts, trying manfully not to gag.

Chapter 29

Addie took a deep breath and blew it out slowly. She let the embroidery she had been pretending to stitch at fall next to her, and then allowed herself the luxury of closing her eyes and leaning her head back. Lord, she was tired. Tired from keeping her posture impeccable so as not to have to listen to yet another of Mrs. Raines's discourses on the importance of an upright carriage for the health of the internal organs. Tired from Wallace's endless scolds, the thought of which made her grit her teeth, but which, she reminded herself, were delivered only out of kindness. Tired from getting up before first light this last week to supervise Fitzwilliam's training. Tired from being constantly shown up as poorly dressed, poorly accomplished, and poorly blessed in natural beauty by Miss Haverford. Tired from wondering what, if anything, that lovely young lady was to Fitzwilliam—and indeed, what her own status was with regard to that gentleman. And to top it all off, Justine, always her confidante and source of support, had apparently not one thought in her head besides the complete excellence of Drew Mannering in every conceivable arena. If she weren't so fond of Drew herself, she could almost find it sickening.

And, if that was not enough, she had just endured a most tedious scold from Honoria. The subject: *The Behavior of Ladies at House Parties, Addie.*

Ladies, at house parties, Addie, it had gone. *They sew, they knit, they walk out to admire the grounds. They make excursions into town to buy ribbons and the like. They make pleasant conversation, they play cards. Sigh. They ride out gently. They perform upon the pianoforte or harp, or sometimes even sing prettily, when requested, although, here, in all good conscience, she* was *forced to beg that Addie would not attempt it. They do not, however* (glare), *slink off to the ornamental dairy in the dark of night to plant gentlemen facers, or draw their corks, or whatever it is you do! They also,* she had added, for good measure, *only, mind you, do not force gentlemen to take doses of Glauber Salts or adhere to bizarre regimens, almost costing them all the talents of a most highly accomplished French chef. Nor do they rendezvous with aforementioned gentlemen in bedchambers and force them to hide under beds!*

But before Addie had been able to open her mouth to inquire as to how Honoria came by her intelligence, Honoria had gone on to say that the last bit of behavior was *exactly* how Maude Bateman had managed to lose her left shoe at Althorp in, oh, it must have been, 'eighty-two (or possibly 'seventy-nine, but then it would have been Anne, her sister, so, no, it must have been 'eighty-two), and never had been able to find another pair that went as perfectly with the green silk, which, as it turned out, had been Eric Creighton's favorite and he had not in the end come up to scratch. And that, quite frankly, the Raines betrothal ring was not at all, not a bit, suited to Addie's hand.

And then her aunt had swept out in a swish of blue satin and a cloud of scent.

All of which, thought Addie, as she twisted the too-heavy, too-ornate betrothal ring that now graced her left hand, offered a perfectly reasonable account for why a person could feel uncommonly tired and even have a headache coming on.

Chapter 30

"Hacked over to Melton," Freddie Barrist was saying meanwhile, as, cheroot clenched between his teeth, he leaned over the table. "Best day of hunting I've had in years. Assheton-Smith said there hadn't been a November like it in ten years. And damned if I don't agree with him." He straightened.

"Ran with 'em a few times myself this year," said the recently arrived William Mannering, Viscount Ardean. "Good shot!" He clapped his brother-in-law on the back. "Didn't stay above a few days," he added. "Went up with Humphries, you know, and he had, ah, other interests in the area. Interests that would have put Suzanne entirely out of countenance had she but known. She's bosom bows with Lady Humphries. Wanted to save my own hide, so I thought it was prudent to get the hell out of there."

"Don't listen, Drew," suggested Fitzwilliam, handily sinking a shot. He crossed to the opposite side of the table. "As what you're about to hear does not sound likely to be a tale of marital bliss and fidelity." He bent to line up his next shot.

"I haven't heard a thing thus far." Drew grinned. "And here I am in the midst of solidly respectable, blissfully shackled company. Ardean's concerned these days only with farming, tenants, and getting back home to the wife; Freddie here's only interested in chasing foxes—''

"Hey! I chased your sister, you impudent young pup," Freddie pointed out, wounded. "Demmed right I did. Best fox I ever ran to ground!"

They laughed, and Drew continued, as he blew chalk dust off his stick. "Sorry, I stand corrected, Freddie. Anyway, surrounded at the moment by two happily shackled men and a remarkably celibate Fitzwilliam. It's inspiring, I tell you."

"Celibacy?" grumbled Fitzwilliam. "Can't say I find it all that inspiring myself."

"Don't have to be. Celibate, you know," Freddie said. "A Claremont engagement ring on her daughter's finger, and I'm certain even that Haverford dragon'd look the other way."

Fitzwilliam balanced his stick against his foot. After a minute he looked up. "Perhaps celibacy has its merits." He smiled. "A fellow, after all, Freddie, doesn't want to end up making such a drastic mistake in the short term that he ends up having to give up hunting season to find sport in the long term!"

"Lord, no! Heard that Humphries had set himself up a little ladybird in Melton, but I wasn't sure whether to believe it." Freddie shook his head at the thought of a man who'd prefer anything to hunting. "Not at all the thing." He shook his head again. "It ain't right. Not at all the kind of sport a fellow's meant to have during the season in Melton!"

The others chuckled their agreement, and Fitzwilliam, having sent his last ball into a pocket, excused himself to go confer with Hedges and Mrs. Jeffcott.

"Another round?" he heard Freddie say to the others as he quit the room. "Good thing he thinks celibacy has its merits, because heard at White's that Bella's choosing between Skowhagen and Foster. Wasn't too happy apparently that Fitzwilliam gave her her congé by letter. Heard he settled a nice little house *and* a fortune in jewelery on her, but she's still out of countenance about the whole thing. Odds are long on Foster."

* * *

Fitzwilliam paused outside the door to the library and leaned his head against the wall. God, he was tired. Addie's regimen had been grueling. And he could hardly agree that it was contributing to his overall fitness, since he had been half-starved, exhausted, sweated in what he was convinced was a disgustingly unhealthy manner, and dosed with what he could only consider quackish brews. Not only was Antoine in a state requiring constant soothing, and the rest of the house party somewhat baffled at his new spartan regimen, but Weston, would likely, given the chance, disavow his coats entirely, the way they were hanging off of him. And, now that the first few days were over, he was bruised and battered from being repeatedly pummeled, under Addie's direction, at the hands of his best friend.

It must be the exhaustion that was contributing toward this uncharacteristic lowering of spirits he seemed to be experiencing. He had never, to his knowledge, had a fit of the mopes before.

So, he mused, Bella had found another protector already. Good for her. He didn't mourn her particularly, but it somehow saddened him that there was no one left who would be truly glad to see him, or conversely, miss him should they not see him. No one for the moment, anyway. Until, he supposed, he began paying someone new to be glad to see him.

"Oh, Lord Claremont! I mean, Fitzwilliam. I'm so very glad to see you!" said Miss Haverford, floating down the hall, looking positively ethereal in her morning dress of lavender wool.

He had to smile at her choice of words, given his thoughts of a moment ago. "What can I do for you, Miss Haverford?" he asked, smiling down at her.

She gazed up at him with those beautiful violet eyes and somehow managed to attach herself to his arm. "I must beg you to give me a tour of the portrait gallery, my lord. I have heard that although it cannot match that at Claremont House, it is of excellent quality, and only you, Mrs. Jeffcott assures me, can do it justice.''

"It would be my pleasure, ma'am,'' he said, still smiling down at her, as, tucking her hand into the crook of his arm, he led her toward the portrait gallery. "Although you must assure me, Miss Haverford,'' he added teasingly, "that you will not try to take advantage of our relative isolation. That my virtue is safe with you.''

As he said it, he was half considering giving it a try. Perhaps it was the celibacy, after all. And just maybe a few stolen kisses shared with the beauteous Lavinia Haverford would help banish his megrims. Which, he decided instantly, was a mark of how low he felt, as under ordinary circumstances, his first instinct, as he had told Drew and Freddie and Ardean, would have been to run in the opposite direction. But she *was* pleasant enough, and so very beautiful, and going to great lengths to make it clear what an exemplary countess she would make. Unlike Addie, he reflected, who would no doubt be feeding Glauber Salts to the grooms and teaching the parlor maids to mill down anyone in their paths.

"Well, Miss Haverford?'' he asked, looking down at her with a smile. "What do you say? Can I trust you?''

To which she giggled, and looking up in such a way that he knew signaled interest, replied, "La! But you are the most shocking flirt, Lord Claremont, ah, I mean, Fitzwilliam.''

Which lighthearted reply, although she could not know it, immediately damped any ideas that had been forming.

Kenston House
Two, February, 1814

My Dear John,
   All goes well here. Fitzwilliam has proved himself a willing, if not especially skilled student. I have begun by putting him on Captain Barclay's regimen with the result that having gone a regular course of it, his fitness is much improved. I realize that you and I still differ as to the efficacy of the Glauber Salts and the sweating liquor, but once again, I cannot express disappointment with it, as his stamina and his wind seem much improved.
   I have also learned, to my surprise, and having known him my entire life am disappointed in my observational powers for not having realized sooner, that it seems he is ambidextrous, with a dominant left hand. I have little experience with left-handed boxers, but Father, I know, was adamant that one is at cross-purposes to attempt to teach them to lead from the right. They must learn, he always said, to come from the left. So it must be, I think, largely a matter of training him to come from the other direction.
   To this end, he spars daily with Mr. Mannering, who shows himself a solid and steady opponent, but is neither a man of science, nor, as I know Mr. Walters must remain, a man of brutish propensity. Fitzwilliam's science is somewhat improved, and his wind and courage, much so. I have noted, that when leading with his left hand, his distance is considerably better judged (or at least, less ill-judged) than before, and consequently there is less idle sparring, and he strikes more effective blows. He dealt two excellent rib-roasters yesterday that left Mr. Mannering wincing and gasping for breath. I have asked them to refrain from hitting each other in the face, as these injuries, drawn corks, etc., will likely prove themselves difficult to explain away to the assembled company.

I am optimistic of continued improvement, but still uncertain about his ability to have the best of Mr. Walters. You, John, must, I think, referee that match. And I would welcome, it goes without saying, any advice forthcoming from you on training left-handers.

The weather continues unusually cold here, as, I trust it does in London. Honoria and Justine send their love. I remain yours affectionately.

Addie

Kenston House
Two, February, 1814

Dearest Lizbeth,

    You cannot mean that! Is Glendower even aware that you know such words, let alone that you would put them to paper? I trust not. Because although I must profess myself ardently opposed to the practice in general, I think it would be indeed fitting in the specific, were he to beat you soundly!

    You have already apprised me, do not forget, of your disappointment in having been mistaken as to the identity of my intended husband, Lizbeth. Nonetheless, there can be no call to heap such invective (and I hesitate to mention, cant) upon Mr. Raines's innocent head.

    As to the rumors that are circulating, Fitzwilliam and I did indeed come upon Mr. Raymond Walters as we walked together at Vauxhall, but as to what he told you, I must take leave to disagree. Mr. Walters was, although it distresses me to mention such a thing, deep in his cups, acutely castaway, in fact, and in company with a woman who was less than virtuous. In short, I would give little credence to any version of events you are to have had from him.

    I should, my dear friend, have been most happy to receive your correspondence, except that I truly cannot like the aspersions cast within upon my intended husband, and must ask that you desist in the future. These are words that once we are contentedly wed, as are you and Glendower, and surrounded by a family, I can only think you will come to regret.

    And as for Fitzwilliam, I think that you should know that Miss Lavinia Haverford and her mother have joined our party and all is well to smelling of April and May for the two of them. So, please, Lizbeth, I beg you, let me hear no more on this score.

    Despite my discomposure, I remain, your loving friend.
        Addie

Chapter 31

"I think," Fitzwilliam announced to the assembled company after dinner, which he noted, with some bitterness, had consisted of pheasant soup, stewed trout, larded partridges, apricot tart, curried lobster, game patties, boiled capon, ginger ice cream, preserved cherries, and raspberry cream for the rest of the company, but muttonchops and stale bread for himself, "that perhaps we should have our own Frost Fair. Indeed, it has been quite a while since I have been in residence here long enough to provide an entertainment for the village."

"What an excellent notion, Lord, er, Fitzwilliam," replied Lavinia Haverford, who had just trounced the company at Jackstraws. "And as you are a single gentleman, and as the Misses Winstead have their fiancés to occupy them, and such good fortune cannot be my dear Lavinia's to claim, I hope you shall not gainsay her the diversion of acting as hostess in this event," Mrs. Haverford inserted.

Fitzwilliam looked momentarily taken aback. "I had not thought, I, ah—" he began.

"Not publicly, of course, *that* would be vastly improper,"

Mrs. Haverford hastened to assure him. "But in accepting the responsibility of being charged with the planning."

"Oh *do* say *yes*, my lord," Lavina begged prettily. "For I shall like it beyond anything."

"You will have no cause to regret acceptance," Mrs. Haverford assured him. "My Lavinia is *quite* the planner."

As Fitzwilliam gravely accepted the offer, Addie thought about how well-suited the two of them were. Lavinia was almost as coolly beautiful as he was, and clearly was eminently suited to be a countess—unlike herself, a woman who had sunk not only to lurking about boxing salons, but to writing about it for commerce. *And* who had allowed Fitzwilliam unthinkable liberties with her person. The first time just moments after he had told her that he'd no intention of marrying her. Lavinia, she decided on a repressed sigh, would never have allowed such ridiculous passions to get the better of her.

Beside her, Wallace fretted about the possible repercussions of such folly to their health, and his limpid brown eyes fixed on her made her feel even worse.

"I cannot see *great* harm in it, as long as one is prudently dressed and does not remain out of doors for an excessive amount of time," his mama counseled. "It is only a *minor* risk, after all, Wallace, and one must, I have always said, *live* life. No, I think even one with a delicate constitution should be able to withstand a little. Mayhap an hour or two."

"But you do not think it is too cold for you, my dear?" Wallace worried to Addie. "I hope you will not think me presumptuous if I point out that the evening vapors bring out, I tend to think, qualities you cannot wish to display. A certain, snappishness, the blame for which of course cannot, my dear, be laid at your door, brought about as it is by noxious agents that abound in nighttime air. And there is your frailty—"

"What a lucky woman you are, to be sure, to have found such devotion from so eligible a gentleman. And at your age!" remarked Millicent Haverford, interrupting, and Wallace preened.

Honoria laughed gaily. "Addie? Frail? Really, I hadn't

thought you such a dry boots, Wallace!'' she said. ''Why the gel is as hardy a soul as I've ever met.''

And . . . Addie waited for Honoria to take Wallace to task on the issue of the snappishness, only to be disappointed.

Lavinia Haverford smiled delicately behind her fingertips. ''Then I shall ask you to do some of the, er, more *arduous* work, Miss Winstead, take some of the weight off the gentlemen's shoulders, so to speak,'' she said, pleasantly. ''As you are so *hardy*. I must confess, that although I shall vastly enjoy such a thing as holding our own Frost Fair, I am not made of such stern stuff as you appear to be.''

Addie glared at Honoria. Really, was it entirely necessary to have made her sound like a plow horse? she wondered, as Justine said, diplomatically, taking up Addie's hand, ''You do rarely succumb to illness, Addie, love, but on the rare occasions when you do, you manage it with excellent grace.''

Was *no one* going to defend her on the issue of the alleged snappishness? she wondered, directing a glare at her relations. Apparently not. ''Well since I *am* so hardy,'' she said, ''I think I shall put it to good advantage by taking some air before retiring.''

Fitzwilliam stood. ''I shall fetch your cloak and join you. I am, after all, thought to be *almost* as robust as you, Addie,'' he added.

''Not afraid of my snappishness, then, Fitzwilliam?'' Addie asked with a raised brow, somewhat . . . snappishly.

''Out of countenance already, are you? And to think, you've not even been outside yet,'' Fitzwilliam retorted.

Mrs. Haverford, who clearly could not like Addie's ease of manners with their host, interjected, ''My Lavinia, although she is not so rugged, does enjoy a stroll before retiring.''

At which point, the entire party decided to join them, with the exception of Mrs. Raines, who chose to go and prepare a steaming bowl of water infused with herbs for her son to inhale upon his return, and Lord Ardean and his wife, who opted to stay by the fire. Such decision caused Honoria to level an assessing gaze at Lady Ardean, and Addie guessed that she was trying to decipher whether such care was because they believed her to be increasing, thus foiling Drew's chances of having his brother die without having produced an heir.

Justine apparently had formed the same suspicions regarding their aunt's thoughts, and as she took Addie's arm, she whispered, "I'm surprised she hasn't suggested separate bedchambers during their stay."

Which caused Addie to blush, even as she laughed.

They walked outside, warmly dressed, up and down the little paths that were brightly lit by the moon. Fitzwilliam led the way with Honoria on one arm and Mrs. Haverford on the other. And he, Addie decided with a grin, could not be having anything except a capital time, as Honoria and Mrs. Haverford sounded to be engaged in a rousing disagreement as to whether it was Margaret Poyntz who had worn the unattractive slippers at her wedding to the first Earl Spencer in 'fifty-five, or Aurelie Bingham at hers to the second Earl Spencer in 'eighty-one.

Addie followed with Wallace, who had on his other arm a clearly simmering Lavinia Haverford. Miss Haverford repeatedly thought of points of interest regarding the proposed Frost Fair that she could only think the earl would like to know with all despatch. Behind them, Drew and Justine lagged behind a bit, conversing with Freddie and Madeleine.

They all admired the beauty of the grounds at night, and discussed at length the Frost Fair. Until, eventually, Lavinia, pleading the cold, asked Fitzwilliam if he would be so good as to escort her indoors. At this, Justine, who appeared to her sister to have one eye on Addie and one on Lavinia, said that she also was vastly chilled and would welcome the tea tray, and the entire party decided to return.

As they approached the door to the terrace, Lavinia keeping a firm grasp on Fitzwilliam's arm, Addie cried out that she had dropped her bracelet. Fitzwilliam offered, as he drew Lavinia to a stop to send a footman, but Addie insisted that she more than likely knew almost to the spot where it had dropped and that it made no sense at all to send a footman out into the cold as it would likely take him twice as long to locate it.

"Then I will escort you," he said, and Lavinia gave her an assessing look. "I know these paths well."

"There is no need, Fitzwilliam," Addie said sternly. "It is not a particularly dark night, after all."

"I must confess that were it my bracelet, I should accept Lord Cl—Fitzwilliam's offer to send a footman," Lavinia said with a shiver, still, Addie noted, holding tight. "I am not very brave about being by myself at night, but then, we have already established that I am not nearly so strapping as you, Miss Winstead."

"You are always most sensible, my love," her mother said.

"I only know that I *must,* and it is a matter of grave consequence, suspend my head over a steaming bowl within minutes," Wallace warned.

"Go, Wallace," Addie said. "I beg you will not suffer adverse consequences on my account. I shall anyway be back in a trice, and there is no need, as I have pointed out, for anyone to accompany me."

Drew then offered to take a look, and Justine to assist, and Freddie suggested sending out the hounds. "Demmed fine hounds. Sired by Rutland's y'know! Just let them sniff at some other gewgaw, my dear. An earbob, or such, and they'd find it."

"What a lot of fuss about nothing," Addie exclaimed.

"I would like to blow a cloud, anyway. And even one so *hardy* as we have established you to be should not be jauntering about by yourself at night, Addie." Fitzwilliam said in a tone that brooked an end to the disagreement. "We shall no doubt find the bracelet and have you indoors in a trice. Does that answer?"

Everyone agreed that it did, although it was with clear reluctance that Lavinia relinquished Fitzwilliam's arm, while Wallace trotted into the house with what appeared to be great relief.

"There is no lost bracelet, is there, Addie?" Fitzwilliam said, no sooner had they gained the lawn.

And she replied, "And I don't believe, come to think on it, that I've ever seen you smoke a cheroot, Fitzwilliam."

He smiled, relaxing into her company. "Snappish, are you? I guess we both felt a need for a few minutes of solitude before the ritual of the tea tray. I feel myself the recipient of more attention than I would necessarily like."

"I rather thought you did like it," Addie said shortly.

He grinned. "Is that jealousy, Addie?"

"Jealousy, Fitzwilliam? I think not."

"Mrs. Haverford cannot seem to recall for more than five minutes at a time that I cannot abide being called Claremont," he said, after a moment. "It's Claremont, I mean, Fitzwilliam, this, and Claremont, I mean, Fitzwilliam, that, all day."

"Is that so awful?" Addie raised a brow in question.

He bent silently, and picked up a stone, which he threw, hard, toward the frozen lake. They stood and listened as it hit the ground and bounced a few times on the downhill slope. His face was hard. "The name does not, somehow, seem to bring out the best in people," he said lightly. "But it may be your name someday, too, y'know. Then *you* tell *me*."

And Addie could not help but feel wounded by the bitterness in his tone. She was, after all, going to great, even sacrificial lengths, to ensure that such a thing did not come to pass. And this ridiculous wager was not *her* idea, to be sure. "Hardly likely," she said, dryly. "And if it is solitude you desire, Fitzwilliam, shall we go our separate ways?"

"We shall not," he said firmly, thinking the odd thing was that he almost felt he could be solitary *with* Addie. Which made no sense. "I am sure you must have something to say to me that cannot be said in company. Some criticism to my left, which I understand is still not nearly punishing enough, or some such." He tossed another rock.

"No." She tilted her head appraisingly. "I think I said quite enough on that topic this morning."

"Well, then," he said quietly, turning toward her, "let us go on to another. Do you know that I am reminded forcefully of the last time we were out in the cold together?"

And Addie felt that familiar lurch of confusion. She could never, it seemed, understand what he was thinking. Just a moment ago she had been wondering whether he was in love with Lavinia Haverford, and now, here he was, weaving that silken, sensual spell around her again.

"Really, Claremont? I mean, Fitzwilliam," she replied in as unconcerned a voice as she could muster. "I do believe I must have forgotten that."

He laughed, and leaned back against the high stone wall of the terrace above them. "I doubt that," he said, once again withdrawing the little silver flask from his pocket. "But then I'm a conceited fellow, as Raines will no doubt be happy to tell you." She eyed the flask distrustfully as he uncapped it and handed it to her. "Go ahead. For the cold. And do not think it has escaped me, Addie, how that old fuss-jaw you think you are shackling yourself to watches every drop of wine you take."

She shook her head no, to the flask. And he said quietly, "It wasn't this that made you drunk, you know, last time, Addie. It was this." And before she knew what he was about, he had pulled her roughly into his arms and was kissing her, thoroughly and hungrily, and yet, surprisingly gently. The fine wool of his greatcoat enveloped her, and his gloved hands held her firmly against him.

Very likely he was right, she thought fuzzily, and then, *I really must get Wallace to kiss me. Maybe it will be just the same as this.* And then, *is he doing this with me because he's stuck up here, with no mistress, and Lavinia Haverford won't allow it?* Before, that is, she stopped thinking altogether and abandoned herself to his warm mouth, and fierce embrace.

But then, as suddenly as he had begun, Fitzwilliam broke away. "Take a drink," he said, leaving Addie—who was still swimming up from a pool of sensation that she would rather not leave—a few steps behind.

From their spot just below the terrace, she could see the light spilling out from the French doors. Someone had apparently left at least one of the doors open, and she heard the unmistakable tones of her future mother-in-law separate from the thread of general conversation and float out into the still night. "... and it turned out, you know, that she had a"—here her voice lowered so that Addie, glad for any diversion from their previous activities, had to strain to catch her words— "*blockage!*" she all but whispered.

Then she heard Millicent Haverford gasp. "No!"

"A blockage!" Wallace's voice echoed faintly.

"Yes, indeed!" Gretchen Raines said, triumphantly. And then, confidentially, "Too much cheese! It turned out that she was just consuming *cheese* whenever the notion hit her! Cheese in the morning! Cheese at lunch! Cheese at dinner!"

Her voice had risen in her excitement, and Fitzwilliam laughed. "I'd be taking that drink were I you, Addie," he said, softly.

"And sometimes even cheese with the tea tray!" Gretchen Raines almost shouted in her excitement.

"Perhaps I will," Addie allowed, taking the flask a mite too quickly.

"Just don't ask me for cheese to go with it," Fitzwilliam said, which struck them as unaccountably hilarious, and they both doubled over, trying to suppress their laughter so as not to be caught.

"Good Lord, I feel like a schoolgirl," Addie confessed, taking a slug. "Not, mind you, that I ever told bouncers about losing jewelry and snuck about eavesdropping at doorways and drinking spirits with gentlemen as a schoolgirl," she added quickly, lest he get the wrong idea.

"No, I know exactly what you mean, Addie, because I feel like a school*boy*. The thing of it is," he said, accepting back the flask and capping it and replacing it in the pocket of his greatcoat, "that the schoolboys, you must know, always want to kiss the schoolgirls—"

Addie knew she should put a stop to this conversation and the dangerous road down which it was leading, but simply could not bring herself to do so.

"—except that *they* are notoriously inexperienced at it, Addie. And *I* am about to kiss you very well, indeed."

She could have sworn that she backed up a step, but conceded that it must have only been in her mind. In fact, when he put his hand out for hers, she might even have taken a step toward him. And possibly wet her lips with the tip of her tongue. She swallowed. "I wish you would not, Fitzwilliam."

His voice was lazily amused when he replied, "You would rather I kissed you poorly, then?"

"No, I did not mean"—she took a deep breath and tried to collect herself—"I *trust* you will not—"

"You have misplaced your trust, Addie," he murmured.

She couldn't see much of his face because the moonlight was behind him, but she could feel him, the solid, warm strength of him, and smell him, the spicy clean scent of him. And she could hear his quick, sharp intake of breath in the moment before he pulled her into his arms again. And she would have resisted, indeed, knew she *should* have resisted, but somehow, could not.

And then he was kissing her again. His lips slanted over hers and his fingers were in her hair, and she knew in some far distant, entirely separate portion of her mind, that she could not walk back into the drawing room and take tea with the company this night. And then he parted his lips and his tongue gently, teasingly touched her lips. She could feel a sizzle ignite down to her toes.

Fitzwilliam was no longer lazily amused. "Dear Lord," he murmured against her mouth, which tasted intriguingly of the brandy, before beginning a slow, sensuous invasion of hers.

And Addie's arms went around his neck, seemingly of their own accord, and she leaned in to him. She could feel the unsteadiness of his breathing, and his heart thundering against her chest. He pulled her body more firmly against his, and she arched back as his lips took hers again. He moaned, or, Addie had to concede, it might have been her, and his hands went around her back, molding her against him, and she felt him asking for something, wanting something. But not sure what, she simply opened her mouth under his.

"Dear Lord," he said again, but she hardly recognized his voice, it was so hoarse, and his body was shaking. Nothing had ever felt better, or more dangerous, than his embrace.

And then, suddenly overcome by a fit of conscience, lest she feel more than she ought, and unease at the feeling that he wanted more from her than the satisfaction of his physical needs, he put her away from him. More abruptly than he had intended.

They stood looking at each other.

He was breathing unsteadily, as though he had just come in from one of his prescribed uphill runs, Addie noted. And his eyes, even in bright light, she guessed, would have been entirely unreadable.

"What do you want," she whispered, backing away another step, "from me?"

So she had felt it. His confusion. That he'd wanted more. "I don't know," he replied.

"What is there between you and Miss Haverford?"

"I don't know," he replied again.

She stared at him. She had never seen him like this. All her life she had known him as polished and collected, impossible to ruffle, and generally lazily amused by everything. Now, looking down at her, he seemed for once lost and uncertain. He was not even leaning negligently back against the wall, as she would have expected. She could feel even from a distance how tightly coiled his body was.

"Do you love her?" she whispered, wondering if she truly wanted to hear the answer.

"No," he replied succinctly.

"Fitzwilliam?" she asked, heartened by his last answer.

"Yes, Addie?"

"Do you want to best Raymond Walters?"

He paused a second. "I don't know." His voice was barely audible. "Do you want me to?"

She shook her head as her eyes filled with tears. "I don't know," she whispered back.

He reached for her, but she backed up hastily. "No! Don't touch me." She was bordering on hysteria, she knew, but was damned if she was going to let his touch seduce her again. "In fact, don't touch me again," she whispered before turning and fleeing back to the house, where, she ran through the drawing room and up the stairs without so much as a word to the astonished company.

Chapter 32

"Has Miss Winstead been eating an immoderate amount of poultry of late, Wallace? She seems somewhat, unbalanced, and an excess of fowl, well, we all know what *that* can lead to," Fitzwilliam heard Gretchen Raines say after the momentary silence that had greeted Addie's abrupt trip through the drawing room.

He sighed and leaned back against the wall. He certainly needed a minute before he could walk back in there. If poultry was Addie's problem, surely an excess of muttonchops was his. Perhaps he should ask Mrs. Raines whether muttonchops were known to overheat the blood. The lady would surely have some opinion on that score, although overheated blood was almost certainly not her area of expertise. He nearly laughed.

But truly, what *was* he doing? Why on earth could he not seem to convince himself to keep his hands off of Addie? And, of late, when his hands weren't on her, it was all he could think about. Getting them there.

He closed his eyes and tried to recall her as his tomboyish childhood companion, but to his surprise, he could no longer summon that picture to mind. Even when she came to the

ornamental dairy in her boxing-instructor mode, she seemed
every inch a desirable woman to him, as she stomped about,
hands on her slim hips, bossing him around and critiquing
his—according to her, anyway—less-than-satisfactory progress.

He thought of her as she had looked tonight: the quiet beauty
he had only recently come to see, her simple clothing, her ready
laugh as they had shared that illicit drink under the terrace.
That thought, quite naturally, led him to the other illicit things
they had shared under the terrace, and how she had felt against
him. And what it was that he had wanted from her.

He opened his eyes and looked about at the moonlit gardens
sloping down to the lake. This was the only house, in truth,
the only place, he had ever cared for. He had never brought a
party here before, and he could not particularly figure why he
had chosen to do so now. While no one, he reflected, could
fault him as a landlord at any of his properties—his tenants
and dependents were well taken care of, and his estates were
all overseen by reliable and hardworking stewards—none of
them touched anything in him the way this place seemed to.
Something about being here made him relax in a way he never
did elsewhere. And with that, having Addie here, she just
seemed to . . . *belong,* he thought was the word. And when she
had been in his arms, against him, despite his almost overwhelming wanting, there had been something else, a feeling of
a certain peace, a connection, that had felt just beyond his
grasp. Had he not had such a restless soul, he decided, he would
almost have been able to imagine finding that peace within
himself and within her, down the years.

But he did have a restless soul. And that was that, he thought,
folding his arms, still staring down toward the lake. If he had
needs that he'd not even seen until tonight, goodness knew,
she did too, and he was not such a selfish flat as to be able to
overlook that. But perhaps that was exactly what he had done
by forcing her into this wager, he thought uncomfortably, all
to assuage his own feelings of guilt at not having done right
by her. She needed the freedom to find the part of herself that

chafed under convention, certainly, not to have to hide it. And likely to attend the odd mill or two, he thought, almost laughing. And certainly Wallace would, *could,* never give her that.

But she also needed, he understood instinctively, a true and constant husband. A straying spouse would all but destroy her. And that was one thing he could never promise. While Wallace, well, he would be faithful, if nothing else. He should let her go, he knew, release Addie to accept the security Wallace could offer and turn his own eyes to Lavinia Haverford, or someone like her. Lavinia was beautiful, she would make an excellent countess, she was willing—hell, more than willing—and she would accept marriage à la mode, with a husband who had other interests without so much as the blink of one of her lovely eyes. Expected it, most likely. And perhaps most importantly, there was no conceivable way that she would awake this mysterious, troublesome part of him, the one that wanted more, that had surfaced this night.

"Where do you suppose Clarem—ah, *Fitzwilliam,* has got to?" he heard the musical tones of that very lady inquire.

"No doubt searching further," he heard Drew reassure her. "Very thorough fellow, Fitzwilliam is."

He looked down for a moment at the little gold bracelet that he had had the foresight to slip off Addie's wrist. With a deliberate motion, he wrenched the clasp, and then, holding it in his closed fist, returned to the drawing room.

"I've found it, but I'm afraid it's broken," he announced to the company at large as he entered the warmth of the room. He looked around, feigning surprise. "Where is Addie?"

Drew raised an eloquent brow at him.

"Ah, retired, for the evening one assumes," Honoria supplied, dryly. "Although she was somewhat less than forthcoming as to her destination."

Those two, anyway, knew something had occurred. And Fitzwilliam guessed that Honoria, at least, had taken no more than a second to assess the fact that he did not smell like a man who had just smoked a cheroot.

"Without so much as *trying* the herbal steam Mother so

painstakingly prepared for her, which, one is certain, she can only regret come morning.''

"Quite ill-judged," Lavinia Haverford sympathized, smiling at Wallace. "One can only hope that Miss Winstead does not take ill. I, myself, am feeling a slight tickle in the back of my throat, and I spent a much shorter time out of doors than she.''

"A honey poultice," Wallace recommended gravely.

"I've an excellent receipe," began Gretchen Raines, leaning forward in her excitement.

"Don't worry, Gretchen." Mrs. Haverford smiled sweetly, so as to suggest that she did not mean a word she was saying. "I am certain Miss Winstead's manners are not always so ragged. She"—her eyes were now fixed on Fitzwilliam, and he knew that this was for his benefit—"tore through here like a veritable *hoyden,* without so much as a 'Good evening'!" She sniffed.

"She was most distressed at not being able to find the bracelet," Fitzwilliam said firmly. "A gift from her late father, I believe, so her upset is, perhaps, understandable."

"Indeed . . ." Honoria began ominously.

"Oh, well. I suppose it is," Mrs. Haverford allowed, "understandable under the circumstances. Why, you should *see* how rude my Lavinia is, given the proper conditions. Downright rag-mannered!"

"Indeed! I can only hope then to witness such a display," Fitzwilliam replied, suppressing a grin. "I think I shall go and give the bracelet to a maid to bring up to Miss Winstead."

But, having quit the room, he instead tucked the bracelet into his pocket.

Chapter 33

"Don't be such a flat, Drew," Fitzwilliam said the next morning as they faced each other in the ring. "Of course it ain't love."

Why, he wondered, had he told Drew anything? He should have known, given the current sodden state of Drew's heart—and brain—that he would come up with some maggoty notion to explain what had clearly been no more than an odd start last night.

They were sparring lightly and waiting for Addie, who was uncharacteristically late down to the ring, and he had felt the compulsion to spill some of the tale.

"And how d'you know?" Drew inquired, sounding stubborn. "Except, of course, for the pigheaded notion that *Claremont men don't fall in love,*" he parroted, his voice a credible imitation of Fitzwilliam's.

"I just know."

"Right. Like I said, Claremont man stuff."

"Exactly."

And then Drew hit him. Harder than usual.

"What was that for?" Fitzwilliam asked from the floor.

"Just seeing how good your defenses were. Off your guard, and all that."

"The hell you were!" Fitzwilliam stood and glared. And then with a quickness and accuracy that he could only think Addie would have applauded, he applied an excellent left to Drew's mouth.

"And that? What was *it* for?" Drew asked, attempting to staunch the blood flowing from his split lip.

"I'm not sure," Fitzwilliam admitted, advancing on him.

"Sublimation of other desires, I'd guess," Drew murmured.

"And *your* other desires, Drew?" Fitzwilliam asked silkily, and he knew, nastily. "Are they being met?"

And then they were at each other in earnest, exchanging blow for blow in a surprisingly even bout, until—

"Drew! Fitzwilliam!"

They stopped, midflail, and sheepishly turned to face Addie. She was standing inside the door, her arms folded over her chest, looking furious, as though they were two recalcitrant schoolboys. She also looked, Fitzwilliam noted with no small measure of guilt, exhausted. Sleep presumably had been long in coming the previous night.

"What on earth are you two doing?" she asked calmly.

"Ah, sparring?" suggested Drew.

"Yes. I can see that much." She walked closer. "I don't suppose either of you has given any thought to how difficult your faces will be to explain?"

They both flushed, and she knew they had not even realized what a sight they presented. Fitzwilliam's nose was spouting blood, and he was sporting what looked to become an excellent bruise on his left temple. Drew's split lip was still dripping, his right ear was bleeding, and his left eye was in a fair way to turning black. "Right. You both look a mess," she said severely. "You also seem to have forgotten my first lesson—"

"That Glauber Salts are vile?" Fitzwilliam suggested with a glint of humor.

"No, no. That sweating liquor is best drunk without a half bottle of port as a chaser?" Drew said merrily.

They were both laughing now, once again in charity with each other. "That even an excellent French chef can make underdone muttonchops taste loathsome?" Fitzwilliam contributed.

"That if you are an earl, no one at your house party will dare to remark it if you decide to adopt a bizarre regimen of taking stale bread and ale at every meal?" Drew offered.

"That the first requirement of becoming any kind of boxer is to learn to keep your passions in check," Addie said quietly. "When you don't, science immediately goes out the window, and no boxer can afford that. That's why Jackson is so good. Haven't you ever noticed that nothing ruffles him? That there's no anger in his sparring?"

They both nodded, looking, once again, sheepish.

"And now," she continued, "for today, I think I'd suggest dispensing with the sparring. Take a four-mile run. And then think of a good reason why you both look this way."

As they moved toward the door, she said, "And, Fitzwilliam?"

He looked at her.

Just a ghost of a smile hovered about her mouth. "Excellent left," she said. "Much improved. Now, get running."

And then, without sparing them another glance, she strode purposefully back to the house.

Chapter 34

"Do you mean they were actually hitting each other, really hitting?" Justine asked, sitting up sleepily in bed. "What time is it?" She rubbed her eyes.

"Almost seven." Addie moved a little farther onto the edge of her sister's bed, keeping her fingers around a folded letter in her pocket. "Don't worry, he's fine. He's going to be a little battered about the face, but fine. I sent them on a four-mile run."

"I almost hesitate to ask this, but Fitzwilliam? How did he fare?"

"Actually rather well," Addie said, as Justine yawned hugely. "Under different circumstances, I would have been impressed by his progress."

"What do you know! So, why do you suppose they were doing that?"

"I've no idea." Addie shook her head. "None. And the odd thing is that not two minutes later they were perfectly in charity with each other. Laughing together, in fact."

Justine looked perplexed. "Just like that?"

"Exactly."

Justine shook her head. "I shall attempt to get something out of Drew later, and I will certainly inform you if I learn anything. But truly, Addie, I don't hold out any real hope of understanding them. So, we may as well move on to another subject," she said, fully awake now.

Addie groaned, but Justine would not be deterred. "I hate to mention it, love, but you are looking a trifle, ah, peaked this morning. And after you—after last night, well, is there anything peaked you want to talk about?"

Addie laughed. "No. And your tact is, as usual, appreciated, my dear."

"I was going to come to you last night to make certain you were all right, but Drew thought I should"—Justine raised her hands and let them fall—"should let you be. Was he right?" Her forehead wrinkled in concern.

Addie took her hand. "Tell Drew a fervent *thank you.*"

"You must have been pleased to have the bracelet back anyway. I hadn't realized that was from Father."

What bracelet from Father? Addie wondered. "Ah, yes, it was. And I am. Glad to have it back," she replied quickly.

"So what do you have planned for today, Ad?" Justine asked. "Drew tells me that he, Fitzwilliam, Freddie, and Ardean are going shooting. Not much sport, I shouldn't think, as any birds foolish enough to have stayed in the neighborhood are, no doubt, too frozen to escape, but he says that Freddie is chafing at the lack of sport. And that the dogs, anyway, will enjoy themselves. Miss Haverford, I know, wants to spend the day planning for the Frost Fair."

Addie laughed. "Today, Justine," she said, "I plan to write letters to Lizbeth and Jackson and spend some time with Honoria, who I've barely seen since our arrival. And, oh, yes, get Wallace to kiss me."

Justine bolted upright. "I know I heard you correctly. Do you care to explain?"

"Which part?"

"The, ah, kissing part. Wallace."

"Are you saying it is odd that I would want my future husband to kiss me?" Addie asked.

"No," Justine replied slowly. "But there was something in the *way* you said it."

"I need to see if I, ah, like it," Addie said forthrightly, although *like* didn't seem quite the right word to describe what happened to her in Fitzwilliam's embrace.

"Oh, dear. I do see," her sister replied, pulling her knees up to her chest and hugging them against herself under the blankets. "But surely he has kissed you?"

Addie shook her head. "Not a real kiss."

"Oh, dear," Justine said again.

"Exactly," Addie said with something close to a smile.

"You won't, you know."

"I might," Addie insisted.

Justine shook her head with a great deal of firmness. "I know you won't, but I suppose you need to see that for yourself. I shouldn't tell Honny of your plans, though, were I you. She won't like it. Not a bit."

"No." Addie stood. "No, she wouldn't. But first, breakfast, I think. *Au revoir,* Justine." She waved from the door.

Justine laughed. *"Au revoir,* Addie," she replied. "And best of luck."

Before going down to the breakfast room, Addie went back to her own chamber where, sitting on the edge of her bed, she pulled the letter that had arrived the day before out of her pocket, and read it one more time.

London
Eight, February, 1814

Addie, my dear,

Many thanks for your last letter. Before I respond to the information contained therein, I have some of my own that I feel it imperative to share with you: The bout between Raymond Walters and Fitzwilliam will, of necessity, have to be postponed, or in a more likely event, dispensed with altogether.

I trust that even without this missive, you will soon be, if you have not already been, apprised of this intelligence either through Mr. Walters himself or his second, who I understand to be Tom Edgerton. It seems—and here I must own, only to you, Addie, and not to Anonymous—that I lost control over my passions while in the ring with Mr. Walters. A most unusual circumstance, as you know. And I should think that due to some injuries he suffered—not severe, but not trifling either—he shall lack the ability, and possibly the inclination, to again enter the ring for some several weeks to come. And may possibly find himself overcome by a desire to reach the conciliation that I, shall we say, suggested, and that he found so repugnant previously.

I realize fully now, in the cool light of dispassion, that I should not, perhaps, have allowed myself to give in to my baser urges in this matter. But it did, when I looked at it from the direction of the harm he has done you—and can continue to do you—seem quite the thing, to give him a most thorough pummeling. As you must know, my dear, I look upon you as being as dear to my heart as my own beloved niece. And I find myself in the unusual and lamentable position of having been able to discern no excellence of heart at all in the man. So, I am afraid, under the circumstances, I cannot entirely bring myself to regret my actions in most strongly suggesting that he might find himself inclined to issue an apology.

On another topic: I was most surprised to read your news of Fitzwilliam being a dominant left-hander. That is the type of detail, and I trust I am not overstepping myself when I say this, that I rarely overlook. I must, therefore, stand before you, humbled by your superior observation. I can only, in my own defense, plead that the fellow was so poor in the ring that I am not certain I ever saw him throw a punch! Please do keep me informed of what the change in Mr. Walters's immediate plans will mean.

I trust it shall relieve your mind to learn that my stint as the ersatz Anonymous continues, with, I think I can say, no one the wiser. I find the boxing part comes easily, as I am certain you can imagine, but adding the on-dits continues to be difficult, although I believe I am beginning to become quite good at it. To that end, Mrs. Glendower has been most punctilious in sending me daily messages, for which I am grateful.

How, though, do you manage to make sense of her letters? I have never thought Glendower to want for sense, for all that he is not an excellent pugilist, but she, well, her letters are impossible to decipher. The simplest one is crossed and recrossed, and, truly, Addie! The woman appears to use no punctuation at all!

Despite that, I remain yours affectionately, as always.
                                                            John

Addie refolded the billet, and standing and shaking out her skirts, placed it carefully in the drawer of her night table before exiting and descending the stairs.

Chapter 35

"Adelaide!" Wallace, who was alone in the breakfast room, which Addie took to be a sign, rose to greet her with a pleasing alacrity as she entered. He took her hands in his, and she smiled at him. "It is indeed a good morning," he said. "And you, a pleasing sight."

"Thank you, Wallace," she replied, genuinely touched by his pleasure in seeing her. "And good morning to you also."

At least, with him so much nearer her own height than Fitzwilliam, she did not have to crane her neck up at him, she thought, resolving to put that fact in her letter to Lizbeth. Her friend, though, was bound to underestimate the importance of going through life without a stiff neck, Addie decided. And perhaps it did pale a bit next to say, enduring passion, but, well, a silver lining was a silver lining.

She smiled at him again. It felt odd being the only two people in the breakfast room, and she realized that it was the first time they had been alone together since coming to Kenston. Perhaps they would rub along better without the omnipresent company of his mama. It was unfortunate, then, that Gretchen Raines was planning to live with them. "Did you sleep well?" she asked, choosing a seat near his and motioning for him to again take his. "Coffee, please, but no food just yet, thank you," she said to the footman while Wallace took his seat. "And then you may leave us until others come down."

Wallace, whose brow had clouded at her question, did not seem to notice her rather high-handed ordering of the servants. "I did not," he returned, stirring at his gruel. "I passed an extremely restless night, I'm afraid. I feel a congestion coming on, and"—he looked at her accusingly—"I was *most* concerned about you having been outside for so long last evening without having taken a steam treatment afterward."

Oh, dear. She smiled at him in what she hoped was a conciliatory manner. "I am sorry, Wallace. I know your mama went to a great deal of trouble. I realize that I owe everyone an explanation for my conduct last night. I was upset over the bracelet," she explained, marveling as she did, at how easily the lie seemed to trip off her lips, "and I-I just wasn't thinking clearly."

Wallace, having finished his gruel, was now taking his tea. Black, Addie knew, because milk and sugar introduced impurities to the system. Having stirred it his customary three times he sipped slowly, and then said, "That is exactly what I am concerned about. This tendency toward excessive emotion. These strong passions." He looked at her, his gaze suddenly and surprisingly heated. "Adelaide," he said urgently, setting down his cup, "there is something I must say."

And she was moved by his intensity to put her hand over his. "Yes, Wallace?"

"I must ask, no, beg, that you will consider—No! I've no right to ask this of you yet. I cannot!"

"Wallace," she said, gently, never having seen *him* display such strong passions. "Surely it is all right. Whatever you have to say will be between us. We are, after all, soon to be husband and wife."

He stood, and paced awkwardly for a moment, until, stopping in front of her, he passed a hand over his thinning hair. "Adelaide," he began, his voice hoarse with emotion, "I truly can claim no right to ask this of you. But since you have given me leave''—he suddenly went down on his knees before her and looked up into her eyes beseechingly—''to speak my heart and my mind, my dear, and your goodness, your generosity in granting me such a liberty does not, I assure you, go unnoted—''

Whatever can he want? she wondered.

''Please,'' he burst out. ''I must beg of you, *give up poultry, Adelaide!*''

''P-poultry?'' She looked down at him.

''Yes, my love. It''—he stood and began to pace again, faltering, while Addie watched, still much bewildered—''it—that is, Mother, she, ah, thinks it has made you, ah, *unstable,* ah, just a *touch,* of course,'' he finished in a rush.

''Poultry has made me *unstable?''* she repeated dumbly.

He resumed his position before her on his knees and possessed himself of her hands. ''Yes. It is one of her greatest fears. Poultry instability. She can no longer countenance the match, she says, if you are to continue consuming fowl. Please, my dear?''

''Wallace,'' she said, suddenly, leaning down.

''Yes, Adelaide?'' he breathed.

''Kiss me.''

''Wh-what?''

''I said, kiss me.'' She wet her lips with the tip of her tongue.

''I thought that was what you had said!'' He stood up like a shot.

This is not going well, she reflected. Why did she seem to have no effect at all on this man who was to be her husband? Fitzwilliam had let her know in no uncertain terms that he considered marriage to her only slightly better than an eternity at Almack's, at best, yet he would likely have had her clothing halfway to off by this point in the conversation. She sighed.

''. . . most improper.'' Wallace was huffing. ''And *exactly* the type of thing Mother has told me to watch for in a fowl overconsumer!''

''Wallace,'' she said firmly. ''We are to be married. Drew and Justine kiss, I know for a fact—''

"Well, I think we know from whom *he* gets his moral guidance, and let me assure you, *that* man, Claremont, Fitzwilliam, or whatever he calls himself, is, as I have told you before, old friend of the family or not, nothing more than a base—"

"Please, Wallace, don't let's argue. Do come back," Addie interrupted softly, motioning to the floor in front of her where he had knelt.

He looked at her mistrustfully.

"Please?"

"Very well." He came back and knelt once again.

She put her fingers gently over his lips. "Just a kiss, Wallace. Just one."

"I don't know," he said, but he was calmer now. "To own the truth, Adelaide, that is the type of activity that a man does not engage in with his wife. It simply is not seemly."

"With whom, then, does he engage in it?" she asked, joking, only to have him turn such a fiery red that she feared he might momentarily require the use of Honoria's vinaigrette. "Oh, dear," she said, "I didn't mean—I am sorry, Wallace ..." She trailed off, almost as embarrassed as he. It had never occurred to her that Wallace would have had a mistress. *Damn!* Did they *all?* And why, in this case, did she not care?

"Very well, Adelaide," he said. "If you truly desire it."

But she could see he was still dubious, that it was a concession. "Wallace," she said, lowering her voice.

"Yes?"

"I will do it. I shall give up poultry."

He leaned closer, and she could sense a quickening in his interest. "Really?"

She nodded. "No chicken, no duck, no goose."

He was coming closer still

"No pigeon, no squab, no grouse—"

"Truly?" He put his hands on her shoulders and paused.

So she nodded and continued. "No partridge, no pheasant, no woodcock, no lark." Oh dear, she was running out.

"No capon!" he whispered, as his lips closed the distance to hers.

"No capon," she agreed, just before their lips met.

It was not altogether unpleasant, she thought, and if she had never been kissed so hotly and so well, she might *almost* have enjoyed it, although she could wish that his lips were a tad dryer and perhaps firmer. There *was* an awkward moment when their noses bumped, and, to be sure, she felt no urge whatsoever to press herself against his body, or to open her lips under his, or for the moment to continue forever. Nor, she reflected, did he seem to be unduly laboring under any of those emotions.

Hmm. Perhaps that was the entire problem. Too much thinking. Yes, that was it! She was doing altogether too much thinking. When Fitzwilliam kissed her there seemed to be no room for thought, only sensation, and it was no doubt, in this case, the thinking that was preventing a maelstrom of burning and melting from going on. Indeed, that was clearly the problem, she decided as Wallace removed his lips from hers.

"One more? Wallace?" she asked softly. *And this time without the thinking.*

"Addie . . ." he began to protest, but then, at something in her eyes, acquiesced.

Much the same. Although this time she could not help but notice that there was a certain lack of technique. *Good Lord! What have I become?* she scolded herself, truly horrified. A few short weeks ago she had never even been kissed, let alone realized there was a technique to it, and now here she was, *comparing gentlemen!*

"So you *do* see, now, Adelaide," Wallace said, intensely, having broken the kiss and taken hold of her hands once again, "why this experience is deemed unsuitable for ladies of breeding?"

"Well, I, ah—"

He nodded sagely. "It is only natural that you would be overcome by the passions. Especially as you are no doubt already riled by last night's larded partridges. It offends every sense of delicacy. In the future, I shall attempt to spare you this as much as possible."

She gulped, wishing that this entire incident had not made

her feel so much like crying on any number of counts. "Thank you, Wallace."

"And, Adelaide?"

"Yes, Wallace?" she whispered.

"Snipe. You forgot snipe."

"So I did," she agreed. "No snipe."

Which tender lovers' words Fitzwilliam could not hear, as he stood as though rooted to the spot outside the door to his breakfast room.

He should have known that even such a cold fish as Raines would take advantage of having Addie wearing his ring. His ugly ring. But it had never occurred to him, not for a moment, that she would desire those attentions. But there she'd been, clearly leaning down to Wallace Raines, smiling, and, unless he missed his very practiced guess, encouraging the fellow in his forwardness. No, the attentions were all too obviously not unwelcome.

And here, he had almost convinced himself that she had felt what he was beginning to. Both that extraordinary heat *and* that sense of something else. Hell. He well and truly felt like a knife had been inserted into where, in another man, his heart would have been.

Suddenly, not at all in the mood for underdone mutton and stale bread, or even less so than usual, he turned on his heel and left.

London
Ten, February, 1814

Dearest Addie:

*Well! Simply the most shocking! The most wonderful,
incredible! Well! It is indeed news. The Earl of Stanhope,
you must know, has returned to Town. Of course he has,
or I would hardly be telling you this, since that, of course,
is where I am, and naturally where one does belong, and
where you would be, if you were not off on this Mad
start with that Odious Wallace Raines, and the Divine
Fitzwilliam! And I never could have thought, indeed,
would have believed that you would be so foolish as to
miss this! But returned he is, and with his charmingly
outrageous countess, and well! You can never believe,
but she is shockingly unfashionable in her dress—not at
all what one would have pictured for him—and delightfully, amusingly, radical in her notions, trés outré, an
Original, and Stanhope, has, equally shockingly—scandalously, some say!—given up all of his former amusements, or at least most of his former amusements (all of
those not discussed in polite company, anyway) but I
shan't mention that he has, or that he had them at all,
because it would be all things inappropriate with you an
unmarried woman. But as you are engaged, I think I can
at least tell you that he had had them, although not what
(or who) they were! But, incredibly, he is done with them,
and quite lives in her pocket (her rather drab pocket, for
all that she is a taking little thing, one cannot but see
her, but one quite aches to take her to Madame Boucharde!) but, incredibly, the man does not seem to notice.
He is quite smitten, most unfashionably so, and does
not appear to give two cents for how unfashionable an
appearance it presents—he danced only with her at Sally
Jersey's little ball the other night, three dances, and then
they left so early that it was practically unseemly. Sally
was scandalized. The new countess does talk of the most*

bizarre things, although she does it delightfully—reforms, etc.—to which, of course, I don't really listen, but naturally only pretend to, because one does not like to appear rude, and you never know when that type of thing will come back to haunt one. But this is the thing: When I apprised Jackson of all of this, do you know what he wrote about? BOXING! Barely a word about her dress, or how unfashionably devoted Stanhope is, or how they leave all entertainments as early as possible, or her radical ideas, or, well, anything! He rabbited on and on and on and on and, well, you get the idea, about punishing rights, and footwork, and toeing the scatch, and all manner of hideously tedious things, quite mentioning that dull old stick Sandringham as often as he did Stanhope, while entirely missing the point of the column! And when the Dowager Lady Elsingham told me, well, bellowed at me, really—one likes to be precise—at the Roundtree's musicale, that she had put it down halfway through, without even finishing, even though the thought of Stanhope in his shirtsleeves, never mind stripped, practically makes her have the vapors! Why, I almost cried with the misery of the realization of what a travesty this column has become, I don't mind telling you. And I am certain you must feel the same. And he has accused me of writing confusing letters! So, please, Addie, I beg you, have done with this ridiculous engagement business, force Fitzwilliam to have you, and return to Town, before that Jackson fellow ruins everything! Has the man no idea of how to write about boxing? Apparently not, although, one would think he should, as Glendower, goodness knows, is forever prosing on about his skill in the ring!

With love and concern, and the sincere hope I shall live to see you rid yourself of Wallace Raines and return to again take up your pen, saving us all from the tedium of Jackson as Anonymous, oh, and yourself from life as Mrs. Raines, I remain, as ever, your loving friend,

Lizbeth

Chapter 36

"One, of course, cannot like to mention it, but she *is* looking downright haggard," whispered Mrs. Haverford to Gretchen Raines as the two women sat before the fire in the Yellow Salon, gossiping over their stitchery. "Now, Lavinia," she confided, "never looks haggard because—"

"I am sure she does not," interrupted Gretchen Raines dismissively. "But the point is"—she paused rather dramatically—"that if Miss Winstead cannot, or will not"—she sniffed—"regard her *own* health with proper care, the question that begs is: what can recommend her to watch my Wallace?"

"And I well understand your concern," Mrs. Haverford replied in a low voice. "Wallace is a precious lad. Most precious, to be sure. I still think, however, that you should encourage him to remove Miss Winstead from here, and with all haste. It is as plain as a pikestaff that Clare—er, Fitzwilliam exerts an influence over her that cannot be at all salubrious. That strange predilection for strenuous exercise—why he and Mr. Mannering all but beat each other senseless with their ridiculous regimen of boxing exercise! Did you *see* the bruises?"

"And what an odd regimen of food! While he does seem to

possess an excessive fondness for mutton,'' Gretchen Raines mused, ''he does not appear to partake of fowl, which one can only think is to the good. But it *is* true that such devotion to mutton is to be wondered at. And it is always chops. . . . *Not*''— she paused to sniff—''the most wholesome cut of the mutton!''

''Well, he *is* an earl,'' Millicent Haverford said doubtfully.

''And what has that to say to anything?''

''The bloodlines, Gretchen,'' Millicent admonished. ''With the excellent bloodlines, earls are not prey to the weaknesses of system that plague the rest of us. And he certainly does *appear* to be in the pink of health.''

''Nonsense, Millicent,'' Gretchen Raines returned roundly. ''Utter nonsense. Appearances, as we all know, are deceiving. And look at Claverstock. A duke, no less, and *he*, I don't mind telling you, perished from ill-humors of the blood due to an excess of jellied eel! And if he did not look fit as anything only the day before, well, then I don't know anything.''

Mrs. Haverford's tones were chilly. ''Dukes,'' she replied, ''do not, Gretchen, expire for such paltry reasons. No, no. I quite recall, it was the influenza that did it for him.''

Gretchen Raines's look was knowing. ''*That* was what they put about, true enough. And if you choose to believe it, well . . .'' She shrugged. ''And by the by: Lavinia,'' she said, turning a basilisk stare upon Mrs. Haverford, and effectively putting an end to the debate, ''*did*—I note—take seconds on the partridge.''

''Partridge,'' that lady replied hotly, ''*agrees* with Lavinia!''

''So you may think now,'' Gretchen Raines said obliquely.

As of one accord, they both looked out the window at the terrace where Lavinia and Fitzwilliam made a pretty tableau. She was attired in a fur-lined pelisse, the violet color of which brought out her eyes and set off her dark hair exceptionally, her mama had noted. She was holding Fitzwilliam's arm, very properly, and one presumed, elaborating on her plans for the Frost Fair. She pointed toward the lake and he, in turn, pointed to another spot, and, engaged in animated conversation, they walked together to the edge of the terrace, apparently better to survey the vista.

"A beautiful pair," commented Gretchen Raines.

"Indeed," replied Mrs. Haverford, permitting herself a small smile of satisfaction. "Indeed."

"As were Hugh Orvis and Marion Delacey," Honoria said, entering the room and taking a seat. She took out her tambour frame and set to work stitching. "Beautiful. Everyone commented upon it, if you recall, Gretchen," she said, somehow managing to convey to Millicent Haverford that *she* would not remember, not having traveled in the same social circles before her fortunate marriage. "Indeed, one had only to see them together and it was invariably all one could think of. But then, after the Incident—more an Episode, really, I suppose—one rarely thought of it, their beauty, that is, since it paled in contrast to his unfortunate predilection for—Well, no need to relive it, I suppose. Suffice it to say that it is best forgotten and, really, if they hadn't looked so well together in the first place, it all could have been avoided. Or one hopes so, anyway!"

Mrs. Haverford raised a brow.

Gretchen Raines sniffed disapprovingly. "*That,* Honoria, had nothing at all to do with how they looked together. No. It was her careless disregard for chewing the proper number of times that *led* to the Incident, well, more an Episode, as you say, and as for his unfortunate predilection—Well, indeed, you are right—it is best forgotten. *If* one can."

"As I said," Honoria agreed, changing her thread.

"Even now, one doesn't like to think of it," Gretchen Raines said with a shudder. "It quite put me off of apricots and *anything* to do with seashells for years, and I vow, I still have trouble with porcelain figurines!"

"Naturally," Honoria agreed. "It is only to be expected."

"But what," inquired Mrs. Haverford, looking back and forth in her confusion, "on earth does this Incident, or Episode, however you want to phrase it, have to do with how my Lavinia and Fitzwilliam look together?"

"Suffice it to say, Millicent, that you are happier not knowing," Honoria advised.

"Dear me, yes," concurred Gretchen Raines. "Dear me, yes."

Outside, Lavinia Haverford pointed out the area where the musicians would be. Skating, of course, would be on the pond, which would be cleared of snow in the morning, and refreshments would be dispensed over here. And right where they stood now, the two of them would receive guests from the village.

His eyebrow almost went up at what could be seen as her presumption, but he suddenly remembered Addie smiling down, Wallace Raines on his knees before her, and turned his own expression to a smile. "You have done an exemplary job, it would seem, Miss Haverford," he said. "It won't do for you to think that I work all my guests shamelessly into the ground. Now that the planning is over, you must permit yourself some enjoyment. And I think," he said, lightly, "that I must extract a promise that you will do no more work for the rest of your stay."

"La, my lord, you refine on it too much," she replied. "There is little I like as well as planning entertainments."

"And you certainly excel at it, if this is anything to go by. You must tell me, Miss Haverford," he said conversationally, leading her down a path that curved around the frozen pond, "you do not by any chance make a practice of attending mills?"

She stopped and stared at him. "No, Clare—er, my lor—*Fitzwilliam*, I do not. Why would I? Surely a mill can be no place for a properly reared female?"

He smiled down at her, his look enigmatic, and she frowned.

"That is, unless—Would you like me to?" she offered. "I suppose then I—"

"No, Miss Haverford," he said, firmly, but with a grin. "I would not like you to. Mills, as you so sensibly pointed out, are no place for a properly reared female. Now," he said, deliberately leading her farther into the gardens, "let us talk of something else."

"Yes, my—Fitzwilliam." She smiled and looked up at him from under lowered lashes as she equally deliberately allowed herself to be led away from the house.

Ah, now they were in familiar territory. He knew exactly what *that* look had meant. He breathed. This was much better than with Addie. Safer. Infinitely more like the dalliances he was used to, even if this one might result in marriage. At least it would be exactly the marriage he had always expected.

"Miss Haverford. Lavinia." He looked down at her beautiful face, upturned toward his own, and his voice dropped, seductively. "Were I to kiss you—"

"Mama," she interrupted, "would like that above all things."

"Ah. But I shall not kiss your mama," he returned, smiling.

She trilled a little laugh. "La, you are amusing, sir."

"And you, Miss Haverford?" he asked quietly. "Would *you* like it above all things?"

"I should," she replied, surprising him by moving closer with a boldness he would not have expected. "In fact, my lord," she said, with a smile, "I trust it will not be too forward under the circumstances, to say that I have been quite expecting this moment."

"Indeed?"

"Yes." She was slightly breathless.

"And why, if I may, have you been doing that?"

She laughed softly, leaning a little closer, so he could smell her perfume. Lilacs or lilies, he thought, in some corner of his mind, something cloying, with an *l*, at any rate.

"It is only to be expected," she said, "You and I, well, we are after all, shall we say, well-suited. And you are, Mama has told me, a man of strong passions. As was, she tells me, your father before you."

"Was he!" replied Fitzwilliam, smiling lightly.

"Yes," she replied firmly, perhaps failing to note that it had not been a question. "And not to put too fine a point on it, my lord, but,'' she continued, before frowning and looking up at him, ''perhaps I go to far?''

''Not at all. Please, speak your mind, Miss Haverford. I would have it no other way.''

''Thank you.'' She looked down for a moment and took a breath before looking back at him. ''I should not, you know, expect a man of such *heated* passions to give up his, ah, *other interests,* shall we say?''

''Very handsome of you, ma'am,'' he replied, looking into her lovely eyes. ''Am I to take it then that you do not feel any warmer emotions for me? No, ah, resentment at the idea of a husband with *other interests?''*

She laughed. ''Heavens, no! Although you are very well, certainly, Cl-l—er, Fitzwilliam—And I do think while I should enjoy being wed to you above all things—and to ally our families with the nuptial tie must be desirable to all parties—it is not, I believe, seemly to feel strong emotions in a marriage.''

''What then, does one do in a marriage?'' he asked.

She looked surprised. ''Be a good wife: Run the households, entertain, be decorative,'' she said, clearly reciting, ''and''— a touch of color came into her cheeks—''bear heirs, of course.''

''Of course.''

''And Mama will be in alt for me to be a countess, naturally.''

''Naturally,'' he replied in grave tones.

''And I should do quite well at it, I would think.''

He inclined his head in agreement. ''Without a doubt.''

''And it will be no sacrifice,'' she continued. ''You are all that is amiable and certainly well-favored—at least when your poor face has not been battered by Mr. Mannering,'' she said, reaching up to gently touch his bruised forehead. ''In fact, we make an extraordinarily handsome couple; everyone has remarked it. No, indeed, we should be quite envied.''

''Indeed,'' he replied. ''Your honesty becomes you, Miss Haverford. And naturally, it is pleasing to learn that you would not consider wedding me a sacrifice. But as we seem to be having the tree with no bark on it, so to speak, perhaps I should point out that I have not *asked* you to marry me.''

She smiled. "You will."

"Is this a proposal, then, Miss Haverford?" he asked, brow lifted.

"Don't be ridiculous, sir," she replied with a little laugh. *"That* would be vastly improper."

"Of course."

"Now, were you not about to ... *do* something, my lord?" she asked, managing to look quite fetching as she did. "I confess, I was quite looking forward to it."

He laughed and bent his head briefly to hers, brushing his lips quickly across her upturned mouth.

That is not at all how he kisses me! Addie reflected from her place by her bedroom window, which, fortunately or perhaps unfortunately, depending on your viewpoint, offered her an excellent vantage over their little tryst. Certainly they seemed to be enjoying themselves, she thought. Strolling with their beautiful heads bent together, and then stopping for an earnest-looking conversation. Followed by that sweet, chaste little kiss. She sighed. The way a man would, according to Wallace anyway, kiss his wife.

What are we all doing? she wondered. She had kissed Fitzwilliam. She had kissed Wallace. Fitzwilliam had kissed Lavinia Haverford. Where would it end? Hard to know, really. Honestly, at this point she would hardly have been surprised to find Honoria kissing Antoine, the French chef.

She looked again at the two letters in her hand. She had been about to go in search of Fitzwilliam to tell him that they could cease his training, when she had happened across this charming little tableau: the two of them together in the bare winter garden, apparently creating their own heat. And these days she—unfortunately, perhaps—knew all about that type of heat.

It was much the best thing for everyone, for her, especially, she knew, to end this sojourn. To be away from Fitzwilliam's courtship of Lavinia Haverford and the pain that was slicing through her. But she simply couldn't bring herself to do it just yet. *This will likely be my last time together with him,* she thought. *Soon we will both be wed to other people, and things will never be the same again.*

And so, she went down to the drawing room, having decided once again not to mention Jackson's letter for the moment.

And well it might have remained undiscovered in her drawer had Justine, not ten minutes later, gone searching for the reticule she had lent Addie two nights previous.

She hadn't meant to read it, of course. And once started, she told herself most firmly that it would only be the first few words and then she would put it down. But somehow the first few words had turned into the next few, which had turned into a sentence, into a paragraph, into the whole thing.

When she did at last put it down, with no small measure of guilt for having read it in the first place, she went immediately in search of Drew.

"Hello, my love," that gentleman said, looking up when she had located him in the library, where he was finishing yet another in a seemingly endless string of games of billiards with his brother and Freddie Barrist. "How glad I am to see you. These two fellows are beginning to wear thin on my nerves, William prattling endlessly on about crop rotation, or flotation, or some such, and Freddie bemoaning his lack of success on this morning's shooting expedition. Not to mention yesterday's, and likely tomorrow's."

Lord Ardean then expressed his heated disagreement with that assessment, asserting that he had not, indeed, uttered a single word about farming that day. To which Drew had replied that he was *thinking* about farming to such an extent that even his thoughts were provokingly dull.

At which point Freddie burst in with the assertion that it was not on his *own* account at all, mind you, that he had been put out about the morning's lack of success, but on the *dogs'* behalf.

Bored senseless, they were, he explained, and well on their way to suffering a clear canine *crise de nerfs,* tails drooping, ears floppy, noses disconcertingly still.

Then Ardean had called Drew a distempered young jack-of-warts, and Drew had replied that his brother was nothing but a stuffy old bottle-head. And just as Ardean had looked set to retort with an equally mature and civilized rejoinder, Suzanne Ardean had stuck her head around the door frame and inquired as to whether her husband cared to join her for a walk.

"He would," Drew answered for him. "And Freddie here would like to go commune with the dogs for a while, so that Justine can come here and be soundly kissed."

Justine turned a fiery red at this, but the rest of the company laughed good-naturedly, and indeed, departed.

When he had done making good on his words, and most satisfactorily, Justine drew back for a moment. When Drew would have pulled her back against him, she stilled him with a hand on his arm.

"Growing tired of me already?" he asked with a smile. "And here I was, thinking that I should ask you to marry me!"

Justine laughed. "No such thing." She smoothed her hands over her now sadly crumpled dress. "I wanted to speak with you, though."

"About what?" Drew took her hand and, looking serious, drew her down to a seat on the sofa, next to him.

"Addie," replied Justine. "Has she spoken to you and Fitz-william about Jackson's letter?"

"Not that I know of," Drew replied. "What letter, Justine?"

"The one that I, ah, found. In her drawer." Justine colored. "In which he says that Raymond Walters will be calling off the challenge."

Drew's brow went up. "Not a word," he said. "How interesting."

Justine frowned. "Why do you suppose she hasn't told him—You?" She bit her lip. "Or, for that matter, me?"

Drew smiled gently. "I think we already know that answer, my love."

"But shouldn't we *do* something, Drew?" Justine was still biting her lip, looking so enchantingly concerned that Drew was hard-pressed to concentrate on Addie's and Fitzwilliam's problems.

"No," he said, forcing his mind, heroically, he could not help thinking, back to the issue at hand. "I think, my sweet, that we have to leave them to make their own discoveries."

"Where *is* Fitzwilliam, anyway?" Justine wanted to know. "I had thought to find him with you."

"Out in the garden," Drew replied. "Kissing Miss Haverford, I'd wager."

Justine's jaw dropped. "Kissing Lavinia!" she said, shocked. "Should we not—How awful!"

"Oh, I don't know." Drew smiled at her. "As I'd also wager that he's finding it a profoundly unmoving experience, it might well be just what he needs."

"Do you really think so?" Justine could not keep the doubtful expression off of her face.

"Actually," Drew said conversationally, drawing her a fraction closer, "d'you know who Miss Haverford reminds me of?" At Justine's shake of her head, he continued, "Fitzwilliam's mother. Do you remember her?" At Justine's nod, he continued. "Lavinia's more grasping, of course, and knows what she wants, but she has a similar lack of fire. She's decorative, but no match for him, as his mother was not for his father. And the ghost of *that* marriage is one that, believe me, he needs to exorcise in his own way. So I shall just have to resign myself to being duly pummeled by my best friend—who, incidentally improves daily. And I think the wisest course of action is for us both to feign ignorance of the intelligence you have just brought me, until one of them comes to their senses. And now," he said, "since this great sacrifice is, in part, on behalf of your sister, my love, I must extract payment. Come and be kissed some more."

To which plan, it should be noted, Justine acquiesced with a great deal of enthusiasm.

Chapter 37

Addie, meanwhile, feeling in need of a little familial comfort, had gone in search of Honoria.

"Well, Adelaide, we really must have a coze," Gretchen Raines said, no sooner had Addie entered the drawing room. "Now hold this wool for me. Not like that! Over your hands."

A coze with Wallace's mama was the last thing Addie wanted at the moment, sick as she was feeling over the tender scene she had just witnessed in the garden. But she could hardly say so, so she smiled instead, taking the wool as instructed, and replied that that would be delightful above all things.

Her future mother-in-law began to wind the wool into skeins. "Hold it higher, please," she said. "Good. Now, tell me, Adelaide. In what society would you like to become active, after the wedding, once you are removed to Derbyshade."

"Ma'am?" Addie asked, hoping that her arms would not fall off before Gretchen Raines wound her way through the veritable mountain of wool.

"You know: good works, female society. That type of thing. Surely your aunt has made certain that you are conversant with your proper role once wed?'' Gretchen Raines said, directing a disapproving look at Honoria.

"Goodness knows, I tried, Gretchen. I tried," Honoria said with a tragic lilt to her voice.

Addie cast her a frown.

"The sewing circle!" Mrs. Raines suggested. "Of a certainty you will want to join the sewing circle."

"I would be honored, naturally, but I should warn you that I am not, actually, much of a hand with a needle, ma'am," Addie admitted. She could practically feel Honoria's triumphant expression.

"I myself am an execrable seamstress," Madeleine Barrist contributed, looking up from her sketchbook and giving Addie a complicit look. "Hideous! I cannot so much as darn linen, and my household has survived these many years regardless!"

"Sketching!" Mrs. Raines said brightly, catching sight of the sketchbook. "You do, of course, sketch, Adelaide?"

Addie had to work to suppress a smile as Madeleine again caught her eye. "Of course. Just not well," she added, and she heard Madeleine smother a laugh.

Mrs. Raines was looking quite put out. "Gardening Club, then," she suggested. "We do not, of course, actually *garden*, but we do direct the gardeners. And quite firmly, too, you can be sure."

"I suppose I could do that." Addie's tones were dubious, as she recalled her conversation with Justine about her horticultural abilities.

"Lavinia," Mrs. Haverford said, "has a *way* with horticulture! And"—she directed a reproving look at Addie—"*she* sketches wildflowers!"

"Very nice," Mrs. Raines said approvingly. "A lovely hobby for a young lady of quality, I always think."

"Oh, look, Addie," Honoria said in innocent tones, "that vase of flowers behind you! They are looking quite wilted, and I swear it, they were at the peak of their blooms not ten minutes ago, before you sat down! Perhaps not the Gardening Club, after all."

Addie glared at her aunt.

"As long as you don't have the same effect on the *gardeners,* there shouldn't be any reason for you to stay away from Gardening Club, my dear," Madeleine contributed.

"Yes. Well ... There is, of course, embroidery...." Gretchen Raines trailed off, looking dubious.

"Have I mentioned that *Lavinia* embroidered all the cushions for the sofas in our Oriental Room?" Mrs. Haverford said.

"And did *I* mention that Marion Delacey embroidered?" Honoria wondered. "Couldn't keep the girl away from her stitchery. That, of course, was before the, ah, Incident."

"Episode!" Gretchen Raines corrected.

"Of course," agreed Honoria. "At any rate, I shouldn't suppose she kept it up."

"Gracious, no!" Gretchen almost dropped her ball of wool. "Musical Wednesdays!" she remembered with apparent relief. "You will, *of course,* want to join our little Society for Musical Wednesdays. Strings only, naturally."

" 'Fraid not," Honoria supplied before Addie could have a chance to respond. "Unless of course you have a Society for Recovering-From-Your-Headache Thursdays!"

Addie stared openmouthed at her aunt.

Madeleine Barrist kept her head bent over her sketchbook, but Addie was perfectly well aware that her shoulders were shaking.

"Lavinia never has the headache. And *certainly* not on Thursdays!" Mrs. Haverford took the opportunity to mention.

Which intelligence caused Fitzwilliam a moment's pause as he escorted that young lady into the drawing room following their walk. He, in fact, would have guessed that under certain circumstances, Lavinia would have the headache rather a lot.

"Oh, dear," Mrs. Raines fretted. "There *must* be something!"

"Tree-climbing!" suggested Fitzwilliam blandly as he steered Lavinia solicitously toward a chair. "Having grown up with Addie, I am conversant with all her talents!"

"Excellent suggestion, Fitzwilliam," Honoria said. "Have you a Society for the Proponence of Tree-Climbing, Gretchen?"

"Oh, dear! The very thought makes me quite faint," Lavinia said languidly, leaning more heavily on Fitzwilliam's arm.

Gretchen Raines was frowning at Addie. "I'm afraid, ah— No. No, we do not!"

Why are they doing this to me? And why is Honoria looking quite so much like the cat that ate the cream, so to speak? "Ma'am, I do not climb trees, I assure you—" Addie started to say, but was interrupted by Fitzwilliam.

"Not anymore, Addie? Really? I must own myself quite surprised. Dietary regimens then!" Fitzwilliam suggested, shooting her a grin, that, despite everything, made her heart crash against her ribs. *God, he's handsome.* "Do you have Mutton Mondays, perhaps, in Derbyshade?"

At this, Madeleine Barrist suffered a choking fit so severe that she had to excuse herself from the room, which Addie could not help noting, she accomplished rather speedily for someone in the throes of a coughing spell.

The rest of them stared at Fitzwilliam as he made his way across the room to fetch a cup of tea from the tray for Lavinia, who now reclined languidly in her chair.

"We do not!" Gretchen Raines replied frostily as she gathered up her now-finished skeins.

"Pity," Fitzwilliam replied. "Addie, you can be sure, would be in great demand there."

Gretchen stood, her wool firmly stuffed into her workbasket. "And now, if you'll excuse me, I must go in search of Wallace! I like to remind him to take his draught and a constitutional around this time of day."

Addie stood also. And, shooting Fitzwilliam what she trusted was a withering glance, followed her future mother-in-law out of the room.

"We had a housekeeper once who ate only fish on Fridays," she heard Mrs. Haverford muse behind her. "Popist! But I never have heard of Mutton Mondays, my lord. Have you, Lavinia, my dear?"

Addie shut the door firmly behind her, effectively cutting off whatever intelligence Lavinia's musical tones were imparting.

Tree climbing and Mutton Mondays, indeed, John Fitzwilliam, Addie thought.

Chapter 38

No one in our cast of characters slept particularly well that night.

Not Fitzwilliam, certainly. He tossed and turned, attempting to get comfortable, and trying mightily to recall the feel of Lavinia Haverford's lips under his, so as to assess why it was such a profoundly dissatisfying experience. He piled pillows up behind his head. And thought of the marriage Lavinia had so blatantly offered him. And then unpiled them. And thought of his parents. He rolled onto his right side. And thought of Addie marrying Wallace Raines. And then to his left and thought of his parents. He punched his pillow and settled on his back. And reminded himself of how easy the life that Lavinia offered him would be. He stuck his foot out of the covers and then rolled onto his stomach, burying his head in his arms. Then he untangled his feet from the covers and reluctantly thought about his father. Then he thought about Addie—her constant presence in his house, and her smile, and *her* lips under his, which, incidentally, he could recall clearly, with no trouble whatsoever. And her body pressed against his, and how much he had wanted to pull her to the ground next to the terrace, snow-covered though it was, and show her precisely what she was missing by wedding that Friday-faced gapeseed.

And then he swore to himself and got up to settle in the chair by the fire with the decanter of brandy that Hedges had strategically left for him, wondering seriously, for the first time, whether he had progressed enough to best Raymond Walters.

Not Addie, who was wrestling with some confusion of her own. And some jealousy, some dread, some worry. And some *most* unladylike yearnings. Enough said.

Not Wallace. His sinuses were constricted. Distressingly, he recognized the possibility that he may have a corn developing on the little toe of his left foot. And he was not a little disturbed by what his mama had told him about Adelaide's dearth of ladylike accomplishments and her likely reception into Derbyshade society.

Not Justine, who was not a little worried about the tangle her sister was in.

Not Drew, whose face still hurt, and who was uncomfortably aware of Justine sleeping a few corridors over, and who could not seem, no matter how hard he tried, to stop wondering whether her nightgown was of the sensible cotton variety, or of the filmy, silk variety.

Not Honoria. No, indeed. *She,* for some obscure reason, was craving apricots, and frankly, wished that this entire, rather tiresome business would wind itself up to the satisfaction of all parties, so they could finally return to Town and start the pleasingly arduous business of shopping for trousseaus.

Not Gretchen Raines, who was having some very grave doubts *indeed* about the suitability of her future daughter-in-law, and who felt certain that Wallace's bedchamber, facing north as it did, was drafty.

Not Mrs. Haverford. She was busily attempting to remember whether as mother-in-law to an earl she was entitled to a coronet on her coach.

Not Lavinia, who was quite disappointed that no proposal had materialized: she had been all but certain it would when she had allowed that kiss, and could not help but wonder whether she had made a grave miscalculation. She brushed her fingers over her lips where Fitzwilliam's had so fleetingly been.

Not Ardean and Suzanne, who were actually taking their responsibility to produce an heir quite seriously indeed.

And not the Barrists. Madeleine missed her children and, anyway, found it quite impossible to move at all, what with the pack of hounds that Freddie had sharing their bed. And as for Freddie . . . Well, all right, so *one* person at Kenston House was, in fact, sleeping soundly. And snoring loudly to prove it.

And, oh, yes. It should also bear mention that on the road north, in three different inns, the members of three different parties—the Glendowers, John Jackson, and Raymond Walters—all traveling unbeknownst to each other, were also passing the night in various degrees of restlessness.

Chapter 39

Addie slept late the following morning, and when she did arise it was with a feeling of lassitude.

Which was no more than Fitzwilliam suffered, when he awoke, stiff and cramped, still in the chair, his head aching abominably, his throat dry, and the brandy decanter considerably depleted—er, empty.

When they all came together at breakfast, there was a general lack of spirit among the company. Even Honoria and Mrs. Haverford could hardly be bothered to snipe at each other. The only exception coming when Gretchen Raines had suggested to Addie that she should partake of Wallace's tepid soured milk instead of her usual *hazardously unhealthy* coffee. Addie had demurred, and Mrs. Haverford had suggested that *her* Lavinia always accepted helpful criticisms in the spirit in which they were offered, and Honoria had replied that *Lavinia*, then, should partake of the soured milk. Mrs. Raines had retorted that *Lavinia* did not stand in *need* of helpful criticisms, or, for that matter, soured milk. And Honoria had pointed out that *that* was *exactly* what Rita Redcliffe, Lady Ardmoor, had believed, and the entire household had ended up with *mice* in the clothespresses!

All in all Fitzwilliam, who suddenly had things weighing heavy on his mind, could only be grateful, as the host, that they would have the frost fair to keep them entertained tonight, and then the entire party would begin to break up within the next few days. The only lowering part was that he would actually miss the boxing matches. He was improving markedly, certainly, and there was something to be said for being ordered about by Addie, which he had quite come to enjoy. Although the same, quite frankly, could not be said for the diet, he decided, poking dispiritedly at his muttonchop.

Ordinarily, the house party would not have been so much in each other's company and so lacking for entertainment, since just *his* arrival, let alone that of a houseful of guests, was generally of a nature to set off a veritable frenzy of calls and the leaving of cards. Which was inevitably followed by a sudden surge of routs and card parties in the vicinity, not to mention dinners, dances, and musical evenings.

But the weather this winter, and certainly this month of February, had been the worst anyone could remember, with the frigid temperatures and heavy snows effectively putting a stop to all of the socializing that normally took place, and had indeed contrived to render them practically isolated. Which circumstances, he was certain, were bound to have contributed to creating almost a frenzy of curiosity in the village, thus ensuring that everyone who was able to attend tonight would do so. To that end, the weather had been unusually cooperative the last few days, with, at least, no new snowfall of significance. And his men had cleared as many roads and paths as they could. So, all in all, they were expecting a heavy turnout.

By afternoon, all was in readiness. Lavinia, looking coolly beautiful, had directed the last of the preparations with a firm hand. Until, having indeed, proved herself at every turn, up to the task of running Fitzwilliam's households with a pleasing elegance and grace, she went upstairs to make herself as ready as the house and grounds.

He, clad in his heavy greatcoat, stood on the terrace, observing the servants carrying out the last of the preparations and awaiting the rest of the guests, who, like Lavinia, were making their final toilettes. He had insisted, over that lady's protests, that they open the great hall for refreshments and dancing. She had been hesitant, being of the opinion that such democracy, inviting persons of inferior rank into the actual *house,* could not be at all the thing. But he had been firm: as master of Kenston, it was his duty and his pleasure to open the house to his tenants and neighbors. So, in front of him, the lawns stood in readiness: the pond cleared of snow for skating, an area for musicians, booths of games, bonfires, and pots of steaming punch. And back in the great hall, all was in a similar state. It was decorated and garlanded; blazing fires burned in the great fireplaces to counter the fact that the windows and doors had all been left open. More musicians would be playing here, and there would be dancing. Silver bowls of punch and spiced ale were being filled, and all manner of delicacies being laid out.

He reflected on the evening ahead of him, while he surveyed the snow-covered expanse of lawns. Drew and Justine had just exited the house, and he could see them, warmly bundled, walking the grounds, inspecting everything and talking animatedly together.

Addie, he made no doubt, had affected a quick toilette. He could picture her: her brown hair smoothly pulled back in its customary knot, her dress simple. And she was, no doubt, snatching the opportunity, before descending, to curl up with the copy of *The Gymnasiad, or Boxing Match: A very short, but very curious Epic Poem. With the prolegomena of Sciblerus, tertius, and notes at variorum,* that he had seen her smuggling out of his library and up the stairs. He smiled at the picture in his mind. Wallace, though, he thought, would soon put a stop to *that* reading material, unless he missed his guess, since it could hardly be deemed suitable by such a conventional mind.

And as for himself, well, he was about to greet his guests with a beautiful woman at his side.

He truly felt like the lord and master for once. As his father had been. Except, of course, that his father, right about now, would, no doubt, have been taking advantage of the dressing interlude to have taken some maid to his bed. Or his wife's bed, or one of the guest chambers, or the stables, or any of the numerous closets in the house, Fitzwilliam thought ruefully. And when he thought of Lavinia's company, her conversation, her very perfection, hell, he could feel the temptation himself. She was not unbearable. Certainly she was amiable; certainly she was beautiful. She just happened to bore him senseless.

God. He leaned his hands on the balustrade, still staring absently at Drew and Justine, now walking together under the ice-kissed weeping willows. He could feel it there, inside him, the propensity to end up that way, like his father. And it wasn't, he realized with some surprise, a restlessness born of relentless desire. Hell, he passed the comeliest maids daily without so much as a lecherous thought. It was boredom. Boredom and dread. That this was it, the rest of his life. He ran a hand over his impeccable cravat, which suddenly felt tight. He could take this fork in the road. It would be all too easy. Life would be ... predictable. He would know what every day would bring. Only in gaming and thinking up larks with his friends, and in women, would he find variety.

Or, he could take another direction. He could go upstairs right this minute and tell Addie that she was marrying him. And not so he could do his duty by her, but because he wanted her, needed her. That she was his lifeline to being the person he wanted to be. They could finish reading *The Gymnasiad* together. And then ... Well, perhaps they wouldn't finish *The Gymnasiad* first. Since just the thought of what he hoped was to follow made him want to groan, and, if he were to be honest, on some level it was all he had thought about practically since she had descended that carriage in his driveway, with Wallace rattling on about chilblains. Or maybe, more likely, he conceded, he had been lost since that first moment his lips had touched hers at Vauxhall.

And then Lavinia was joining him. Smiling. Talking with animation. And looking absolutely radiant. For what seemed to him like hours, they greeted guests—with the democracy that Lavinia found so alarming, but which Fitzwilliam, in fact, enjoyed.

He was, through it all, acutely and troublingly aware of the expectations being created. Both in her heart and in the minds of his guests, by having Lavinia by his side. There were, in fact, several coy references by various ladies of the neighborhood to the fact that it would be lovely once again to see a mistress at Kenston House. And they were not, he trusted, referring to the type of mistress he had so recently had. To these sallies, he had replied only with a smile. And what Mrs. Hughes later confessed to Lady Carbury, could only be considered one of his more enigmatic ones, at that.

He was equally acutely aware of Addie, in the same Hungarian wrap she had worn at Vauxhall, the mere sight of which made his stomach tighten with longing. She was here and there—skating, inexpertly but enthusiastically, with Suzanne and Ardean, talking with Madeleine, mingling with his guests, listening to Freddie discourse on hounds, laughing with Drew and Justine, walking with Wallace. And assiduously avoiding *him*. At which, he promised himself, she'd not succeed for long.

Chapter 40

Addie *was,* in fact, avoiding Fitzwilliam. Assiduously, as he had guessed.

The sight of him side by side with Lavinia Haverford made her ache. There could be no doubt that Lavinia was regally beautiful in her blue velvet pelisse, edged with fur and clasped at regular intervals from the throat to the demi-length bottom. It was cleverly devoid of ornamentation except for the tassels in the center, and topped by a sable pelerine, so as to better highlight its wearer. She was also excessively gracious in her greetings, and would have been perfect in her role, Addie could not help thinking, if only there had been some, well, *substance* to her.

Somehow, that was what hurt the most. She could almost have accepted it with greater equanimity if Fitzwilliam had fixed his affections on Bella or some other passionately unsuitable choice. But Lavinia Haverford was so—*suitable* was the word that came to mind. So perfect. So bland. She seemed to possess no substance other than her beauty and ambition. She was not awful in any way. Nor was she particularly good or spirited or passionate or interesting, either. Certainly not deserving of so magnetic a man. Much, in fact, like, Addie thought, feeling guilty at the disloyal idea, Fitzwilliam's mother had been.

She would tell him before this night was over, she resolved, that he stood in no further need of boxing lessons. Continuing the charade served nothing, except to keep her from getting on with her life.

She pasted a smile onto her face as she set herself to approach Wallace. He was heavily bundled, and was, with his mama, in animated conversation with a footman, apparently about the contents of the punch. "There is, you are quite certain, no Arrack in here?" she heard him quiz. "Arrack, you do realize, good sir, disrupts the digestive processes most distressingly!"

None, he was assured. But not, seemingly, to his satisfaction. His mama sipped it, and, with a vigorous shake of her head, handed the cup back to the footman. "I trust you have not partaken of any of this, Adelaide," she said, as the footman departed to fetch more tepid soured milk, as per her instructions. "It is positively *loaded* with Arrack! *Loaded!*"

"No indeed, ma'am," Addie said, trying gamely to suppress the memory of the full cup of the stuff Drew had pressed on her as she came off the ice. "Wallace?"

"Yes, Adelaide?" he asked, looking at her.

"Would—would you dance with me?" she asked, knowing that she sounded plaintive, but desperate for some warmth from him.

His mama gasped and was, Addie knew, about to give vent to her shock at how inappropriate it was for Addie to be doing the asking.

But Wallace surprised her. "Yes, let's do," he said, taking her arm. "Please have the footman bring the milk inside, Mother," he said, quite commandingly, for once.

"Certainly, Wallace," Gretchen Raines replied, looking non-plussed as Wallace led Addie indoors. "As you like."

The dancers were in the middle of a set, so Addie and Wallace stood by the side of the room and passed the time in fairly easy conversation. Like most of the dancers, they remained in their outdoor garments, as the doors and windows had all been thrown open so as to make this room seem a part of the general festivities. And it was, despite the great fires, cold in there.

Justine was dancing with the son of one of Fitzwilliam's tenants, and Madeleine Barrist had taken the floor with the local squire. Honoria was being energetically, if not expertly, partnered by Freddie Barrist, and Mannering and Suzanne were together. Fitzwilliam was going through the paces with what looked to be one of a steady stream of giggling local misses he was obliged to lead out.

When that dance drew to a close, and the musicians struck up the next, Addie and Wallace took the floor amid the shuffling of partners. It was a country dance, and Justine, this time with Drew, was in their set. And Addie could not help but be aware, despite her best efforts—and with a stab of pain, also despite her best efforts—that this time, Fitzwilliam, on the opposite side of the floor, was partnered with Lavinia. Somehow, despite this knowledge, she managed to enjoy the dance to a small degree. Wallace was a passable partner, certainly, and some half hour later when it ended, she was feeling a greater degree of equanimity.

"Oh, look," Wallace said, as they exited the floor. "There is the footman with my soured milk! Do you care for some, Adelaide?"

"Actually," said Fitzwilliam coming up behind them, "Addie is promised to me for the next dance."

"Gammon Fitzwilliam!" she responded heatedly. "I am no such thing."

"This dance is claimed?" He raised a brow at her. "Host's prerogative, Addie," he said.

She shrugged, saying, "Very well, then."

"Ah, a gracious acceptance," he replied, smiling. "I like that."

"Now, Mr. Raines," Lavinia said as graciously as Addie had not, "you must allow me to sample this tepid milk drink about which I have heard so much."

"Certainly, dear lady," Wallace said, taking up her arm. "You are interested in dairy remedies?"

"Oh, vastly," Lavinia assured him.

"Well, this one, I think you shall find, is quite smooth on the palate as well as efficacious for . . ." Wallace was saying as he led her away.

Addie and Fitzwilliam stood awkwardly together, looking at each other, waiting for the music to begin. And then, suddenly, he said, "Do you know, Addie, I have a better idea." And before she could reply, he took her arm, and skirting the edge of the great room, led her briskly, and without further ceremony, down the hallway and into his library.

It is warm in here, was her first thought. *And dim.* The fire burned low in the grate and a few sconces were lit, but the room with its dark paneling and heavy velvet drapes was softly illuminated. And although they could hear the sounds of the revelry, even as Fitzwilliam shut the door behind them, it felt hushed after the noise of the great room. He unbuttoned his greatcoat and tossed it carelessly on the billiard table, his eyes not leaving hers. And at his gesture, she removed her wrap and laid it over a chair.

"Well," she said briskly, feeling awkward.

"Addie," he said quietly, hesitantly. For once there was none of the lightheartedness, the teasing that went on between them.

She looked at him, her heart pounding, and knew that this was the moment to tell him that they no longer had a reason to be there.

"I—Fitzwilliam, I, ah—" she began, but he held up his hand.

"Let's dance, Addie," he said quietly. "We have never danced the waltz together, and do you know, I suddenly want to. Above all things."

She raised a brow as she, for one, could tell clearly that the music had not yet begun. "And suppose," she said, "that it is not a waltz?"

He smiled, and her traitorous body reacted. Too strongly.

"It will be," he replied, softly, "because I told them to make it one. Host's prerogative, remember? Listen."

She listened as the music started up. "So it is," she owned.

"And? Do we dance?" His gaze still held hers.

She somehow summoned the resolve to break it and looked around. "Certainly, if you wish it we can go back. I had something to tell you, though, and—"

"No. Here," he said, taking her hands and drawing her close, effectively cutting off her words. "We can hear the music well enough. And I also have something I wish to tell you."

"You do?" she asked, her voice barely above a whisper, while her mind swirled with possibilities.

"After the dance," he replied, placing his hand about her waist and taking her hand in his other one.

She placed her left hand on his shoulder. When he led her into the dance, she followed him effortlessly, their bodies seemingly of their own accord, in perfect harmony through the twirls and spins. Despite the energetic nature of the dance, Addie felt as though they were not even moving. She had danced the waltz many times. But never like this. Never alone in a room with a man. And never, as he had pointed out, anywhere with *this* man.

Although he held her in quite the accepted fashion, she could not but feel that there was something vastly improper about this. That they were doing something more than dancing. She was aware of the lean strength of his arms, and the smell of him, as she never had been with any other man during this dance. And his hand at her waist seemed to burn through the fairly substantial fabric of her dress.

"Addie," he whispered suddenly, pulling her closer. So close in fact, that no space remained between their two bodies, never mind the requisite twelve inches that the patronesses at Almack's insisted on so stringently.

And frankly, Addie was beginning to understand exactly why they did. "Yes?" she whispered back, her voice almost refusing to cooperate, as they all but stopped moving, despite the fact that the music did not. Oh God, it was happening again between them. Their bodies swayed slightly, together still, but there was no longer any pretense of them continuing the dance.

He looked down at her upturned face. "You're wearing the earrings," he whispered, still holding her tight about the waist with his left hand, but freeing his right to touch her earlobe, gently.

"Yes," she said, not sure where to put her suddenly freed right hand.

And all Fitzwilliam could think of was to eradicate any centimeter of space that kept his body from being pressed fully against hers. She felt—*God!* He lowered his mouth to hers. Slowly. And he waited a heartbeat before parting her lips with his own. But his kiss was hardly gentle, and this time did not start off with the challenging air that had previously been between them. But then, her response was hardly gentle either. After a moment, and with great effort, he lifted his head. It had been too long that he had wanted this.

"God help me," he whispered, "but I want—I want—" And unable to finish, and sure anyway that this time she could feel exactly what he wanted—and he was *glad* of it—he instead decided to show her.

And she, were she to be perfectly honest, did know. And she wanted it, too.

But not a moment after his arms had gone more firmly around her and his mouth once again sought hers, the door was flung open. Light from the hall spilled in. And noise. Still, it was a few seconds before either of them noticed. And even then, Fitzwilliam's lips lingered a moment over hers, communicating, he hoped, a message.

He raised his head and, blinking as his dilated pupils adjusted, he looked toward the door, where an angry Wallace Raines accompanied by his clearly outraged mama, stood.

"Wallace!" Addie said, trying to catch her breath and simultaneously detach herself from Fitzwilliam with as much dignity as she could.

"Well!" Wallace said, advancing into the room, his mama a close step behind him. "Adelaide!"

"It's not—It's not what you—" Addie started to say and then stopped. There was not much use in denying, certainly, that she had been well and truly wrapped around Fitzwilliam. And this might, anyway, well be for the best.

"I had come in search of you, Adelaide," Wallace said stiffly, "because Mother and I had decided to tell you that we no longer believe we shall suit after all. I see, however," he said, eyeing them, particularly Fitzwilliam, who was still keeping possession of one of Addie's hands, "that breaking the news gently shall hardly be a necessity."

"I am sorry, Wallace," Addie said, feeling awful. She detached her hand and crossed the room to him. "I do understand, but I want you to know how sorry I am."

"Yes, well!" Wallace looked at them. "Our not suiting, Adelaide, was on account of what I can only consider—despite what I think to be some extensive tutelage, both on my part *and* on Mother's—some alarming, and yes, deplorable tendencies in your person: your fondness for poultry and noxiously unhealthful drinks such as coffee and champagne. Miss Haverford, by the by, pronounced the soured milk most delightful! Your refusal to carry a handkerchief. Your lack of interest in preserving your own health. And Mother"—he glanced at his parent and her nod seemed to encourage him—"Mother, has been almost sick with worry about what she perceives to be your lack of ladylike accomplishments and with concern over your likely lack of success in Derbyshade society!"

"Oh, Wallace," Addie said. "It's damnably true about the accomplishments. But still, I am so—"

"No!" he exclaimed, taking a few steps inside the room. "Let me finish. But what a fool I've been! I should have realized that coming here, to the home of a known libertine, a rake, could only result in scandal! How long, if I may presume to make so bold as to ask, has this been going on?"

"It hasn't—" Addie began, just as Fitzwilliam said, "Since—"

They stopped and looked at each other. Addie took a deep breath. Awful, actually, did not *begin* to describe how she felt. "I never meant to hurt you, Wallace," she said. "I-I understand your feelings, however, and I shall send a notice terminating the engagement."

"Well! Young lady, it is certainly fortunate that my son had already decided not to have you! Before—well! *This,*" Gretchen Raines said with indignation. "In fact, it shall be something of a wonder if his delicate sensibilities are not overset for *months* on account of what he has seen. And—" It was clear that she was set to continue in this vein for quite some time, and doubtless would have had Wallace not interrupted.

"No, Mother," he said, with quiet dignity, "*I* shall take care of this. I shall send notice, Adelaide. And you!" he said turning to Fitzwilliam. "You are truly reprehensible! To have been making free with a guest under your roof. A defenseless young lady—"

"Addie? Defenseless?" Fitzwilliam asked with genuine amusement. "I hardly think—"

"*And* you have toyed with the affections of so gentle a soul as Miss Haverford," Wallace continued.

And before Fitzwilliam could open his mouth in his *own* defense—although, he admitted, there was not much to say there, if anything—Wallace's fist crashed out, finding him full in the face and sending him to the floor.

"Jesus!" he said a second later, spitting out blood, but fortunately no teeth, he reflected, as he struggled from his position prone on the floor to sitting. "Addie—" he began.

But she was staring at Wallace, her expression transfixed. "Wallace!" she cried. "What an excellent left! Your economy of movement, your precision of aim! Tell me, can you do that with your right, too?"

Wallace, looking quite surprised at this sudden enthusiasm, ignored the question, and, much on his high ropes, said, "And please be certain to return the ring, Adelaide." With that, he tossed a clean handkerchief in Fitzwilliam's direction and departed, saying, "Come, Mother."

That lady bestowed upon Addie one last icy glance and followed her son as he strode from the room.

Addie stood looking after them. Then, slowly, her eyes met Fitzwilliam's. He groaned and resumed his prone position.

Chapter 41

A short time later, the blood having been staunched, but no particular conversation exchanged, Fitzwilliam and a subdued Addie also departed the library.

They exited the house from the front, Fitzwilliam having decided that their disappearance would occasion less comment if they simply joined in the festivities on the lawn. But before they did, Fitzwilliam, who was desperately aware of the unfinished business between them, pulled her into the shadow of the portico.

"Addie," he said softly, determined not to waste time, but conscious of the rather unromantic blood-stained handkerchief he still held. "I—that is, we, I want—" But no sooner had he begun than a voice interrupted them.

"Well," it said, lazily, *"whatever* have we here?"

And Raymond Walters stepped out of the shadows.

"Oh, Christ," Fitzwilliam blasphemed. "You, here? Walters? This is all we need." And he reached into his greatcoat.

And not a second later, what Addie could have sworn was a shot whizzed by, and Raymond Walters fell, clutching his arm.

It *was* a shot?

"*You shot me!*" Raymond Walters howled.

Just as Addie said, "You sh-shot him?" She stared up at Fitzwilliam.

"So I did," Fitzwilliam confirmed lightly as he slid the pistol back into his coat.

"You could have killed him!" Addie exclaimed, suddenly feeling faint.

"No chance of that," Fitzwilliam replied, his tone grim. "Get up, Walters. You're bleeding on my drive."

"I'm dying."

"The merest scratch."

"You *shot* him," Addie whispered again, thinking that her legs might well and truly give way, they were shaking so.

"But why? Why did you shoot me?"

"You've caused Miss Winstead one too many problems," Fitzwilliam answered.

"But I came—Damn it, man, I came here to apologize! And what the hell is going on?" he demanded, still sitting and clutching his arm. "Devilish queer! First *she,*" he said, raising both arms to point a shaky finger at Addie. "She's sneaking around Mayfair at an unholy hour of the morning, dressed like a servant." He let his arms drop, still holding the right. "But she clearly ain't. A servant."

"Was she?" Fitzwilliam's eyes met Addie's, a question in his. At the slight incline of her head, he said, "Ah, go on, Walters. Do."

Raymond Walters was highly indignant now. "Well, I admit it. I thought she was a lightskirt. But, damme it, what else should I have thought, under the circumstances? And then! Well, *then* I find the two of you kissing on a bench off of Lover's Walk at Vauxhall, and, again, what was I supposed to think? And *you* say she is your fiancée, and I admit"—he glared defiantly up at them—"that I was not as respectful as I could have been. But I was in my cups, for heaven's sake, man, and I *did* truly believe—well . . . And then, Fitzwilliam, you *did* knock me down! And *then* it's in the paper that she's engaged to that Raines fellow. And you all slope off out of Town. Together. And Jackson beats me bloody, *suggesting* I apologize. And I come here to do it, and you two are practically all over each other in the dark, and *you!* Well—You *shoot* me!''

''Oh, lord,'' Fitzwilliam said, starting to laugh. ''I do owe you an apology, it seems.''

''It does rather seem so,'' Addie agreed.

''If I don't die first,'' Walters said, darkly.

''It *is* just a scratch,'' Fitzwilliam said, firmly. ''But I am sorry, Walters. I thought you were here to . . . Suffice it to say that I really could not allow one more person to hit me this week.''

Walters had peeled off his coat, despite the cold, and, still sitting on the ground, examined his arm. ''I suppose you're right,'' he said grudgingly. ''About it being a scratch.''

''Come indoors. My man will fix you up in a trice,'' Fitzwilliam said, helping him up. ''And I *am* sorry. But, Walters?'' he said.

''Yes?''

They were facing each other now.

''That was for Bridgeton.''

''I was young and foolish. And I paid for that,'' Walters replied, meeting his steady gaze. ''Believe me, I did.''

''I do believe you,'' Fitzwilliam replied. He held out his hand to shake, but upon realizing that Walters's right was hanging limply by his side, said, in brisk tones, ''Come. Let us get you fixed up.''

''I own myself more than a little surprised that Jackson did not write to tell you I would be coming to attempt a conciliation,'' Raymond Walters said, as they turned toward the house. ''He said that he would do so.''

Fitzwilliam stopped and looked again at Addie, who, he could not help but feel, had been unusually silent during their exchange.

She felt the color surge into her face.

''Addie?'' he asked, quietly.

"Well, actually"—she looked down, scuffing her boot in the snow—"he—"

"Do you mean to say you knew?" Fitzwilliam demanded dangerously.

She nodded.

"Addie?" he said again, still dangerously.

"Yes?"

Even in the poor light, he could see that she was pale. "I just shot a man. And exactly how many extra days," he asked, "of undercooked muttonchops *did* I consume?" And then he started to laugh as they helped Walters into the house.

Chapter 42

And no sooner had they got Walters delivered into the capable hands of Fitzwilliam's valet, but there was a commotion at the foot of the stairs.

"I don't know what else I could have expected," Fitzwilliam murmured, looking over the stair rail onto the hall below. "Yes, taken of a piece with the rest of this day, it must make perfect sense."

For there, in the entryway, in a state of high agitation, waving a piece of paper around and yelling at a clearly perplexed John Jackson, was Lizbeth. "But you *ruined* it," she was screaming, modish traveling bonnet dangling, ebony curls disarrayed, sables slipping fetchingly off her shoulders, and a spark of anger lighting her cheeks. "Even the Dowager Lady Elsingham is reading about horse racing instead! Here it all is—in black and white." She brandished the page. "Here it is. Pages practically upon pages, on the fight between Lord Sunderson and the Marquis of Grangeley. Hitting and punching and all manner of *disgusting* things. *That* is all in here. In *detail!* But the Marquis of Grangeley's wife left him for his own groom! And do you know why? Because he *was too much of a nipfarthing to spend so much as a groat on purchasing her a single new gown this year. And* because do you know what his preferred footwear is when he is at home? *Women's dancing slippers with emeralds studded into the heels!* Talk about an expense! And is there a word about *that* in here? No! Not one!'' She paused for breath, and Glendower drew her aside.

"Now, Lizbeth, my love," he began, soothingly.

Fitzwilliam, for one, had no intention of hearing the outcome of *that* conversation. "Let us go, Addie," he whispered, "down the back stairs. Truly, I wish to be private."

"You do?" she whispered back, looking up at him.

"Oh, yes," he said, taking her hand, and her blood seemed to thrum from the warmth of his touch. "Assuredly."

But at the bottom of those stairs, they found Honoria. "Addie! Fitzwilliam!" that lady began, seeming not to notice that they were hand in hand. "You must come with me at once! I most particularly wished to speak with you both on account of the—"

"Not now, Honoria," Fitzwilliam said. "I am coming to love you dearly, but if you stand in our way a moment longer, I may have to shoot you."

Honoria gaped at him, but did not move.

So Addie was compelled to say, "I think he means it, Honny."

"Just answer me this, Fitzwilliam," Honoria said. "Do *you* wish me to accompany you on your wedding journey?"

Fitzwilliams eyes met hers over Addie's head. "Not unless you wish to be shocked," he replied with a grin.

At which Honoria stepped aside. "Excellent!" she said, clapping her hands once they had departed. "Oh, how simply excellent!" And went in search of Justine and Drew to impart the happy news that Fitzwilliam, the Dear Boy, had just threatened to shoot her.

Chapter 43

The problem, from Fitzwilliam's perspective, was that the Frost Fair, which was turning out to be one of the most extraordinarily successful entertainments ever to be held in the vicinity and which, indeed, would be talked about for many years to come, still raged on. Everywhere.

The ornamental dairy, he decided, was their best hope for privacy. And so, taking a rather circuitous route, he brought her there. True, in its present incarnation as a boxing salon, it perhaps lacked the piquant charm one would wish for the scene of a proposal, he thought. But on the other hand, there was something singularly appropriate about the place.

Once they had achieved the relative serenity of the dairy, he took her hand and led her up to the ring. Ducking under the rope, he held it for her to do the same. Although they could still *hear* sounds of merriment from every direction, the place at least appeared blessedly empty. Having achieved the center of the ring, he stood, holding both her hands and looking down at her. "What do you think, Addie, shall we pull the gloves on?" he asked, smiling lightly.

She smiled in return. "Not afraid?"

"Only a little," he said, looking down at her intently. " think though," he said, after a moment, "that upon reflection I would rather love you instead."

"You would?" she whispered. "Truly?"

"Oh, yes," he said, pulling her up to her toes and the delightfully against him. "Oh, yes."

Then his mouth came firmly and hungrily down on hers, and things continued in this delirious vein for quite some time Until he lifted his head, and said, quite seriously. "This is it Addie. You and me. There is no ill-conceived wager, no Ray mond Walters, no Wallace Raines. No talk of duty. No secret left between us." He cupped her cheek. "Will you marry me?" he asked, the words coming out, she thought, as if warmed like honey in his mouth. She looked up at him, and he took he hand, pressing the palm against his chest, and said, "From my heart, Addie. No other women. Only you. There hasn't bee another since I kissed you at Vauxhall. You, you make m what I want to be."

Her eyes filled with tears. "Really, Fitzwilliam?" she whis pered.

"Oh, yes," he said. "I'll spend years groveling if you wis it, for pretending to myself and to you that it was out of som ridiculous sense of duty that I wanted it."

"Your parents . . ." she started to say.

But he did not allow her to continue. "*We* are not my parents Addie. I know that now. *They* were a frightful mismatch. We're not. You, in fact, are likely the only good thing my father eve did in his life. And I'm a bigger fool than he was, because almost let you go."

"Oh, Fitzwilliam," she said softly, tears in her eyes.

"No, Addie," he said, equally softly. "Call me John."

"John," she whispered, trying it out.

And the sound of it on her lips caused him to groan as h pulled her down to the floor.

"I like that," he whispered back, before kissing her, thor oughly.

She smiled. "As do I."

"And incidentally," he said, rolling them over so that she was better nestled under him, but careful to keep his full weight off her, "as my wife, you know, I'm offering you freedom. I know you will use it properly."

"What do you mean?" she asked, suddenly still, as she looked up at him.

"Take it, Addie. Wear breeches, smoke cheroots, attend every mill and prizefight you want, as long as it is with me. Go to Jackson's rooms, keep being *Anonymous* if you desire. Don't feel obligated to suppress the originality in you that I have only just come to see. I hope you will not."

"Really?" she whispered. "Do you mean that?"

"Truthfully, I am *not* much enamored of cheroots. But the breeches," he said, his hand sliding up her leg and causing her a quick intake of breath, "well, *those* could be interesting. So, will you, Addie? Marry me?"

"Yes," she whispered. "Yes."

"I love you," he whispered back as he lowered his head.

"I hear there's a mill next week in—" she began.

But he interrupted. "No, Addie. Not just yet," he said against her lips, before his mouth once again claimed hers in earnest. When the necessity of breathing caused him finally to lift his mouth, he continued. "I must insist that I am the only man that you see without a shirt for just the next few months. After that, well, you decide."

"I'd like that—F—John," she said, her hands sliding up to untuck that garment.

"Good Lord," he said, against her mouth, his hand still on her leg. "Don't do that!"

"Why?" she whispered, her hands sliding up his bare skin.

He groaned. "Because we are going to wait, Addie," he said fiercely. "I *was* going to seduce you, but I've just decided: not until you are wearing my ring."

"I don't want to wait," she whispered. "I've waited too long. *Please* seduce me, John."

And those, Fitzwilliam could not help but think, were by far the sweetest words he had ever heard. As he looked down at her, half under him, flushed and heavy-lidded, he was exerting every ounce of self-control he had ever possessed. "You don't?" he asked, praying that his voice wouldn't crack.

"No." Her eyes met his, and they were clear, no shadow of regret.

"In that case"—he slipped his signet ring off an unsteady hand—"perhaps this will suffice. It *is*, technically, my ring, after all."

"Yes. It is." She smiled up at him as he slid it onto her finger.

"Well then, Miss Winstead," he said, exulting in the feel of her body under his as he slid his hand back up her skirts, "let us get to it. Although," he said, his lips sliding down her neck, "I'm not certain exactly who is seducing whom."

Which is exactly the position in which Lavinia Haverford found them not a minute later when she and Wallace Raines stepped into the dairy for a look round.

And she then ran, indulging in a fit of strong hysterics, up to the house, with Wallace running after her, calling, "Now, Miss Haverford, you have had a shock, to be sure. Let me give you some of Mother's elderberry tisane. It is just the thing. Had some myself earlier."

But still Lavinia spilled, not particularly coherently and in great sobbing gulps, the tale of what she had seen, to the rest of the house party who had assembled themselves in the drawing room, now that the Frost Fair had wound down.

". . . And it—it seemed to be a *boxing ring*, of all things! In the ornamental dairy! And Miss Winstead, *your* sister!" she rambled to Justine, in clarification. "And Claremont—I don't give a *fig* what he likes to be called—they were, they were *lying in it.* And k-kissing! In a shockingly abandoned way. And his *hands*," she cried, truly shocked, "were *up her skirts!*"

And then she was much distressed, as her news appeared not to concern the vast majority of the assembled guests in the least.

"Excellent!" announced Honoria upon having this intelligence imparted. "Then we shan't disturb them just now. Really, one could not have hoped for a better outcome!"

"Goodness!" said Drew, kissing the back of Justine's hand, and *she* just smiled. "She still had her skirts on?"

"Capital thing," supplied Freddie Barrist. "Didn't think old Fitz to be so slow off the mark, though. Still had her skirts on!"

"Ah, young love," agreed his wife complacently.

"How nice. Come my dear. It's late. Let's to bed," suggested the Viscount Ardean to his wife.

"Only to be expected," announced Raymond Walters, adding darkly, "but I shouldn't tax him about it if I were you. Don't seem to take it well. Shoots first, asks after."

"Well, it *is* about time," said Lizbeth. "High time! Is it not about time, Glendower?"

He nodded. "Yes, dear."

"Good man," said Jackson.

Only her own mama, Wallace, and Mrs. Raines, in fact, were at all sympathetic, Lavinia was horrified to discover.

Although the elderberry tisane, she had to admit, *was* quite soothing.

Epilogue

Ah, Monday again, and sweet it was, with the mysterious *Anonymous* returned to form.

"Well!" The Dowager Lady Elsingham said, removing her quizzing glass from her eye and looking across the breakfast table at her companion.

"Eh, Corabel?" Sophronia Pettiford asked.

"I SAID, 'WELL.' "

"WELL?"

"I-SAID-'WELL.' " her employer roared.

"THAT'S WHAT *I* SAID: WELL?" Sophronia sounded quite irritated.

"I WAS REFERRING—" Lady Elsingham screamed.

"PREFERING, DID YOU SAY?"

"I SAID REFERRING!"

"DID YOU?"

"YES!"

"SO *YOU* SAY."

"I THINK, SOPHRONIA, AND I HESITATE TO MENTION IT, THAT YOU NEED YOUR EARS CHECKED!"

"NOTHING WRONG WITH MY EARS, CORABEL. IT IS YOUR WHISPERING. IF THERE IS ONE THING—"

"THAT YOU CANNOT ABIDE—"

"IT IS A MEALY MOUTHED WHISPERER. YES!"

"I KNOW THAT," Lady Elsingham finished.

"WELL, WHAT IS IT, CORABEL?"

"IT IS CLAREMONT," Lady Elsingham howled.

At this, Sophronia sat up straighter. "WELL! WHY DID YOU NOT SAY SO!"

"HE APPARENTLY ACQUITTED HIMSELF SOME- WHAT BETTER!" Lady Elsingham yelled, passing over the paper.

"OH, MY. AND HIM JUST MARRIED!" Miss Pettiford said, somewhat breathless. "OF COURSE, ONE DOES NOT LIKE TO THINK OF HIM ON HIS HONEYMOON—"

"NO, INDEED!"

"INDEED, NO!" Miss Pettiford clasped the paper to her bosom, considerably more breathless.

"GOODNESS, NO. IF YOU WOULD JUST PASS THE PAPER OVER HERE, SOPHRONIA, I WILL JUST READ IT ONCE MORE!"

"ALOUD, IF YOU PLEASE," Sophronia commanded. "OF COURSE ONE'S MIND DOES NOT THINK OF HIM 'PEELING'—"

"NO, INDEED! NOT 'PEELING!' VASTLY IMPROPER!"

And so saying, the two ladies each reread the article in question and then retired for their naps.

A few blocks away, Claremont himself, still known as John Fitzwilliam, fourth Earl of Claremont was, once again, reading the very same thing, but this time with a much greater degree of equanimity. "Have I ever mentioned, my love," he inquired, raising his gaze from the newspaper and looking heatedly across the table at his wife, "exactly how much I admire that ratty maid costume of yours? This article brings it to mind. Perhaps," he suggested, putting down the paper altogether, "we should go upstairs, and you can put it on. Or better yet, leave it off."

ABOUT THE AUTHOR

Jessica Benson lives with her family in New York. She is also the author of LORD STANHOPE'S PROPOSAL. Jessica loves to hear from readers, and you may write to her c/o Zebra Books. Please include a self-addressed stamped envelope if you wish a response.

Contemporary Romance By
Kasey Michaels